THE PROBLEM WITH LUST

THE SEVEN SINS, #2

LILY ZANTE

AUTHOR'S NOTE

The Problem with Lust is the second book in **The Seven Sins,** which is a contemporary romance series of steamy, angsty and emotional stories featuring characters who are loosely connected.

All books in this series are STANDALONE.
Other books in The Seven Sins:

Underdog (prequel)
The Wrath of Eli
The Problem with Lust
The Lies of Pride
The Price of Inertia
The Other Side of Greed

Sign up for my newsletter and get a FREE book:
https://www.lilyzante.com/news

CHAPTER ONE

MAX

"Hot Gina's in town?" Al asks. There's a hint of jealousy in his voice.

I wipe the grease off my hands with a cloth and nod, a huge smile spreads across my lips. "She sure is."

"You let me know if she—"

"Yeah, yeah, I know." He wants to hook up with her friend, *any* friend of hers, Al says, but he's joking. He's been with Sammy for years and has eyes for no one but her. Sometimes, like on a Hot Gina weekend, a sliver of excitement passes over his expression, but I know it's only fleeting. He would never risk losing what he has with Sammy to have what I have.

Besides, I don't know about Gina's friends. We don't waste time talking about insignificant stuff. Come to think of it, we don't talk much at all, not immediately when we see one another. Gina is unique. She has the sexual appetite of a man. She's a bona fide nymphomaniac, and I've known a fair share of them to be able to confirm this. She's coming home for the weekend, on leave from the military, and that means forty-eight hours of sex.

She calls, and I answer on the first ring.

"Haven't you left yet?" she cries. I hear the anger in her voice, and it adds to my frustration. I'm already mad at Enzo because a customer walked in last minute and needed something to be looked at and Enzo told me to deal with it.

Forget about going home to freshen up. "I'm coming," I tell her as I walk over to my locker.

"I should be coming," she grumbles, clearly not amused.

"You will be, over and over again," I promise her as I pull out a clean shirt. Absence makes the heart grow fonder, some people say, but I can tell you that absence makes the dick grow harder.

"How long are you going to be?" she asks. "I have pizza slices all over me."

"All over you?"

"On me, like I'm a plate. I'm not wearing anything either."

I hiss out a breath, and in the same instant my cock hardens.

"Gimme ten minutes," I tell her as I unbutton my shirt and quickly take it off.

"Hurry up! I feel like an idiot lying here like this."

I can see I'm going to have to make it up to her big time when I get there. I quickly whip out a clean T-shirt from my locker. "I'm going to have to take a shower at your place—"

"I have to wait for you to take a shower too?"

"No. no. Just lie back and spread your legs. I'll take good care of you first, and that's a promise."

"That's more like it." I can imagine the huge grin on her face as she says this.

"Don't move a muscle," I order. "See you on Monday," I say to Al.

"Come over to Waquito's. Rumors are Cardoza's going to be there."

I scowl at him.

"The boxer. The heavyweight champion of the world. Chicago's New Ho—"

I raise my arm in a dismissive gesture. Al is a huge fan of Elias Cardoza—the local underdog who surprised many by winning the belt. "Gonna be busy, dude. Probably not going to get out of bed."

"Goddamn lucky son of a bitch," he mutters good-naturedly and loud enough for me to hear.

I rush out the door and over to my bike.

Weekends like this are few and far between. With my regular friends-with-benefits setups—and I have one or two lucky women here in Chicago—it's just an instant gratification before I return to my place after. Or she leaves to go to hers. We never spend the night together. It's an unspoken rule.

With Gina it's different, because she only gets leave once in a while and it's usually only for the weekend. With her, we spend the whole weekend together.

We fuck like rabbits.

It's beautiful.

CHAPTER TWO

TRINITY

"You're doing amazing, Dylan. Absolutely amazing. I love this drawing." School only started a few weeks ago, and this scrawny, skinny little boy has already stolen my heart.

Each morning he comes to my classroom looking a little rougher, dirtier, hungrier, and sad, but by the end of the school day, his eyes are all lit up, and there's a smile on his face. But also, by the end of the day, he's in no hurry to go home, unlike most of the others. He drags his feet as if he doesn't want to leave.

I shouldn't have favorites, and I try not to, but as I'm slowly getting to know my new class of seven-year-olds, something about this child makes it impossible for me not to reach out. This isn't about having a favorite, it's about me adding something to this kid's life to make him smile.

"Oh, look," I say, pulling a banana out of my bag. "I

forgot to eat this at lunchtime. I'd hate to waste it. Would you like it?"

He eyes the banana without blinking "You could have it tomorrow, miss."

Smart kid. "I could, but I'm worried I might squash it by the time I get home." I hold it out to him. "It would be a shame to let it go to waste." This is the third time I've done this in the past few weeks, and it's getting to a point now where I deliberately don't eat my fruit and save it for him.

"Can I eat it here?"

It's the first time he's asked this. I don't want him to stay too late because I know his mother will be waiting for him. "Here? Won't your mom be waiting for you?"

He shrugs, and seems reluctant to take it. "Well, sure, you can eat it here," I say.

No sooner has he peeled the banana than he wolfs it down greedily. It disappears in about three seconds. I hold my hand out for the banana skin.

His mouth is still full, but he nods, a sort of 'thank you.'

"Off you go, and don't forget your reading."

He rushes off, and I stare after him long after he's disappeared from sight. I worry about him, but I'm also not sure if I'm reading too much into things.

"Are you still here?" Ed, my colleague from the classroom next to mine, walks in.

"I'm killing time before I pick Benji up from the vet. What's your excuse?"

"Prepping my lessons for next week." He walks up to my desk with a smug smile, obviously pleased at himself. "How is your soulmate?"

I grin at the term of endearment he uses for my cat. Though, he's not far wrong. My furry friend and I have shared many a cozy night in front of the TV. "Benji is well, but he doesn't like going to the vet."

"Is he sick?"

"No. He's getting up there though, and it's his usual yearly check-up, all the blood work, etcetera. He's going to be in a stinker of a mood when he comes home," I state, and am glad that I have my crochet class later to escape to.

"You give that cat too much importance."

"He rules the roost. What can I do? He's the best company."

I'm no better when it comes to leading an exciting life. Ed is staying behind on Friday to prepare next week's lessons, and I have a crochet class.

Sex, drugs, and rock 'n' roll is an alien concept for both of us. We're both similar in some respects. It's probably why we get along so well, aside from the fact that he usually passes by my classroom for a quick chat on most days.

"Any plans for the weekend?" he asks, straightening his tie.

"We have a trip to the Nature Sanctuary over by North Pond."

"*We?*" There's a spark of uneasiness in his tone.

I relax and sit back, trying hard not to smile. "My adult art class."

His expression smooths to a smile. "I can't believe how you give up your weekends for these things, Trinity. Your life is already hectic enough."

"Best way to be." I volunteer on Monday evenings to teach art to adults with minor learning difficulties. This weekend the other teacher and I have organized a picnic at a local nature reserve. We never work weekends, but this has become a yearly thing. I don't mind giving up most of my Saturday for this. It's something different for the students and they're all excited about it.

Ed looks at me the way he usually looks at me; with curiosity, as if he can't quite figure me out. But there's something else behind those irises today. He looks especially nice this evening in a dark shirt. He's almost always in a white shirt and the contrast of him in something dark makes him look slightly sexy, at least, to my eyes.

He and I are on the same page. He's not overly pushy, and I'm not overly flirty. In fact, I'm *never* flirty, though I do take a few seconds longer to gaze at him today.

"Isn't teaching seven-year-olds enough?"

"I love my job, but you know me, Ed—"

"Do I?" he asks. His comment stops me momentarily, and suddenly I'm not so sure what he means.

"What do you mean?"

"Do I know you, Trinity? I don't think I do. We've been friends for what, two years now? And I still don't think I know you that well."

This naturally begs the question of how well does he need to know me?

"Maybe..." He clears his throat and then seems to hesitate.

"Maybe what?" I ask. Does he have a point to make, or is he still making small talk?

"Maybe you're just too nice for your own good."

"Meaning what exactly, Ed?"

"Spending a weekend going on a picnic with your art class?"

"It's only for a few hours and on one day, not the entire weekend," I correct him. "You teach Sunday school," I point out. "And you do that every weekend. I only teach art classes on a Monday night. I'm not as selfless as you, when it comes to these things."

"It's just a few hours on a Sunday," he clarifies.

I'm still not sure where he's going with this, but Ed has a way of going around and around in circles and can take forever to get to the point. But I'm used to it now.

"How about you? What are your plans?" I ask him.

"I'm looking for a new bed."

I widen my eyes a little to show interest. "A new bed?"

He nods. "I'm not sleeping well and my back's starting to hurt. The foam in the mattress is worn out and I can feel the springs more."

"I highly recommend a memory foam mattress."

"A memory foam mattress?" he asks, with interest. "Is that what you sleep on?"

I nod vigorously. "I swear by it."

"I'll take your advice."

We fall silent. Both of us talking about a bed is, and isn't, weird. A bed is an intimate part of the household furniture, or it's a place to sleep. Nobody has ever shared my bed, and I know, through our conversations, that Ed is like me, saving himself for marriage. One life partner forever.

Our gazes lock for a moment so fleeting that I'm not sure if I imagined it. Even though all we've ever done is talk, I sense that Ed likes me.

I like him too.

He's sweet.

This is nice enough, and pleasant enough, and it is *enough;* talking, and getting to know one another. He makes me smile whenever he walks into my classroom for an end-of-day chat.

Maybe we'll talk for another year or two before he

makes a move. That suits me just fine. He's good-looking, well, *pleasant* looking, I'd say. He's no Chris Hemsworth. He's skinny and angular, with thinning hair, but, more importantly, his eyes don't drop to my chest during our conversations. I am aware that most men can't shift their eyes away from my ample bosom, because I see this with the dads at parents' evening.

Ed is nothing like that.

He's the type of man I can see myself with. The type of man I am saving myself for. He plays it safe, as do I. Life isn't exactly riveting, but it is smooth-sailing, which is fine by me.

I hear some of the sob stories from a few of my teacher friends—broken hearts, a trail of cheating boyfriends, jealousy and heartbreak. If that's what love is all about, I don't want it. I don't want to risk wading through a load of boyfriends before I find 'the one.'

No, thank you.

I'm saving myself.

"Well, if you ever have a weekend free, maybe...maybe we could ...uh...go for a pizza or something," he offers, looking at the floor as he shuffles from one foot to the other.

"A pizza?"

"Or something. Just you and me."

"Oh." My heart sinks a little, and I'm not sure why. It's definitely not a heartbeat skip, more like a feeling of it sinking slowly to the pit of my stomach.

"Like, maybe next weekend or the weekend after that," Ed continues, his face looking slightly shinier now.

"Sure." I say, feeling confused as to what he's asking.

"Have a good time at the picnic," he says quickly, then leaves.

"Enjoy your mattress hunting."

So, that was it. That was the thing he'd been wanting to say all along; it just took him longer to say it.

I'm still not sure if that was a date, or a maybe-date, or pizza with friends. He and I don't really get together outside of work, though he did come to the Christmas get-together with the crochet class last year, and he met Christina, my best friend. It turned out to be a good night, now that I remember it.

Ed surprised me, and it reminds me that he can be good fun socially.

One day, who knows? Maybe Ed and I will end up sharing a memory foam mattress together.

CHAPTER THREE

TRINITY

My heart almost stops when my car stalls at the light. *Not again.*

I turn the key again and it splutters and dies. Then I hear a loud crash, as if a tank has suddenly hit me, and I jolt forward from the impact. Luckily, my seatbelt stops my face from hitting the dashboard.

What the hell?

I turn and look over my shoulder. Car horns are blaring, and I undo my seatbelt.

"What's wrong with you?" I hear someone shout.

I look at the rearview mirror and see a guy get off his bike and walk towards me. When he takes his helmet off, I see the angry expression on his face.

My heart lurches as I slowly get out of the car. I hate confrontations, even though this isn't my fault. He crashed into the back of me, and yet I feel nervous. This isn't a particularly busy road, but traffic is jacked up a few cars behind me. Slowly, annoyed-looking drivers start driving around us.

I walk to the back of my car and inspect the damage. It looks bad. My bumper is lying on the ground, and there's a huge ugly dent in my trunk.

"Damn it, lady! What the hell happened?" An angry voice behind me makes me jump. I turn around to face him. He reminds me of a bully, and I hate bullies.

"The...the car stalled," I manage to say, after which my brain registers that he looks a little Chris Hemsworth-ish, except that his eyes are brown, not blue.

I turn my back to him and survey the damage again, then I glance at his motorbike to assess how bad the damage is to that. But his bike looks perfectly fine, and now that I find myself staring at him, he looks fine too. No injuries.

"The lights changed, why didn't you move?" he growls.

"Hey!" My temper flares. He's got some nerve. I have no idea why he's so mad. If anyone should be mad, it should be me. "Don't you go getting mad at me," I snap. "This is all *your* fault."

He opens his mouth to say something but I waggle my finger at him, motioning for him to stay silent. To my surprise, he does.

"My car stalled," I continue. "It does that sometimes. I don't know what's wrong with it, but *you* bumped into the back of *me*."

He swipes his hand over his forehead, then looks at his watch, obviously not interested in my explanation. "You shouldn't be driving it if there's a problem with it."

Somewhere in the back of my mind, I realize that if my car hadn't stalled, we wouldn't be having this conversation. "But you crashed into me," I remind him, trying to sound as indignant as I can.

"I crashed because you stopped! You're not supposed to stop at the lights."

"I stalled!" I throw back, shocked by his refusal to accept that this was his fault. He narrows his eyes at me, and then looks at his watch again. I survey him carefully. He's really not hurt at all, and his mouth and vocal chords are in perfect working order. "You look like you need to be somewhere. We should swap insurance details," I tell him. His face hardens and he doesn't say anything.

Unfazed, I pull out my notebook, find my insurance details, and scribble them down. In the background I can still hear car horns honking and people shouting for us to get off the road. This isn't ideal, being stranded here, and I'm conscious that Benji is waiting for me at the vet's. I'm in a hurry too.

"Here," I hold out my piece of paper to him, but he doesn't move to take it, and he hasn't written anything down as far as I can see.

"Can I have your details?" I ask again, but he looks at me as if I've he doesn't understand.

- - -

MAX

Hot Gina's sent me a selfie of her lying naked on the bed, and this woman is asking for my insurance details.

Fuck. Fuck. Fuck.

I maintain eye contact and try to figure out how I'm going to get out of this situation fast. It doesn't help that my cock is steel-pipe hard.

"Can you please give me your insurance details so that I

can get off the road and get my car towed to the garage?" she asks, and she's starting to sound a little irritated. I can't do what she's asking, and I really need to get the hell out of here pronto. She's wasting valuable time.

"Well?" she asks, folding her arms when I don't say anything.

I don't know how to get out of this, so I clear my throat and try for diplomacy. "I'm really not sure this is entirely my fault."

She laughs. "You're something else. How many times do we have to go over this? *You* crashed into the back of my car."

"But you're to blame for that."

"I stalled." She shouts, and it's the first time I've heard her raise her voice. I'm temporarily dumbstruck. "Why are you having problems understanding this?" She whips out her cell phone and starts dialing. "Let's see what the cops have to say."

"Whoa." I step forward and grab the phone out of her hand.

"Hey! Give that back."

I hold the phone away from me, but out of her reach. "Don't call the cops."

"Give me back my phone, otherwise I will report you for assault."

"Assault?" I step towards her. "Really?" I step right up to her so that we are only inches apart. A blush creeps across her face. I notice that she's a little rounded. Voluptuous, some would say. Curvy in all the right places. And she has a huge pair of tits. The thought is too much for my cock to take, on top of everything else.

If I step any closer, I'll probably brush against them. I'm tempted, but then she'd have a good reason to report me for assault. I'm not wired like that, though. I'm no douchebag. I like sex and I appreciate women, but I'd never make an uninvited move.

"Hey, no. I didn't mean it like that." I take a step back, and so does she. I hand her back her phone, and give her *the look,* in an attempt to disarm her. Her face is fully red, and I can't tell if she's annoyed at me or if she's just reacting from The Max Factor.

I haven't fully deployed it with her; I haven't given her my usual intense look that burns into her eyes, nor dropped my gaze to her lips and then lower, taking in the entirety of her figure. I'd normally finish with a slow stare all the way back up, from her legs, to her chest, to her mouth, to her eyes, looking at her in a way that lets her know I'm interested. It works for most women.

But I'm not interested in this one. She's not my type. Seems to me as if she's maybe in her thirties because of the way she's dressed. Frilly blouse and a flared-out purple skirt. *Purple?* Who the heck wears purple anymore? Doesn't that color belong in the '70s, or something?

"You crashed into me," she states, before moving back another step. I'm not going to win this one, and I kind of already know that it's my mistake. I can't wriggle my way out of it. I begrudgingly have to agree, because she's right. "Okay. Sure." I raise my hands in a defeated way.

She scowls at my tone. "You *did.* There's no disputing the fact. Insurance details?" she asks, before looking at her watch.

Ever the deflector, I ask her, "You gotta be somewhere?"

"I'm in a hurry, so please give me your details."

"Insurance details?" I echo. I can't give her any because I don't have any insurance and if the police found out, I'd be in serious shit.

"Yes," she snaps, as if I've tried her patience.

I glance at my watch again, fully aware that this woman isn't going to let me off as easily as I'd hoped. The dent on her trunk is something I can fix, and likewise with the bumper. She's driving a battered old piece of shit. It's a death trap and if it seems to be stalling regularly, like she says it has, she shouldn't be driving it. But, on the plus side, my bike is OK, and so am I. I just need to get to Hot Gina's place and get my weekend started. "Can I see your details?" I ask, in another lame attempt to buy some time.

She shoves the piece of paper at me. Her handwriting is neat and tidy, probably just like her. Thinking about it, I'm the one who's damaged her car, and my bike is fine, and yet she's not the one who's getting angry. I am. And it's all because my dick needs to be someplace else.

"I work at a garage, and I can get this fixed for you at a good rate," I tell her.

"It doesn't matter what it costs because I'm not paying. The fault isn't mine."

It was worth a try. I could fix that real fine for her, and the bumper, too. The damn thing isn't starting though, and I know for sure that part isn't my problem.

Before I can say anything, my phone pings, and I'm staring at another picture of Hot Gina's breasts.

My cock twitches in appreciation and I'm mesmerized by the visual. The purple-skirted woman in front of me threatens to call the cops again, and I have no choice but to deal with it. "Fine." I tell her. "I can take care of the repairs for you. My fault, so I'll pay." My boss, Enzo, won't be too happy, and I'll have to do it in my own time, and pay for it out of my own pocket, but it will be better to do that than risk getting a fine for not having insurance.

"Why are you going to fix that for me, when we can go through insurance?" she asks.

"I work for a garage," I tell her. "We fix cars all day long."

She stares at me, her gaze all shifty. "You fix cars?"

I take offense at her tone because she says it as if she's surprised, no, shocked, more like, that I'm capable of doing such a thing.

I wink at her, turning my charm up a notch while I give her an approving look. "I'm not just a good-looking guy with a great body. Yes, I fix cars. I'm pretty good with my hands." I wink again.

She shrinks back, as if I've scared her. This is interesting. My lines don't usually scare women off. They get them hot and wet. My cock twitches again, reminding me that it needs to be someplace. Inside Gina, and soon. "Look, lady, this isn't the time or place to be having this conversation."

"Then lets swap insurance details—"

Fuck. Why does she not listen? "I can't," I snap. "I can't because I don't have insurance. If you call the cops, I will get in trouble. *Please,* do not call the cops on me." There's a begging tone to my voice, but I'm desperate to leave and I'm worried that Gina might use one of her sex toys and satisfy herself before I get to her.

"You don't you have insurance?"

"No."

"But why not? That's illegal."

I run my hand through my hair, the helmet in my other hand. "Because I don't. I can't afford it yet. It ran out a few months ago."

She raises an eyebrow again, and fixes me with the kind of look that my dad would when he doesn't agree with something that I've done. But my dad has an excuse, given that he's in his late sixties.

She stares at me as if she's considering my proposal, and then she surprises me with, "How far is your garage?"

I almost smile with relief.

"Not far. I can arrange for someone to tow you back to the garage, but you'll have to drive the car with your hazards on, real slow."

"It might start now," she says, moving towards the driver's side. "Sometimes it's okay after I've left it a while." She gets in, while I stand there wondering what the hell did I do to deserve this on this of all days?

She tries, but the car splutters and refuses to start.

I walk towards her, pissed off with myself for not having insurance, because my financial situation is lousy, but her car certainly doesn't sound roadworthy. "We'll pull you along. No clutch, no gas pedal, just use the brake if you need to."

She looks worried.

"You'll be fine," I tell her. She glances at her watch again, prompting me to wonder if she's got the male equivalent of Hot Gina waiting for her at home. "Why are you in a hurry?"

"I have to pick up my cat from the vet."

"I can take you." I really don't want to. Especially not now, knowing that Hot Gina's waiting for me, but I figure it's the least I can do, seeing that she didn't have to agree to my proposal and I did behave like a jerk initially.

"You'll take me to the vet?"

I'm scared that she might change her mind and call her insurance company, or her parents or friends might convince her to. If I do something nice for her, maybe she won't be swayed. "As soon as we tow your car back to the garage," I say quickly, my heart rate speeding up at the sound of another text notification on my phone.

It's Gina again.

I was supposed to be fucking her brains out right about now, not towing a car back and making a detour to the vet.

"I'm coming," I text back quickly.

CHAPTER FOUR

TRINITY

I've finally gotten the hang of it. Being towed isn't as scary as I thought it would be. The Motorcycle Guy is behind me, on my tail and driving slowly and his friend is in the van in front, pulling my car along with the tow rope.

It's unnerving, the sensation of not having any control; of being at the mercy of someone else, but I don't really have a choice. At first I wasn't sure about agreeing to this guy's proposition—because it benefits him, not me—and if I tell my parents, they'll get annoyed, but what was I supposed to do when he said he didn't have insurance?

I don't like getting people in trouble if I can help it, and even if this guy is stupid not to have insurance, that's his problem, not mine. Besides, the damage to my car isn't so bad, and on top of that, it's an old car. I need to get a newer one, but I'm saving up for a deposit on a house, because that's my first priority. It used to run just fine but in the last few weeks, it's really started to act up.

I keep meaning to replace it, but a teacher's salary only goes so far, and this thing gets me from A to B, most of the time.

I'm relieved that this guy can fix it for me, though. It's lucky that he works at a garage. Lucky for us both.

The van in front slows down, then comes to a stop in the parking lot of a huge red and orange building.

This is where that guy works?

I know this garage. I've passed by it many a time.

I turn off the engine and pull up the handbrake just as they told me to. The guy in the van jumps out and Motorcycle Guy gets off his bike and walks towards him. Soon they're laughing and talking, and when they glance at me at the same time, I know immediately that they're laughing about me.

I get out of the car, eyeing them warily, then fold my arms, the way I usually do, trying to hide my hefty chest. It wouldn't surprise me to learn that they've probably made a joke about my bra size or something.

The guy in the van unhooks the tow rope while Motorcycle Guy climbs into my car and appears to be checking something.

I wait patiently, but my patience is beginning to wear thin especially because I don't have long before the vet's closes.

"Good driving," his friend says, walking towards me. "I'm Al." He holds out his hand. We didn't get introduced when he showed up at the scene because Motorcycle Guy was in such a rush. Come to think of it, he and I never introduced ourselves, either.

"I'm Trinity," I say, shaking his hand.

"Trinity?" I hear Motorcycle Guy's voice behind me.

"Yes?" I reply, waiting for the sarcastic comment which

invariably will be something to do with Trinity from *The Matrix* and her slick-as-oil PVC outfits.

"As in..."

I huff loudly, and I'm certain that my flared nostrils stop him from finishing the sentence.

Standing in between them, I don't miss the looks they exchange. These two remind me of the seven-year-olds I teach. Hard to imagine that these are supposedly grown-up men.

"Do I need to do anything? Check the car in, or sign some paperwork? What you're doing is legit, right? Your boss isn't going to call me and get angry, is he?"

"*Legit?*" Motorcycle Guy grins as if I've made a ridiculous joke. "Do you think I'd do anything like that?"

"You don't have insurance," I point out.

"Ouch," his friend cries, smiling with glee.

"This is legit, lady." Motorcycle Guy advances towards me slowly. I don't like the way he keeps calling me 'lady,' as if I'm someone a whole generation older than him. And I also don't know why that sets my heart racing. I don't feel threatened, but right now I feel as if Chris Hemsworth is looking at me and...well, that makes my heart go all fluttery.

"You...you said you'd take me to the vet's," I manage to say, taking a step back because I can feel some heat coming off this guy. It's insane, and I know I haven't imagined it, because I feel hot all of a sudden.

"If I said it, then I'll do it," he answers. "So, Trinity, huh?" he asks, pulling out a notebook and pen, miraculously from his jacket pocket. He couldn't put pen to paper when I needed his insurance details and it amazes me now that he had any stationery on him at all. "Trinity what?" He gets ready to write. One glance tells me that it's his little black book. Full of women's names, I bet. My body stiffens.

"Shouldn't you be writing my details down on … on…" I look around feeling foolish, "On some official business paper?"

He grins again, then chews his bottom lip as if he's weighing me up, as if he doesn't understand my objection. And then he lifts his chin, looks at his notebook, and then to me again. "Oh…" He nods, his eyes twinkling and making me feel even more silly. He lets out a snort as he glances at his friend. I get ready for complete evisceration. "Did you think I was taking your details down for my own personal use?"

I need to dig myself out of this hole. "I was surprised how fast you whipped out your notebook given that you froze when I needed your insurance details."

I hear Al snort again.

Motorcycle Guy narrows his eyes at me and my heart skips a beat.

"You guys are like the kids I teach," I say, because I need to say something, otherwise I will stand here and simmer under this man's gaze. I don't understand what's going on. I don't understand why the mere act of him looking at me makes my insides tingle, but it does. I've been talking to Ed Moorcroft for over a year, and not once have I experienced anything like what I'm feeling now by having this man look at me. It's not like we've exchanged many words either.

"You teach kids?" Al asks, breaking my thoughts. Motorcycle Guy texts on his phone.

I nod.

"How old?"

"Seven- to eight-year-olds."

Al smiles, as if he's feeling proud of himself for being likened to that age group. "You look like a schoolteacher," he comments, and leaves me wondering what he means by that. "I mean, being all nice and huggable."

Huggable? I say nothing but that word slays me. I know what he means—he's trying to be nice and make polite conversation. I'm not overweight, but I'm not super-slim either. I have curves, and I wish my hips and breasts were one size less, but somehow Al's comments sound disparaging to me, and I'm relieved that Motorcycle Guy hasn't heard because he's still busy on his phone. Al asks me which school I teach at, and I tell him. We make small talk, but the word 'huggable' still grates on me.

I glance at my phone to check if I have any missed calls or messages from the vet's clinic. I don't.

"Paperwork," says Motorcycle Guy, suddenly appearing at my side with a clipboard. "Just sign here, and I'll take care of the rest."

I examine the paperwork carefully, taking my time to read every word. Al sniggers again. "He hates being late for hot dinner," I think I hear him say.

"Shut up." Motorcycle Guy throws back.

I carefully examine the paperwork and the whole time I can feel him staring at me. I sense—but I can't be sure because I hardly know him—that he's doing this on purpose. I've seen the way he struts around. He doesn't walk, he *swaggers*, as if he's too laidback to walk with purpose, as if he's slowing down his movements so that women will admire his butt and his body as he walks past.

He's the type of guy that women flock to, like bees to honey. He's like a huge six-foot something of walking honeycomb.

I wouldn't, though.

I have more sense.

"Can't you just hurry up and sign it?" he growls.

I turn to him and arch my eyebrow. "I'm doing you a favor," I remind him. "I'll take as long as I want."

"I can vouch for him," Al pipes up. "Max is a good guy."

Ahh, so he has a name.

"Are you checking for punctuation and grammar?" he snaps. "I gotta be somewhere, lady."

"His friend waits for no one," Al sniggers again as I continue checking the form. There's no mention of costs, or anything to suggest that I will be paying. Still, I want to make sure that this won't come back to bite me, and I add a line to the paperwork.

I show it to him. "You sign here too," I insist.

"Don't you trust me?" he asks, before pulling the pen and clipboard from me.

"Not much. I don't know you from Adam."

He gives me a who-the-hell's-Adam look. "Whose form is this anyway, yours or mine?" he mutters as he signs so quickly that it feels like he's drawn a squiggle. He tosses the clipboard onto a worktop. "Let's go," he says, and walks away.

"Nice meeting you, Trinity." Al nods.

I'm not sure I can say the same, but of the two, Al is definitely the safer and more friendly. "See you when I pick up my car," I tell him.

Max is already sitting on his bike waiting for me. "Here's my spare helmet." He holds it out for me.

"Where did you get that from?" I'm suddenly nervous.

"From my locker. Why?"

"Shouldn't I ... don't I need to wear some protective clothing?"

His gaze runs over me as if I've told him a joke. "Looks to me as if you're already covered up like a nun."

I press my lips together. I was thinking more of those

leather outfits I see bikers wear. My flimsy fabric isn't going to protect me much if I fall off.

He's about to put his helmet on, then sees me hesitate. "Can you hurry up?" he snarls. "I told you, I gotta be somewhere."

I put on my helmet and then stand for a moment like a dork near the bike.

"Well, get on it, then," he orders. I remember that he's in a rush because he has a hot dinner waiting for him, but my schoolteacherly caution suddenly kicks in and I'm not sure.

I don't trust this guy.

What if we have an accident? Maybe I should just get an Uber to the vet's?

"What's the problem?" Al comes over. I feel more at ease when he's around, and I'm not sure why. I don't feel threatened by Motorcycle Guy, but he sets me on edge. I must be insane to want to get on the back of his motorbike and ride with him all the way to the veterinary clinic. Al seems to understand my hesitation.

"Just throw your leg over, and sit tight. Put your arms around Max," he advises.

I'm already beginning to regret this. I climb on tentatively, then smooth down my skirt. It's flared, and puffs out beneath me. Horrified by the thought of it billowing out and therefore flashing my panties to everyone, I fold down the sides of fabric and sit on them, so that it's as narrow as a pencil skirt.

Max, meanwhile has been silent the entire time.

"Are you ready for her?" Al asks him. I can sense the innuendo in that sentence, and I'm even more anxious to get going.

"Can you hurry up?" I cry, though my voice comes out all muffled.

"Oh, now you want me to hurry up?"

"The vet is going to close in ten minutes."

"Address?" Max asks.

I tell him.

He revs up the bike, and I hold on for dear life.

As soon as the bike shoots forward, I throw my arms around his waist even tighter than before. In no time, we're speeding through the streets, me grabbing hold of him as if I might come flying off if I don't. This is new and dangerous, and a first for me.

I pray he won't go faster, otherwise I'll have to tighten my grip.

I also pray he doesn't crash into the back of anyone again.

And I pray some more that my parents won't see me, because they would not approve. They worry and fuss over me enough as it is.

Max stops momentarily at the lights, allowing me to catch my breath. My insides are all over the place. I'm not sure if it's because I've never ridden on a bike before, or if it's because of this guy. I'm still not sure I trust him, although it's too late for me to do anything about that.

He races off again, and I clutch him even tighter.

Today has been the strangest day ever.

I can't wait to tell Ed.

And Christina, assuming I pick Benji up on time and can make it to my crochet class.

Just as I start to get used to the ride, and even enjoy it a little, the familiar vet's clinic comes into view.

Max slows to a halt in front of it. I'm still holding onto him for dear life. It's the closest contact I've had with a guy since I split up with my boyfriend over a year ago.

Holding him like this, being this close with my legs

apart, and my body pressed against his, feels strangely intimate.

A vibration thrums through my entire body, even though he's turned the engine off. I let go of my vice-grip around him, and suddenly feel hot and sticky.

CHAPTER FIVE

MAX

My cock hurts.

All because Trinity's great big watermelon breasts were pressed tight against my back the entire time. I could feel them through my leather jacket.

I've had more temptation thrown at me in the last hour than I can handle right now. It's bad enough seeing Gina's naked selfies, knowing that she's waiting for me, but with Trinity riding behind me, stuck to me like glue, my mind soars to the filthiest of places.

I can't help it.

I love sex.

It's as important to me as breathing.

Plus, this lady is holding onto me real tight. Any tighter and she's going to bruise my ribs. But at the same time, it makes me wonder what it would be like to have a naked selfie of her.

I'm itching to see her breasts.

Is that so wrong?

I'm relieved when we come to a standstill outside the vet's. Trinity takes her helmet off, and hands it to me.

Her face is all red and shiny, and she rubs a hand across her neck as if she's wiping away the sweat. She must have had a thrill riding behind me. Goes to show that I wasn't the only one getting turned on.

"Thanks for the ride," Trinity says, but her voice sounds a little breathless. She's smoothing down her hair, and wiping her face, and doing all sorts of things while I watch, and she doesn't look so schoolteacherish right now. I'm used to this disheveled look. Nearly all the women I fuck end up looking like this; their hair out of place, their faces hot, sweaty, and red.

But this is the first time it's happened after a bike ride.

Holy shit on a stick. I notice that a button on her blouse has popped open and I catch a glimpse of the top of her bra. It doesn't take long for me to imagine my face buried in between those luscious pillows.

I'm going to screw Gina's brains out as soon as I walk through the door.

"You okay?" I ask, "You look a little... flushed."

She winces, before wiping her hand across her neck again. "I'm a little hot." She fans her hand as if she's trying to cool herself down.

I smile because The Max Factor has definitely worked on her. She finds me too hot to handle. Most women do. "I can give you a bigger thrill next time. You just say the word." The sentence slips out before I can stop it. Trinity's face turns even redder, making me wonder how red she gets when she's having sex.

Suddenly, my mind is there.

In bed.

With her.

I cough, to shake myself out of this automatic visual I seem to easily slip into. Talking to a sexy woman often gets me in this mood, so I'm surprised to find myself getting my flirt on with Trinity the schoolteacher. She's about as sexy as a nun.

"You really rate yourself, don't you?"

And *that* comment uttered in *that* tone kills my sex drive. Before I can find a suitable line to toss back at her, she says, "I hope you're not too late for your hot dinner."

Hot dinner?

I have no idea what she's talking about. And then I bark a short laugh, because I think she's maybe heard Al talk about Hot Gina. I shake my head; that guy and his big mouth.

The teacher walks off, and all I see is that purple hot-air balloon of a skirt swaying as she moves.

Great hips, I notice.

Nice ass, too.

It's hypnotic, watching her sashay away from me.

For the briefest of seconds, I wonder what she would look like naked, and then I slip on my helmet and race to Gina's.

When I reach there, it's just as I feared, Gina's dressed, in that she's wearing her nightgown. I'd bet my last dollar that she's not wearing anything underneath it though.

All isn't lost yet.

"Sorry," I say, leaning forward for a kiss, but she has a slice of pizza in her hand and she turns away, her face like thunder, leaving me to close the door.

I toss my leather jacket to the floor, and rush towards her. She has her back to me, and I wrap my arms around her and pull her against me.

"What took you so long?" she asks, the displeasure in her voice cold and cutting. Taking a bite of her pizza slice, she tilts her neck, shrinking away from me as I take her skin between my teeth and suck slowly. There are no raspy sighs, no girlish giggles. Her fingers aren't making a move for my zipper.

I'm going to have to win her over. I press my hips against her and feel the tingle down below. My cock springs back to life again.

"I was late because I had an accident."

She spins around, surprising me with the look of worry in her eyes. "What happened?" She quickly scans me up and down. "You don't look hurt." Her eyes narrow with disbelief as if she thinks I'm lying.

"I crashed into this woman who stalled her goddamn car at the light."

"Oh, baby," Gina coos, popping the last bite of pizza into her mouth. "In that case, I forgive you."

I smile as she pulls down my zipper. "I tried to get here as fast as I could. And I've shaved, see." I proudly run a hand over my face.

Her fingers skate across my smooth skin. "Sex-Crazy Max," she purrs approvingly. She says she doesn't like the feel of stubble across her thighs when my face is buried in her pussy, so I'm glad I had the foresight to shave this morning.

One less thing for her to be mad at me about.

Her fingers delve into my boxer briefs and I let out a groan.

I pull open her nightgown, and just as I guessed, she's completely naked underneath. Her breasts are already pebbled, and I put my mouth to one while slipping my hand between her legs. She's wet, and I'm in heaven again.

I lift her up easily, and her nightgown slides off as she wraps her legs around me. With my mouth still sucking her breast, I walk over to her bedroom and lay her down on the bed. We're not going to leave this place for the entire weekend, except to use the bathroom and refuel.

My blood races south, and my erection mushrooms. Gina's eyes glaze over as she lies back and watches me undress. Seeing her completely naked, with that huge smile on her face, puts me at ease and plants an equally huge smile on my face.

I walk towards her and she's already opening a condom, getting ready to slip it on me, but my mind suddenly slips elsewhere. I'm thinking about Trinity's breasts, and how much bigger they are than Gina's.

Crap.

Thinking of that annoying schoolteacher bugs the hell out of me.

But then Gina slips the condom over me, and I'm back here with her again.

My lips claim her mouth, and I thrust in slowly.

CHAPTER SIX

TRINITY

'I can give you a bigger thrill.'

What a thing to say.

Who does he think he is?

I turn on my heels and rush away, desperate to get away from Motorcycle Guy.

That man has an ego the size of the Titanic, and any woman stupid enough to get involved with him is asking for trouble.

Just say the word.

I can't seem to drown out his voice, or his words. Or the way his eyes bore into mine.

I hate to admit this but that bike ride was something else. Erotic, almost.

Not to him, most definitely not for him, but I feel weird now that my feet are on solid ground again. My legs feel a little weak.

I fan my face again as I step into the vet's clinic.

At least he got me here just in time because they're starting to close for the day. I settle the bill quickly and coo over Benji.

"Hey, boy. Heeeeyyy." I fuss over him as I take him out of the crate and give him a loving cuddle.

He's slightly frosty at first, but after lots of hugs and sweet murmurings, he snuggles up to me.

I order an Uber to take us home, and when we get back, I sit on the couch with Benji on my lap and play with him, tickling his stomach and apologizing for leaving him at the vet's all day. "Mommy has to make sure you're okay," I say in a baby voice.

I briefly consider missing today's class especially after all the drama, but Christina will be expecting me, and we always go out for dinner afterwards. This evening I'm in need of good female company.

When Benji is suitably appeased, I freshen up, grab my crochet basket and hop into an Uber to the crochet class. I hope that Motorcycle Guy can fix my car quickly because I hate spending money on Ubers.

Why I like my crochet class, and the reason I teach art to adults, is because after spending the whole day with small kids, it's nice to be around adults.

The crochet class is exactly what I need. It's informal, and unstructured, and everyone sits around at leisure, knitting or crocheting, and talking. I wasn't too eager to join at first, but Christina made me go with her, and it's worked out to be a blessing. Everyone is nice and friendly, and we laugh and talk a lot.

The teacher walks around offering help, but this isn't so much a taught class as it is an excuse for a bunch of us—all women, except for one man—to get together and collectively do what we could quite easily do in the comfort of our own homes.

I'm crocheting a blanket using the waffle stitch, where I crochet little squares and then stitch them together. I've been making it up as I go along, and the blanket is about forty inches by twenty. I want it double that in size.

For me, it's a chance to meet with Christina. We've known one another our whole lives. She's like my anchor, and I'm hers. We tell each other everything—our work dramas and issues, our boyfriend problems, and everything else. She's like me, in that she's also saving herself until she gets married. It helps to have a friend who has the same stance because we can then share how we deal with guys who want sex.

We have plenty of stories to tell.

During the class, I tell her the latest about Ed and his mattress saga. She says it's like a serial without a cliffhanger —me and Ed Moorcroft. Then I tell her about the guy who crashed into my car. Later, when we're sitting in a Spanish restaurant sharing a tapas platter, she wants to know the details.

"He crashed into you, and then got angry with you?" Christina asks.

"Yes, but we'd stopped at the lights so we were stationary. My car stalled when the lights changed, and he crashed into the back of me, but it wasn't at a high speed or anything. He wasn't hurt, and neither was I." What had annoyed me the most was that he'd tried to make out that it was my fault.

"I don't understand why you didn't go through your insurance and get it fixed from a reputable place."

"He doesn't have insurance."

Christina's eyes look as if they're going to pop out of her

head. "He doesn't have insurance? How can he not have insurance?"

"Well, he doesn't."

"Then how can you even trust him, Trin?" Christina asks. I know she's right. "Do you trust him to fix your car and do a good job?"

"I saw the garage," I reply, feeling defensive. It seemed to make sense at the time, but telling Christina and seeing her reaction, I'm starting to think that I made a mistake. "It looks reputable," I say, trying hard to make it sound as if everything's going to be fine, making myself believe that Max is a trustworthy guy when the facts tell me he's anything but that.

I stab a prawn with my fork and lift it to my mouth. "He *seems* like a genuine guy. I met his friend."

"And that means what?"

Who am I kidding? Max didn't seem like a genuine guy. He blamed me for the accident and then he told me he wasn't insured.

What kind of idiot am I?

"Your parents won't be happy, Trin. You know how protective they are of you."

"My parents don't need to know." Trust Christina to be the voice of all reason. If I were in her shoes, I'd say the same.

I lost my head a little, I can see that. It's hard to swallow my food, as I realize that the cocky mechanic might have played me like a fool. Maybe I got carried away by his likeness to my favorite movie star; the only guy I regularly fantasize about.

"I don't understand why you're making such a big deal about it," I say, in an attempt to normalize the craziness.

"Because it's not like you," my friend insists. "You always go by the book."

"He didn't have insurance. What was I supposed to do?"

"Again, that's not your problem. Why do you care?"

"I didn't want to get him in more trouble," I say, suddenly growing tired of this conversation.

Christina puts down her glass of wine. "He was cute, wasn't he?"

I dip my bread into the prawny garlic oil and take a bite. Christina's waiting for my answer with an expectant look on her face. I shake my head and lie. "He wasn't cute, not really."

Well, maybe just a little.

He had *something*.

"He's not the type of guy I'd notice," I insist when Christina looks at me as if she doesn't believe me. I said that because a guy like Max is so different than someone like me. A guy like him would never notice someone like me.

"What did he look like?" Christina probes.

The muscles in my jaw tighten because I don't want to talk about Max anymore and I especially don't want to tell her about his likeness to Thor.

It took me until halfway into the crochet class to get over the reaction I'd had from sitting behind him and hugging him during the motorcycle ride and now Christina's asking me about him again.

I shrug. "He was so-so. He was wearing a helmet most of the time."

"Oh, boy." Christina laughs, as if she's not buying my lame reply. She licks her fingers before wiping them on a napkin. "You've told me everything about Ed, right down to his hunt for a memory foam mattress, but you haven't said much about the guy who crashed into you and then gave you a ride to the vet's. I know you, Trinity Weldon. This guy is cute, and I don't think he wore his helmet the whole time."

Sometimes, Christina can read me so well, it unnerves me. "He was rude is what he was."

"That's normal, of course he's going to try to pin the blame on you," she says, dismissing my remark, "but what did he look like?"

I picture him again. "He had blondish hair. Slightly long, not a buzz cut or anything."

"Eyes?"

"Brown."

"Body?"

"I don't know."

"He gave you a bike ride over to the vet, you sat behind him and you don't know?"

"He was average."

"Average? Like Ed Moorcroft average?"

God, no. Max is nothing like Ed Moorcroft.

Nothing at all.

I can't tell Christina how it felt to be riding with Max because she will judge me. I can't tell her, because I still don't understand it myself, how I suddenly found myself so turned on by a man I've just met, a man I barely know.

"Ed asked if I wanted to go out to dinner sometime."

Christina's eyes grow big. "He asked you out?"

"He asked me to dinner."

"I think you can safely say he asked you out on a date."

I wince. "Not exactly. He said we should go out for a pizza sometime." It's hard to tell with Ed because he waffles so much, and he's vague at the best of times. If I did go to dinner with him, and if it was a date, I have a feeling that we wouldn't move forward too fast. Which is fine, because I'm not going to have sex before marriage, and Ed is the same.

There will be no nasty surprises which I've had on a few occasions when the guy I've dated hasn't shared my point of view.

The thought about a date with Ed suddenly makes me uneasy because after months of talking to him, I've never felt anything like how I did after exchanging a few angry words with Max.

That guy has managed to crawl under my skin and root himself beneath the surface. I hope this is a passing moment of craziness and once he's fixed my car, I can wash him right out of my system.

"What did you say?"

"Huh?" My head is full of Max and I've completely zoned out of the conversation.

"What did you say when Ed asked you out?"

"He didn't ask me out. It's just pizza. We could go where we went for the crochet class Christmas party. You could come along," I say, instantly warming to the idea. What better way to emphasize to Ed that it's not a date than by having Christina come with me?

"And be a third wheel?" Christina huffs.

"It's not a date."

"We'll see about that."

Christina's still harping on about Ed but my thoughts are firmly wrapped around the Motorcycle Guy.

I don't know how he managed to do that. How he managed to crash into my car and convince me to let him fix the damage.

I seem to have lost my senses.

CHAPTER SEVEN

MAX

I've barely slept this weekend.

Gina's apartment looks like a bomb hit it; there are clothes lying on the floor, empty pizza boxes, wine bottles and glasses everywhere.

We had sex in every single room, in every possible way. That's what happens when a sex-addict and a nymphomaniac get together. Things get crazy.

But it's Monday morning now, and time to get back to reality. Gina doesn't have to return to her base until later, but I need to hit the garage extra early today. After another night of not sleeping much, I'm surprisingly alert.

"Why do you have to leave so early?" Gina asks, lying on the bed, doing her best to entice me to stay.

"I have stuff to do," I tell her. "I don't want to piss Enzo off." I'm sitting on the bed with my back turned to her as I pull my T-shirt down over my head.

She touches the scars on my back gingerly.

Stupid dares. This is what I tell all the women who ask. They always wince and look as if they can feel my pain. Sometimes I tell them that the wounds were inflicted in some sort of bizarre initiation ceremony when I was a teen and got in with the wrong crowd.

Some women assume I got them in combat, and I let them believe that, even though I've never enlisted.

They run their fingers over them, and some of them even press their lips to them. They think I wear these scars with pride, like war wounds.

I don't.

Because that's not what they are.

She slides off the bed. "Can't I tempt you to stay a little longer?" She stands directly in front of me. I'm putting my boots on, and when I look up, my eyes are level with her pussy.

I lick my lower lip. Even though we've fucked twice already this morning, I can't say no when it's offered to me on a plate.

Temptation rears its beautiful head, but I stand up quickly before my cock gets other ideas.

"Do you ever stop tempting me?" I kiss her on the mouth. Her hand slips south and her fingers start to tease me again, but I push it away. "I gotta fix a car, and I need to get it done before Enzo shows up."

"You're going to love me and leave me?" she adopts a poor-me tone and pouts as I gaze at her lips longingly.

Love?

I won't ever tire of this woman, but what we have isn't love. It's lust.

I feel as if I need to point this out and remind her, because we both know that this is all it is. But sometimes

Gina forgets. Or maybe I'm making too much of her statement.

I decide not to say anything because it's too early in the morning to discuss the fine print of our relationship.

"Let me know when you're next in town," I say, walking away.

She blows me a kiss in return.

I need to get the schoolteacher's car fixed as soon as possible. Enzo doesn't like it when we work on friends' cars using his garage space, tools and our labor.

The schoolteacher isn't a friend, but I owe her a favor, and I don't want to incur Enzo's wrath for taking up space that a legitimate client would. Plus, I'm the one who's going to have to fork out money for the repairs, and I know Enzo double-checks the paperwork for this type of work. I'll still have to pay for the materials I use, albeit at a discounted rate, and the labor will be free because I'll be fixing the car.

Al is already at the garage by the time I get there. He said he'd help me, even though this is an easy enough job to get done. I appreciate his help, though I suspect he wants to know about my weekend with Hot Gina as much as he wants to help.

Sure enough, as soon as we greet each other, he asks how my weekend went. I tell him over our morning cup of coffee, but I don't tell him every little thing. I'm not that shallow, but the morsels I throw him are enough to make his eyes glaze over.

"Does she have a friend?" he asks, like he always does.

"No one with her range of skills."

"If she ever gets bored with you, make sure you tell her about me." He thumps his chest like he's taking a solemn vow. He makes a play of this.

I grin. "Sure, dude." I can't see Gina getting bored of me. We've been friends-with-benefits for years, and what we have works for both of us because I don't see her much. She doesn't live here all year round, and only comes home occasionally. Also, she isn't fazed by the fact that I don't keep in touch with her when she's away. She doesn't expect phone calls, or gifts, or texts, or emails. All she expects is forty-eight hours or more of sex, and I fulfill that function easily.

"And what about Sammy?" I ask, playing along with Al. "How are you going to break it to her?"

That's when his ruse backfires. A smile spreads over his face. "You got me!"

He's not interested in Hot Gina's friends, even if I knew them. Al would run like his butt was on fire if Hot Gina or anyone like her came for him.

He's happy with Sammy.

The rest of it, my adventures, are pure fantasy that he likes to hear about, nothing else.

It's perfect for me. Not so much for a normal guy like Al who's in love with his girlfriend.

Gina and I are in lust, not love.

I don't need a girlfriend. I don't want some needy woman hanging around me, wanting me to do nice things for her, asking me to tell her constantly that I love her. I'm not sure I know what love is. My mom gave me away at the age of four. She tricked me. She left me sitting on some steps and told me she'd be back, but I never saw her again.

It's always made me wonder why. Was I not good enough? Did she not love me?

I was adopted by a wonderful couple who gave me a good life and a solid upbringing, and made everything good again. But then my adoptive mom died when I was a teenager, and I felt abandoned again. It wasn't her fault, but

I loved her. She was the rock I clung onto, fashioned from the memories of my birth mother, but she loved me deeply. And I her.

Somehow, my dad and I got through that dark time, but deep down I've always been wary of love, and what it means.

It means jack.

I connect with people through sex.

Lots of sex.

It's why I have friends-with-benefits in and around Chicago, even though Hot Gina is the main one. But she only comes home every few months and we hook up for a crazy weekend.

"Come on, help me out," I say to Al as I set down my coffee cup and walk over to the car. I examine the dent. It's big, and it's not going to be as simple as I first thought. Then there's the bumper to fix too. I mentally calculate the costs.

Shit.

I don't have enough to pay for this repair upfront. "Can you loan me some money?" I ask Al.

He pulls out his wallet. "How much do you need? I have a tenner."

That's not going to do it. I'll worry about the payment later. My first priority is getting this thing fixed and out of Enzo's garage before I piss him off too much.

CHAPTER EIGHT

TRINITY

"**I**'ve fixed your car."

I'm expecting a greeting. At first the words don't make sense, but the voice is familiar. *Annoying,* in some way.

And then I remember.

It's Motorcycle Guy. A rush of excitement flows through me "Oh," I manage to say, then, "Already? That was fast." It's Monday lunchtime and I feel strangely humbled that he worked on it during his weekend.

I look up to see Ed walking into my classroom. Seeing that I'm on a call, he raises his hand in an apologetic gesture and leaves.

The mechanic laughs. "I fixed it on my own time but it's ready for you, and as good as new, well, as good as I can make it. Pick it up when you want."

"I'll come over once school finishes."

"Cool."

He hangs up just as I was about to thank him because I am surprised by the speed of the repairs. He must have worked all weekend to get it fixed so fast.

When school ends, I rush out, eager to get to the garage, but in my haste, I bump into Ed.

"Going home so early?" he asks, as if it's a cardinal sin. "Your art class isn't until later." His comment immediately gets my back up. "You know my schedule by heart, Ed. Did you want something?"

"I was going to ask you how your picnic with the artists went."

"It was good." It's a vague answer as we stand in the hallway. Ed would have been in my classroom now and we'd be sharing our weekend highlights, instead, I sense that he's wondering why I'm in a rush, and where I'm going. His need to know bothers me.

"What did you do? Did it take up your whole day?"

"I can't stay and chat right now, Ed. I have to pick up my car from the garage."

"Your car? Why, what's wrong with it?" He looks at me expectantly.

"Some guy ran into the back of it on Friday."

His features show instant concern. "No! Really? Why didn't you tell me?"

"I'm telling you now."

"Are you all right?"

"Clearly." I hold out my hands and shrug to indicate that all of me is fine.

"Who was it?"

"Some guy on a bike," I say slowly. I can't figure out if I'm desperate to get away from Ed, or eager to see Max. "I should go. I'm lost without my car." I start to move away.

"I can give you a lift," Ed offers.

"Aw... there's no need, but thanks."

"How will you get there?"

"I was going to take a bus."

"A bus? There's no need. I'll take you." He irritates me more and more by the minute, but as soon as I have that thought, I feel guilty. Ed's a nice guy. A *sweet* guy, and I've never thought of him as being annoying before. Something seems to have happened to me ever since I met Motorcycle Guy. Excitement swirls inside me at the thought of seeing him again. I push the thought away and flash a smile at Ed. "That would be a big help, thanks."

We talk about the weekend as he drives. I tell him about the picnic and how nice it was and he updates me on his mattress saga. I discover that he visited a couple of stores and checked the memory foam mattresses as per my recommendation.

"Did you find one?"

He shakes his head, his eyes on the road in front as he proceeds to tell me about all the mattresses he looked at and what he thought of them.

For some unexpected reason, I find myself glancing at his hands on the steering wheel, and imagine myself sitting behind him on a motorbike. My body doesn't get anywhere near as excited at the prospect. Naturally, my thoughts drift to Max and a fluttery sensation floats inside me in anticipation of seeing him again.

Soon enough, Ed pulls up in the parking lot of the garage, and I catch a glimpse of Max's back. He's in his coveralls. I suck in a breath. My nerve endings are doing a version of the Mexican wave, and a ripple of excitement fans out from my core.

I can't drag my gaze away from him. "Thanks for the ride," I say, forcing myself to turn to Ed. "See you tomorrow." I'm eager to get out of the car and equally as anxious for him to drive away.

"I'll come along," he volunteers, turning the engine off. "I'd hate for these guys to con you into paying more than it's worth."

He can't be serious. "Nonsense," I say, in an attempt to dissuade him. I dislike him treating me like a little woman, as if I'm incapable of dealing with repairs to my car and, more than that, I'm not particularly eager for Ed and Max to meet.

I want to meet Max alone, not have Ed hover over me like I'm a schoolkid he has to chaperone to the bathroom on a school trip. But before I can make my objections known, he's out of the car and standing with his hands in his pockets, waiting for me to get out. I do, slowly, my stomach churning.

"There's your car," Ed says. It's parked up in front, and he starts to walk towards it. I see Max turn to him with a nod of his chin and I rush to catch up with Ed so that I'm by his side. Max glances at me. I see something like surprise when his gaze flits between me and Ed.

He greets us with a "Hey," then, "Let me show you what I've done." It's difficult for me not to stare at his back as Ed and I follow him to my car. I can already feel it happening, the heat creeping along my neck and face. I wipe my hand across it in an effort to get a grip.

"There you go. All fixed." Max steps out of the way and reveals a dent-free shiny-as-new car. It's been polished to make it look so much better than it is.

I examine the bumper, and then run my hands over the place where the dent was. It's hard to imagine that this was all mangled and knocked in a few days ago.

I don't know what he did, but it's impossible to tell that this was so badly damaged before.

"It's perfect," I say. It's impossible to disguise the admiration in my voice. "You did a great job. Thank you."

"Told you I'd fix it as good as new."

"And the problem with it stalling?" I ask, cheekily.

Max wipes his hands on a cloth and shrugs. "I had a look, and I think it could be a problem with the alternator or fuel-flow issue, wear and tear and all that. You'd be better off getting another car, to be honest. If you replace the faulty part, or try to get it fixed it's going to cost you as much—"

"Why don't you take another look at the problem?" Ed asks, interrupting rudely.

"I fixed what I needed to," Max replies calmly, but his face is hard. It's easy to see that he doesn't like Ed's comment.

"But if the car's here, you should have at least taken a good look?"

"No, Ed. It's not a problem," I put my hand on Ed's arm. "It's fine."

When Max's eyes sweep to my hand on Ed's arm, I move my hand away. The corners of his lips turn up. It's subtle, but enough that I can tell. He finds something amusing in all this.

"It's not fine," Ed interjects. I hate the way he's suddenly turned into He-Man, thinking he has to defend me and take control over my car getting fixed.

"It was only the bumper and the dent in the trunk that I was worried about," I grind out slowly. "It's fixed now. Max is right, I do need to get another car."

"I just don't want them charging you for another visit when you have to bring it in again."

"I don't think you understand, Ed. The other problem has nothing to do with the accident damage." I try not to hiss. "Why don't you go, and I'll settle up here?"

"Hey, Trinity!" Al appears, instantly clearing up the tension that has been brewing. Max leans against a pillar with his arms folded and one foot crossed over the other. He looks relaxed, as if he's enjoying watching us. "See what a great job we did on the car?" Al asks me.

I had no idea that he had helped out. "You worked on it, too?"

Al smiles in acknowledgment. "Two mechanics are always better than one."

"Thank you. I hope I didn't mess up your weekend too much."

"We didn't come here over the weekend," Al replies, grinning. "Max was too busy doing something else this weekend."

He grins at his friend like a naughty seven-year-old but Max's hard expression remains.

"He didn't even want to meet Cardoza," Al remarks.

"You met Cardoza? Elias Cardoza?" Ed asks, suddenly excited.

"Yeah, how many Cardozas do you think there are?" Al asks.

Ed's expression lights up. "Where?"

"At Waquito's. Wasn't open to everyone. My girlfriend knew the owners, and they were celebrating ten years in business. Cardoza used to work there. He actually showed up."

"Awesome." Ed squeals like a cheerleader. "What's he like?"

"Cool. The dude is super cool. I got a picture with him, and an autograph."

"Sick," says Ed with glee. I suddenly see a new, highly excitable side to him. "Did you see the fight back in the summer?"

"Couldn't miss it," Al grins. "Was a great fight, wasn't it?"

"Sure was."

"The guy has done us proud."

Al takes a step towards Ed and the two of them bond over Chicago's New Hope; the boxer Elias Cardoza who had a big fight a few months ago.

"Eli Cardoza made history. I reckon most of Chicago must have seen that fight, everyone except for this dude." Al throws a pitiful glance at Max.

"You didn't see the fight?" Ed asks Max.

"I watched the last few rounds," Max replies, pushing off the pillar.

"You missed a great fight," Ed tells him.

"I saw some of it," Max replies, defensively.

"The guy is always *busy*," Al comments, not without a mischievous grin.

"Too busy to watch the Cardoza-Garrison fight?" Ed asks in amazement.

"He was busy then and he was busy now," Al says, then turns to Ed and continues the conversation.

I'm still trying to figure out what Al meant by *busy*. The emphasis on the word gives me a hint as to what Max might have been up to, and I'm suddenly pricked by a needle of jealousy which is completely out of character for me.

Max turns to me. "Need you to sign off some paperwork." He starts to walk away, and I follow, leaving Ed and Al talking about their boxing legend.

"Don't worry about Ed," I say, as Max hands me a form on a clipboard.

"I'm not." He leans against the wall, his hands behind his back, looking a little submissive. It's a pose that seems to be at complete contrast to who he is. He looks at me again, pinning me with his gaze. I try to turn away, and find that I can't, and yet staring at him does peculiar things to me. I force myself to look away and stare down the length of his body instead. When my eyes return to his face, he's smiling. I realize he thinks I'm checking him out.

I quickly turn my attention to the paperwork, and read it as best as I can, which isn't easy because I find it impossible to concentrate whenever this guy's watching me.

"Is that your boyfriend?" he asks, casually.

My cheeks grow hot. "No. He's just a friend."

"He seems pretty concerned about you."

"He's just a friend." I steal a glance at him.

Max nods, but his lips are still curved up at the edges. My heart starts hammering again, the way it does each time he looks at me. I hate that he has this effect on me because I don't understand it. Nobody has ever made me feel uneasy, or self-conscious the way he does. Working with children might be a reason why I'm not used to it, but even so, this is new to me.

I'm determined to conquer it though, whatever *it* is, and so, feeling brave, and because he was nosy in asking me about Ed, I ask him, "What were you busy doing this weekend?"

A part of me already knows that Max was busy with a woman. Ordinarily, I wouldn't ask such a thing, especially of a total stranger, which is what Max is, but I can't think straight or behave like my usual self when I'm around him.

"I was ... busy," he replies, the uncertainty in his words is the only indication that he's surprised by my question. When he doesn't elaborate further, I nod because he's already told me without realizing it. He was with his girlfriend.

Lucky girl.

The thought makes me slightly jealous, which is insane.

As if I care.

I swallow, then take another look at the paperwork, and that's when I see it. "One hundred and thirty-seven dollars and forty five cents?" I bellow, shooting daggers at him. The cost is less than I estimated but that's not the problem. The issue I have is that I wasn't supposed to pay for this repair.

He was.

We agreed it.

"About that," he says, moving to my side. "Uh... I'm real sorry about this, but I gotta ask you for another favor. Is there any chance you could pay for this, and I promise to pay you back as soon—"

"You have got to be kidding me," I exclaim. He looks guilty, and scratches the back of his neck; I see the firm outline of his bicep and my heart sinks because he's taken me for a fool.

"It stinks. I know it stinks. I'm only asking you as a favor."

"I've already done you a favor!"

"I know. That's why it stinks."

"You were supposed to pay for this," I shoot back. "We had a deal."

I start to fill with rage and all he can do is stand and scratch the back of his neck. Christina will decimate me when she finds out, which means I can never tell her.

And Ed? I glance over my shoulder, knowing I can't bring this up in front of him otherwise he'll probably go all Rambo on Max.

"It's a shitty thing of me to ask, I know." Max lowers his

voice to a whisper, before taking a step towards me. He dips his head closer to me and I'm caught up again in that thing he does, when he spins a bubble around me and traps me in it. My inexperience with men puts me at a huge disadvantage with a guy like him. I feel as if I'm in a snake pit just because he's standing so close. Rage and indignation intermingle with something hot that spirals from my belly upwards.

I don't know what to do.

"What's going on?"

I look up to see a man who I presume is Max's boss because he's not wearing coveralls like the other guys, and he speaks with an air of authority.

"Nothing. Just settling the bill, says Max cheerily. "This is Enzo. He owns this place," he says, introducing us, even though there is no need to. I get the impression he's done it to somehow explain why he needs me to pay up when he can't afford to. I'm not sure I entirely believe his reason.

"Happy with the repairs?" his boss asks me.

"Yes, thank you." I am, or at least, I *was*. Max has done a great job but him asking me to pay has left a sour taste in my mouth.

I nod and smile sweetly, then wait for him to leave the room.

"I didn't charge labor, just the cost of materials," he explains and for the first time, his voice has lost that smugness. He seems a little sweeter, a little less sure of himself.

"You weren't supposed to charge me *anything*," I hiss back. "We agreed. *You* collided into the back of my car. It was *your* fault. You don't even have insurance. I only agreed to what you asked as a favor."

"I'm really sorry." He sounds so un-Max-like now that

the change in personality intrigues me. I don't know this guy, and the fact that I'm beginning to know his mannerisms and moods should be a warning.

"I know this is bad, *really* bad of me to ask this of you, but I'm stuck, Trinity. Like *really* stuck."

The muscles in my neck tense. I wish I could close my ears. I wish I could put all this behind me. Every interaction I have with this guy leads me further into frustration. I should never have agreed to anything he said, but each moment I seem to go deeper and deeper into the rabbit hole.

"That isn't my problem."

"No, it's not."

"Then why are you asking me?"

"Because you seem like a nice person."

"Someone for you to take advantage of?" I ask, seething at the idea that he really does take me for a fool.

"No," he says, his brows pushing together. "You're too smart for me to take advantage of."

"So you would have, if you could?"

He makes a sound as if a laugh got stuck in his throat. "No. That's not what I meant. I can't charm you into doing anything for me."

I blink, and wonder what kinds of things he means. "You must think badly of me, and I don't blame you," he continues, "but I rushed to fix your car and I forgot that I'm really tight for money this month. I'm sorry." His voice lowers so that nobody but me can hear. "Please just do me one more favor, that's all I'm asking. It's wrong, I know, and you don't owe me a thing, but I can't pay for these repairs right now."

"I don't owe you a thing," I reiterate. I'm finding this hard to believe. I know money doesn't grow on trees, but this is ridiculous.

"He'll fire me if you don't settle," Max pleads.

"And you think I care?"

His eyes settle on mine. He does this thing when he looks directly at my eyes, and then at my lips. He's only staring, but I feel the slow burn. I feel it in my gut, and in my chest. In the place between my legs. And then I wait for his gaze to drop lower, to my chest, but, remarkably, it doesn't. His eyes snake back up to mine and stay there.

"Didn't you tell your boss that the accident was your fault and that you'd agreed to fix my car for me?" I ask.

"He's not interested in the accident or whose fault it is. He owns a business."

"And I'm supposed to take the hit for all your problems? All I did was stall the car. I can't believe I'm—"

"Ready?" Ed's voice brings me back to reality with a thud.

"Your boyfriend's back," Max whispers, without turning to look.

"He's not my boyfriend."

He raises an eyebrow. "He's acting as if he wants to be." The smugness is back in his expression.

"But he's not," I insist. I should let it go, but I can't, because Ed is suffocating me with his presence, and because I need Max to know that the guy isn't my boyfriend.

"Ready to go?" Ed asks, walking right up to us. His assumption that I'm ready to go, and his interference in something which is none of his business, have been grating on my nerves ever since we got here. Now he's parading around as if we're a couple and my anger shoots up a notch.

I try to suppress my simmering rage. "I thought you'd left."

"I was waiting for you," Ed protests.

"You don't need to wait for me, Ed. I can drive my own car back. Thanks for the ride here, though."

His expression falls a little, and he glances at Max. "If that's the way you feel, see you tomorrow." He's annoyed, but I can't deal with that right now.

I turn to Max. "So now I have to pay."

"I was hoping that Al might be able to loan me some cash, but he can't."

This is all my fault. If I'd gone through my insurance company, and not worried about Max, I wouldn't be in this mess. Christina is never going to let me forget this.

There's no point in debating this any further with Max. The guy is clearly broke. I pull out my credit card and settle the payment, snatching the card machine from him and swiping my card.

"Thanks, Trinity. I really appreciate this. I get paid in two weeks' time, and I promise to pay you back, with interest," he adds, handing me the receipt.

I have no faith in him, and I'm mad at myself for being taken for a ride. I hold out my hand. "Keys."

"Oh, sure..." He pulls them out of the pocket on his coveralls and holds them out for me.

I hate him, and I don't, and I hate that I feel both of these emotions at the same time. Snatching the keys from him, I head towards my car and get in.

He knocks on my window, expecting me to roll it down, probably wanting to say something, probably wanting to thank me again for the millionth time but I am so hacked off about what just happened, that I start the engine.

He lifts his arm and swipes his hand behind his neck. And that's when I see them; a few scars on the underside of his muscle.

Somewhere in the deep recesses of my brain, an alarm

goes off. I've seen those marks before on a few children I've taught. Thankfully, only a few. Thankfully, not Dylan.

Marks which scar forever when a cigarette is stubbed out on human flesh.

My brain insists that it can't be, but I'm pretty sure that's what it is.

Max quickly puts his arm down. I hesitate to drive off but he turns his back on me and walks away.

CHAPTER NINE

MAX

She's nice, and kind, and she doesn't owe me a thing, but that's twice she's saved my butt.

Even though she hates me for it.

I can tell, and that's hard for me to swallow, because women don't usually hate me.

Yet Trinity does. She thinks I scammed her into paying for the repairs. She thinks I'm a joke, and a liar, and a hustler.

But I'm not.

I have every intention of paying her back, and I'm certain that she thinks I won't, but she's wrong. I will pay her back as soon as I can.

But in the meantime, I've had a brainwave of an idea. I wish I'd thought of it before. I might have just found the perfect car for her.

Sometimes people get their cars fixed here and then decide that they would rather get a new one. Sometimes they ask Enzo to take it off their hands, and if he thinks he can sell it for a good price with a minimal cost of repairs, he'll buy it from them. But he'll only sell it onto people he knows, like family and friends, or he'll ask if we know any family or friends who might be looking for a decent car at a decent price.

Enzo says he doesn't want the headache of people coming back to him with something going wrong afterwards because he offers no warranties or post-sale support. It's a little side hustle for the garage, and sometimes, we get a good car at a good price.

We've had a couple of cars here in the back for a few weeks now, and both are better than the deathtrap Trinity currently drives. One of them is a really good car, but Enzo has decided to buy it for his daughter. I call Trinity to tell her about the other one.

"Hey," I say, grateful to hear the sound of her voice. I half-expected that she wouldn't answer knowing it was me.

"Yes?" she asks, clearly wondering why I've called.

"I found a car for you."

"I'm not looking for one."

"But I found one and it's a really good deal. It's in prime condition and not as old as the one you have."

"I don't need a new car," she retorts, "Just the payment that you owe me."

She clearly seems to enjoy busting my balls. "I get paid next week and I'm going to pay you back." I've also been doing a lot of overtime lately in an attempt to make up the extra money I need.

"I'll believe it when it happens."

I'm affronted by her remark. "You don't trust me?"

"Should I?"

"Clearly you have so far."

"I'm just a nice person," she replies. "A nice and gullible person." She sounds frosty today.

"What about the car? It's a really good deal," I tell her. "Why don't you at least come and take a look?" I pause to gauge how she's taking this. There's silence, which means she's at least paying attention. "There was another car, but my boss bought it. This one is really good, too. You should come see it before someone else buys it."

"Like I said, I don't need a new car."

"You can't be driving a car that keeps stalling," I insist. "And getting it fixed isn't worth it."

"Thank you for your concern, but I'd be most appreciative if you would reimburse me. That's more important to me than a new car I don't need."

Her stubbornness annoys me as much as my insistence for her to change cars probably annoys her. But, whether she wants to own up to it or not, she does need a new car, and this one I've got my eye on is going to be a heck of a lot safer to drive than the heap of crap she's currently got. But it's obvious she doesn't want to listen to me.

Screw her.

"You know what's best for you," I say, trying not to sound too angry. I'm only trying to help her out, but she's obviously not interested.

I hang up and decide to let the matter rest.

I wipe a greasy hand across my forehead when Al walks in. "Did you hear?"

"Hear what?" I reply, feeling grumpy.

"It's all over the papers. Cardoza and Garrison. Their managers are talking about a date for the rematch."

"Yeah?" I try to sound enthusiastic.

"He hinted at it when I saw him," says Al, walking in

proudly with a newspaper. He opens it up on one of the worktops.

"You and him are best buddies now all of a sudden, huh?" I ask, walking over to him.

"We talked. He's a normal guy."

"I expect him to be a normal guy. He's not a god."

"Arrgh," Al dismisses me in disgust. "You don't understand what a legend this guy is."

"I get it," I say, looking over Al's shoulder. There's a huge spread on the back page showing Cardoza with his arms up and holding the title belt over his head. "That's from that fight with Garrison," Al explains. "And this," he shuffles back towards the start of the newspaper, "this is me with him!" He jabs the photo in excitement. Sure enough, there's a picture of the boxer with some people and Al.

"Where's Sammy?" I ask him. "Didn't she go with you that night?"

"She was there somewhere."

I peer down and take a good look. "Nice picture."

"I have lots of us from the night," he says, reaching for his cell phone.

"You've already shown me," I remind him and hold out my hand out as if to stop him. "When's the rematch?"

"Soon, I hope. They're still trying to agree on a date, apparently. These promoters like to put on a show."

"Maybe I'll watch it this time around."

"Unless it's a Hot Gina weekend," Al chuckles.

I doubt that. Hot Gina weekends don't seem to have that pull for me, lately.

"Garrison's being a big prick though, and keeps ribbing Eli about his past, you know, that stuff about him being abused as a kid."

I exhale slowly. I remember when that story broke, a

few days after the win. The city of Chicago had some sort of city-wide party for Cardoza. He was welcomed back as if he was a king, and he might as well have been because we don't have many heroes in this city, and Cardoza was a big deal then.

He still is.

I remember hearing the news about his abuse; it broke suddenly, but then also died down as quickly. I was glad. A person's past can make or break him.

Seems to me that Cardoza is a champion not only because he won the heavyweight and other boxing titles that night, but because he rose up and conquered the demons of his past even when they were aired so publicly.

He was at Grampton House, just like me.

I'd read how someone at the children's home messed around with him when he was a kid there, and from that moment on, I've always kept an eye on Cardoza.

I was only there for a few months before I got adopted, and I'm certain that Grampton House was a safe haven for me. Even though I don't have much recollection of my time there, I don't recall anything like that happening to me.

All I remember is playing with kids. I remember the lime green paint on the walls most of all.

I've never told Al that I was at that place, even though I'm sure I mentioned to him years ago that I was adopted. He doesn't need to know that I was also at Grampton House, and he doesn't need to know about my past. No one does, but my gut twists whenever I think about Cardoza.

I admired him, and more so when I'd had a chance to watch the highlights of his big fight. And that news getting out around that time must have been a huge blow for him; it's not the kind of publicity a world heavyweight champion needs, but he seems to have weathered that storm well.

We all have scars of some sort, but he's had to have his examined in the public eye.

That's a new level of superhero right there.

I have scars. They're on my arms and chest and back, but my monsters weren't at Grampton House.

Not all of us have happy beginnings, but the really unlucky ones don't even have happy endings.

I'm still trying to write mine, but Cardoza? He's written it. *Rewritten* it, with fresh new words that mean something.

I'm happy for the guy.

"Coming for a few beers?" Al asks.

I shake my head.

"You doing more overtime?"

"Maybe."

"Come for a couple," Al insists.

I'm no longer in the mood for beers, and I'm not really in the mood for doing any overtime now. Any recollection of my past always dims my mood.

"Lock up then," Al says, waving as he leaves. Enzo has already left for the day, and I sit on a stool feeling suddenly alone.

I wish Hot Gina was coming back this weekend. She understands me more than anyone, and she's my safe harbor; my feel-good place. But she's not around, and she probably won't get leave for another few months.

I look through my notebook at my list of friends-with-benefits. I need a pick-me-up. I need to *feel* something. I reach for my phone and start making calls.

CHAPTER TEN

MAX

It's payday at last.

I have the money I owe that teacher, and on Friday I knock off a little early and go to her school. Luckily for me, Al knew where she worked.

I get there right on time because kids and parents are walking out of the school as I walk in. I ask someone where Miss Weldon's classroom is and follow their instructions.

I'm about to knock on the already-open door, when I see her talking to a kid. So I hold back and wait. Her classroom is all bright colors. Red, yellow and orange, and there are higgledy-piggledy paintings of trees, and houses, and families—at least that's what I assume the stick people and those rectangles and squares are.

She's crouching on the floor, her eyes level with the kid's and it looks as if she's trying to comfort him.

A burst of warmth explodes in my chest. Trinity has a motherly way about her; as if she's been bubble-wrapped in an aura of nice and kindness. I guess that's why she let me talk her into doing what was right for me, that day when I crashed into her and told her I had no insurance.

I doubt that there's a single selfish bone in her body.

I feel like a douchebag when I recall how angry I was when I crashed into her, and now I get why she's so mad that I made her pay.

"Off you go, Dylan," she says, standing slowly. The kid walks away from her, with an apple in his hand.

"Hey," I say, when he walks past me. He looks at me warily, and I notice the holes in his sweater. His eyes look haggard, like those of a fifty-year-old man who has seen better days. The kid looks at me as if he doesn't trust me, so I smile, but step away, letting him pass easily through the door.

"Cool haircut," I say, nodding my head. There wasn't anything else I could find to compliment him on because his shoes are scuffed and his clothes look dirty.

His lips lift a tiny bit, and he glances over his shoulder at his teacher who's watching him. "Bye, miss," he says suddenly, then scoots off.

Trinity's brows push together as I walk towards her with the wad of money rolled up in a brown envelope in my hand.

"The money I owe you," I say, handing it over.

She stares at it, then looks at me. I think she wasn't expecting to see me, and definitely wasn't expecting this.

"Take it," I insist, and she does, gingerly. "You can count it if you want." I turn my back to her and walk around the classroom admiring the artwork on the walls.

I glance over and see that she's counting the money. This makes me smile. I give her a few moments, then ask, "Was that right?"

"It's all there. Thank you."

"Thank you." I walk towards her. "Tell me the truth."

"The truth?"

"You weren't expecting me to pay up, were you?"

"You want the truth?" she asks, putting the money into her handbag.

I nod.

"I didn't expect to ever see you again, and I certainly didn't expect to ever see the money."

"So I proved you wrong?" I ask, as something pinches my insides. She thinks I'm a hustler, and she doesn't mind letting me know. She's a goody two-shoes, a boring, frigid, stuffy schoolteacher, and she thinks I'm nothing but a cheating mechanic. I can see why she would think that because it's not as if I've given her reason to think better of me.

"Clearly."

"Looks can be deceiving." When she doesn't answer, I say, "I'm not a bad guy, Trinity. I wasn't about to cheat you out of your money. I'm honest if nothing else."

"Clearly I was wrong. Thank you for this."

"Did you tell your boyfriend that you had to fork out the money for the repairs?"

"He's not my boyfriend, and I didn't tell him that you asked me to pay. My friends already think I messed up by letting you convince me not to go through my insurance company in the first place."

"Your friends?" It amuses me that she's been talking to her friends about me. "You've been talking about *us* to your friends?"

She throws me a look of annoyance. Ignoring my comment, she says, "Thanks for coming by and settling up." She opens up what looks like a kid's workbook and holds her red pen in her hand before giving me a what-else-can-I-do-for-you look. She obviously wants me to leave, and yet I'm so enjoying being here.

I definitely didn't come all this way just to leave after a few moments.

A knock at the door catches both our attention. It's that idiot who came with her to the garage. I turn back to her, my eyes narrowing as I try to figure out who he is to her.

"Does he always follow you around?" I ask her, lowering my voice. She's adamant that he's not her boyfriend, but I reckon this dude has other ideas.

She doesn't reply, but she also doesn't look too happy.

"Hey," the dude says, walking in with his hands in his pockets. "What a surprise to see you." This is directed at me and I'm not sure how I'm supposed to answer that so I let Trinity do it.

"Max was just passing by," she says.

"Passing by?" the dude asks me. We're both standing up at the other side of Trinity's desk.

"Yeah." I want to tell him to fuck off and get lost, but I miraculously manage not to.

"He says he's got a car at the garage that might be suitable for me," Trinity tells him. Seems to me that she doesn't want to tell him the real reason I'm here.

Ed looks to me for an explanation, but I stare blankly back.

"We could go check it out," he offers.

"Ed, I'm quite capable of checking out and determining whether a car is right for me or not." I see the look on Trinity's face and it's obvious that she finds him as irritating as I do.

I cough lightly. "And of course, I'm an expert on these things, so I can definitely guide her in that respect."

The guy winces, as if someone grabbed him by the balls and didn't let go. "Don't take this the wrong way, but you'd try to sell her anything."

How the hell am I not supposed to take that the wrong way? I turn to Trinity. "I apologize in advance that we're talking about you as if you're not here." Then I turn back to the idiot. "I don't need to sell Trinity anything. She's sensible enough to make up her own mind, and I'm pretty sure she knows what she wants, right?" I glance at her.

She remains tight-lipped. It's nice to see that I'm not the only one hating on this dude for walking in. "I'm not a salesman, dude. I'm a mechanic and my job isn't to make a buck on the car, since I'm not in the business of selling cars."

"Then why are you selling her this one?"

"Ed!" The scraping sound of the chair legs on the wooden floor pierces the air. "This has nothing to do with you."

"I'm only trying to help, Trinity." His voice has a hard edge to it.

"I'm capable of finding the right car for myself."

"I was only offering to look it over with you, but I see you've got that part covered," he says to Trinity before shooting me a look of pure loathing. Then he leaves.

"I've pissed your boyfriend off."

"For the hundredth time, he's not my boyfriend!" she snaps.

"He's possessive, given that he's not your boyfriend."

"I don't know what's wrong with him," she mutters.

I do. That dude has a boner for her and she has no idea, and I'll bet any money that he's going to take forever to confess his feelings for her, but I don't think she's as interested in him as he is in her.

I might not have a college degree in human psychology, but I can read people pretty well, especially when it comes to lust and attraction. I have a good detector for that sort of stuff.

I can tell Trinity is interested in me, though. I had a hunch when she came to pick up her car the other day. But she's also scared of me. Not scared as in *fearful,* but scared as in she finds me *too much.*

I suspect The Max Factor sets her heart racing more than it gets her panties wet.

With her, I only have to stand in front of her and she starts to get uneasy.

We're different. She's not really my type either, but lust is lust. There's something going on between us that makes us both wary, and curious, and that is a great combination for getting together.

She intrigues me for all the reasons that she shouldn't. My type of women wear fishnets stockings and lacy lingerie. Trinity would tell me to go to hell if I ever made a suggestion like that—not that I'm ever going to be in a position to make a suggestion like that to her.

"What's the story with the kid?" I ask, genuinely curious to know.

"There's no story."

"He didn't look too happy."

She twiddles the pen in her hand, but doesn't say anything. So far, she hasn't graded anything in the workbook she's had open in front of her. "Dylan is a concern," she says finally.

"Looks like he could do with a new pair of shoes, and decent clothes. And food."

"Your observation skills amaze me."

I wait for her to offer up some information, but she's being loyal to her kids, and I can't fault her.

"Thanks for coming by," she says, her pen poised as if she's about to write something down.

"Why did you listen to me?" I ask, not ready to leave.

"Listen to you when?"

"When we had the accident? Why did you cover for me, and go with my suggestion when it didn't benefit you in any way?" She didn't need to, and no one does something for nothing. Even with Hot Gina, she takes and then gives. Trinity didn't have to do anything for me, but she did, and she never asked for anything back.

"Did I have a choice?"

Of course she had a choice. She could have told me to go to hell and she could have gotten me in trouble. "You always have a choice."

"I didn't want to get you in trouble."

"But you didn't even know me back then."

"I don't know you now, and I'm still covering for you," she replies.

I nod my head, because she is. Even with the money for the repairs, she covered for me. "Exactly. That's what I mean." That's what I find so intriguing. "We barely know one another, but we can fix that," I say, watching her reaction.

"We don't need to fix anything," she retorts, the color rising to her cheeks again.

"People tend not to do nice things, especially for people they don't know."

"Really?" She sounds surprised. "That hasn't been my experience."

"It's been mine," I tell her.

She looks at me, as if what I'm saying doesn't make sense to her.

"People give to take, but not you," I tell her.

"I really don't understand what you mean."

We really are such different people, after all.

"This is pretty cool," I say, and wave my hand around the brightly colored room.

"Thanks. The children's art work always makes things look pretty."

I come back to my original point. "Even your wanna-be boyfriend can tell we have a thing going."

"We do *not* have a thing going," she snaps, and this time her face flushes a deeper shade. This tells me something, as does the slight wobble in her voice. I'm only making small talk, because I don't want to go home on a Friday night and look through the list of names on my phone, wondering who to call next.

I like being in Miss Weldon's classroom talking to her about her schoolkids. It's a connection of sorts, maybe not as intense as spending the night in someone's bed, but I like this. I like spending time with her, and I don't yet know why.

Now that it's just me and her alone together, I can sense her vulnerability. "But he wishes he was," I point out. Then, "Do you like Ed?" I ask, moving over to her desk, and planting my hands wide. I move my head down a little, and it's almost as if I've caged her in without touching her.

"Do you mind?" she says, placing the pen down hard on the desk. She doesn't seem to like me being so close.

"It's just a question, Trinity. You keep telling me Ed isn't your boyfriend, and yet whenever I see you, he's always around."

She lets out a loud exhale, and from my vantage point, I

can see the slow rise and fall of her chest. She's not wearing a blouse today, but a high-necked dress. Everything about her is luscious, and soft, and just looking at her ignites a spark inside me.

"What are you doing?" she murmurs, almost under her breath. I would walk away if I knew she hated me, if I sensed she felt I was hassling her, but I can detect something between us, and I am determined to find out once and for all if she's aware of it.

"I'm talking to you."

Her dark eyes glare at me. "Talking to me? In that predatory manner?"

Surprise makes me snort. "Predatory?" I've been called many things, but predatory isn't one of them.

"Everything about you is predatory," she spits back.

"If you want me to go, then tell me."

I watch the motion of her chest as it rises and falls, and I wait for her to dismiss me. "You're standing over me, invading my space, almost pinning me down."

"Pinning you down?" This is highly delusionary. "Lady, if I had pinned you down, you'd be smiling." Still, I don't hear her telling me to go.

Instead, her eyes open wider, and her shoulders slump slightly, as if my words have knocked the air right out of her chest. Most women would throw some dirty little words back at me, but Trinity looks uncomfortable.

"How is this predatory?" I ask, with a shrug. I leave my hands planted on the desk. "I'm nowhere near you."

"You're in my personal space."

"I'm at least fifteen inches away, and I'm not even touching you."

"Nobody stands like *that*," she nods at my arms, "to talk to another person."

"Depends on who you're talking to. Depends on what you think about that other person." The fact that she finds it intimidating shouldn't surprise me. I bet she's fairly inexperienced with men; if the likes of her friend Ed are anything to go by.

"Normal people don't stand the way you are."

"I'm not even touching you," and then, because I want to see her reaction, I add, "I wouldn't, unless you wanted me to."

She sits back in her chair, as far away from me as she can. My gaze slips to her lips and rests there. She has the most luscious lips, and I wonder what it would be like to touch her.

I wonder what it would be like to kiss those lips.

"There you go again."

I laugh, because I find her innocence endearing. I'm accustomed to being around highly sensual and sexual women and it's a breath of fresh air to be around someone like her for a change. Someone uncomplicated, not scheming, not after something.

"I don't mean to make you feel uncomfortable, Trinity." I need to back away. It's no fun talking dirty when the other person doesn't want to play. "I wasn't trying to be predatory." Well, maybe a little. Maybe I was testing her limits.

She picks up her pen again. I straighten up and move my arms away.

"Thanks for returning the money."

"No problem. You covered up for me on two occasions. I just wanted to thank you for that."

She tilts her face. "It's okay."

"That was a nice thing you did."

"Thanks for fixing my car."

I turn to leave. "Anytime."

"Don't go crashing into the back of me anytime soon," she says as I walk towards the door. I turn around and there's a lightness in her eyes that wasn't there a moment ago.

"Don't go stalling your car at the lights."

"I'll try not to."

"If you're looking for a used car at a decent price, hit me up."

CHAPTER ELEVEN

TRINITY

It takes me a good few moments to cool down, to recover.

Max didn't stay long at all, I realize as I glance at my watch, but it felt like a lifetime.

I go over and over our conversation, and become aware of every intonation, every nuance in his voice, every double meaning in his words.

My skin prickles when I think of how he stood over my desk, caging me in. And now he's left me feeling all sorts of weird. It might just be me making things up, because of the way he looks, the way he is around me, as if he's toying with my mind and emotions, but after his visit just now, I don't think it's something I'm imagining.

The man is a tease, and he knows it. He's the devil in disguise.

I wish I could talk to someone about how he affects me, but there is no one. I can hardly tell Ed, and Christina won't understand. That man puts thoughts in my head and I don't know where they came from because our conversations aren't at all flirtatious, much. Yet the way he looks at me is.

He doesn't look at me, he *devours* me. I'm not used to being around men like him.

I try once more to get on with grading the children's workbooks, but I haven't made any progress. I can't concentrate because my head's in the wrong place. I shut the workbook and add it to the huge pile I'll have to take home over the weekend.

I need to get to my crochet class and see Christina. I won't talk to her about Max, but seeing her and catching up on our week will make me feel better.

As I leave my classroom, I peek my head around Ed's door. "Goodnight." He's still here, preparing next week's lessons.

"Where's your friend?" he asks.

I sense discord in Ed's voice. "He left."

"You two are getting friendly."

"Friendly isn't the right word." I'm not about to tell Ed about the money. "He's just looking out for me because he thinks I need to replace my car."

"I've said that to you plenty of times."

Ed's made this to be about himself. He seems to feel threatened by Max, it seems. "But you're not a mechanic," I point out. Then, "How about that dinner?"

His eyes widen and he cocks his head as if he didn't hear me clearly.

He'll probably think it's forward of me to suggest it, but I'm only reminding him of the dinner invite he mentioned last time.

"You said something about dinner last time," I say. "We should catch up over dinner, a pizza or something, nothing heavy." I don't want him to think that I want anything more.

I just need someone calm and normal to replace the space that Max has taken up inside my head.

Ed gives me a wide smile. "I was going to ask you, but I didn't know when to pick the right moment."

I can believe that. For a man like Ed, his each and every action is deliberate and measured, unlike someone like Max who probably lives more in the moment.

"Tomorrow?" I say, my head filled with Max. It's like he's left an indelible stain on me.

Ed looks disappointed. "I can't make it tomorrow, sorry. I'm catching up with some friends. I can't even make Sunday."

"How about next weekend?" I suggest.

"That sounds good. Next Saturday?"

"Great. I'll meet you there," I say, before he starts a conversation about coming over to pick me up and drop me off.

"Why don't I just pick you up?"

"Uh... I'm not sure if I'll be at home. I might have plans to meet my mom and dad beforehand. Why don't I just meet you there?"

"Sure, okay," he shrugs.

"The usual place, Nino's?" I ask. It's where we often go to when the teachers have a night out. They serve great food at a good price. I even recommended it to my crochet class and we went there last year for our Christmas party.

"Nino's?" Ed sounds hesitant, as if he had other ideas.

"We always go there, and I love their calzone."

"Looks like Nino's it is," he says.

"Great, well, have a good weekend." I wave as I turn to leave. It's not a date, I tell myself. It's just pizza with a friend.

I go home and lounge around for a while, and make sure

Benji has enough food and water. I'm not in the mood to grade the workbooks I was going to grade at school when Max interrupted me.

For someone who isn't in my life, and who is the complete opposite of me, for someone who isn't even a friend, I seem to have a lot of Max on my brain.

This is why dinner with Ed is a good thing.

I get ready for my crochet class, and I'm already looking forward to the usual dinner with Christina.

I take my usual shortcut through one of the side streets, but when a cat darts in front of me, I brake suddenly and jolt forwards, my heart pounding as if it's going to explode.

Did I accidentally run that poor thing over?

Then I see the black and white tabby dart along the side, and I let out a loud breath of relief.

But my car has stalled. I turn the key again, and the engine refuses to come to life.

Panicked, I try again.

No luck.

In frustration, I bang the steering wheel. I hate being late for anything, especially a class.

I look around me, and the street is deserted. The days are getting shorter and there aren't many lights around here. There are a few buildings scattered around, but they're mostly derelict.

This is the wrong part of town to break down in. Now that I'm stuck, I stare around me in horror. Driving through it, I never noticed how deserted this street was.

I turn the key and pray, but it's in vain because my car refuses to spring to life.

Max is right. I need to get rid of this car. I can't drive this thing any more. It's not safe.

I will the engine to somehow start again. This has

happened before, though the last time, at the accident with Max, it didn't restart then either.

It doesn't look too hopeful, but I decide to give it a few minutes, and then try again. As if I have another option.

In the meantime, I decide to call Max and ask about that car he mentioned.

If it's still available, I'm going to buy it because I've had enough of this.

I call him, but he doesn't answer and his phone goes to voicemail instead.

My heart sinks.

I'm scared.

But I don't leave a message.

CHAPTER TWELVE

MAX

She finds me too much to handle. And that's a fact. After that visit to Miss Weldon's classroom, and making her squirm a little in her seat, I walk away feeling a little heated up myself.

I can't figure it out, the reason I did that to her. Maybe I have an obsession with bigger breasted women.

Maybe.

But I don't think it's purely sexual, because Trinity isn't the type of woman I look at and instantly want. My reaction to her isn't that way inclined.

Much.

But twice she's helped me out when she didn't have to. That's a huge thing for me.

So when my phone goes off, and I see her name pop up on the display, I break away from my kiss. Sadie, one of my friends-with-benefits, moans with disappointment. She's lying on the bed wearing only her bra and jeans. We were just getting started.

"Do you have to answer that?" she asks as I reach over to grab my phone. It stops ringing just as I see Trinity's name show up.

"It's work." I put a finger to my lips, gesturing for her to stay quiet.

"Your workplace has never bothered you before," she mutters, taking off her jeans as I leave the bedroom.

I call Trinity back. "You called?"

"That car...the one you were telling me about..."

Holy shit. She interrupts me at a time like this to talk about a car? I'm not sure what I expected Trinity to call me about but I didn't expect to hear about a goddamn car. "What about it?" I growl.

"Is it still available?"

"Yes," I scratch my chest in annoyance.

"Do you think I could maybe come by and see it?"

"Yes," I reply, because Sadie appears, and stands directly in front of me in her beautiful naked splendor.

"Could I come by tomorrow, do you think, or don't you work on Saturday?"

My mind has fogged over because Sadie's hand is on my cock, and she's trying to free it from my boxer briefs. "Yes," I bite out.

"Yes, what?"

"Uh..." My brain goes limp as my cock grows harder. Sadie's good with her hands, and it takes every ounce of willpower for me not to throw my phone at the wall.

"Should I come by the garage tomorrow, or if you're not work—"

"Come tomorrow," I croak, trying to keep my voice steady and failing when Sadie starts pumping me.

"What time?" Trinity's voice sounds faraway. I can't think. Can't concentrate because Sadie's fingers feel so good on me.

"What time?" Trinity asks again.

I try to clear the haze in my head. I'm working tomorrow, doing some overtime, but I have no idea what time I'll be there. "Uh...all morning," I manage to say. Trinity's voice is bugging the hell out of me. At first I was thrilled to get a call from her, but now that it's just about a car, I'm over it.

Besides, Sadie's fingers are working their magic, and I need to get back to her.

"I'll come by tomorrow, around elevenish. It's just that my car's stalled again," Trinity says, sounding slightly nervous.

"Your car?" I ask, as Sadie leans in for a kiss. Our tongues duel for dominance and my cock stiffens some more. I am desperate to get naked and bury myself inside her.

"I can't get it to start." Trinity's voice interrupts, like a jet of ice-cold water hosing me down. "I think I might have flooded the engine."

"Yeah," I say, while Sadie's mouth trails along my jawline. "Just be careful nobody hits you from behind."

"No chance. I'm on Jefferson Street, you know how quiet that is. I hadn't noticed it before..."

Her voice trails off just as I snap to attention. "You're over by Jefferson Street? Near the old windmill?"

"Yes."

"What the hell are you doing there?"

"I always take this shortcut." Somehow, even with Sadie now raining kisses along my shoulder, I become acutely aware of the possible danger Trinity could be in.

Jefferson Street isn't a safe place for anyone to be broken down in.

It's not your problem, my cock tells me. "Try the key again," I tell her.

"Get off the phone," Sadie whispers as she nips my ear.

Through the fog of my soon-to-have-sex haze, I hear the car splutter and die. "Did you call the emergency roadside service?" I ask her. I need to get off the phone and back to my own business, but I'm worried about her safety.

"No. It's going to be fine," she tells me. "This has happened before. I waited a while and then it was okay. At least nobody's crashed into me this time."

She laughs, as if she's made a joke. For the iciness she showed me when I was in her classroom a few hours ago, she sure seems to have mellowed out.

I wish she'd let me mellow out and enjoy my free time.

"You should call roadside assistance," I urge her.

"Trust me, it's going to be fine."

She's nuts. She's ignorant and has no idea of the danger she could be in. Jefferson Street is where drug addicts hang out. It's where, under the cover of darkness, the drug dealers come to sell their stuff.

It's no place for a sweet-and-soft-as-cotton-candy schoolteacher to break down in.

Sadie's fingers claw into my buttocks, and with her other hand, she pumps me to sweet heaven. Meanwhile her lips are leaving a hickey on my shoulder.

She's a gifted multi-tasker and we're about to have a great time.

"Wait a few minutes, and try the key again," I say, then hang up.

I take Sadie's face in my hands and claim her mouth the way I'd like to claim her down below.

"You took your sweet time with that call," she murmurs, stilling her hand on me. I bite my lip knowing that I can't leave Trinity where she is—no matter how big my erection is.

"Sorry, babe. I have to go."

"Go?" Sadie shrieks as I move away. "Where the hell do you need to go *right now?*"

"I need to sort something out."

"You need to sort me out first!" she yells, following me into the bedroom. I put on my shirt. "I have to help someone." Trinity covered for me twice, and I'm not about to leave her in danger.

"*Right now?*" Sadie's voice reaches a new level of shrill. She puts her hands on those amazing hips, distracting me for a few seconds.

I sure hope that schoolteacher will appreciate what I'm giving up in order to come to her rescue.

"I'll be back," I tell Sadie and kiss her hungrily before I leave.

"You son of a bitch!" is the last angry scream I hear as I walk out.

I reach Trinity about ten minutes later, and breathe a sigh of relief when I see her familiar car stranded on the street.

I climb off my bike, then remove my helmet, to see her staring at me.

"What are you doing here?" she asks, getting out of the car.

"Rescuing you," I say.

"I didn't ask you to rescue me." She gets out of the car and watches me with an expression that is neither pleased, nor grateful that I came here.

"Pop the hood open for me."

"What? Why?"

I left a woman hungry for sex for this? "Do it," I order her, then lift the hood to take a look.

"I didn't ask you to come here," she says, surprising me with her surliness. I didn't expect a great big hug, but I expected a little more enthusiasm on her part.

"Did you call roadside assistance?"

"No, because it's going to be fine. This has happened to me before, I told you."

I examine the engine and everything looks fine. Then I get behind her wheel and turn the key, and sure enough, the car roars into life.

"See," she says, walking over to the driver's side window and peering at me. "Trust it to start the moment you try the key."

"I have magic fingers," I tell her, not feeling too happy myself. Maybe it was a mistake to rush to her assistance. She would have been okay if I'd stayed put.

"I'm sure you do." She rolls her eyes.

"Do you have any idea where you are?"

"Jefferson Street."

"Do you realize *what* this is?" I look around at the closed down buildings, and the empty street.

"It's a rundown part of the city. They used to have manufacturing plants and small businesses here years ago, my dad says."

I turn the engine off and get out of the car. "It might have been that before, but it's a drug dealer's paradise now. This is where people come to sell drugs."

She looks around warily. "I don't see anyone."

"See those buildings? If you walked into any of them, I guarantee you'll find drug addicts lying around completely wasted."

She steps back as if I've just offered her drugs myself.

"I didn't know," she says, clutching her hand to her chest.

"I figured you didn't, that's why I came." I fold my arms as I lean against her car.

"How do *you* know?"

"Because it's common knowledge," I tell her. "What are you doing here anyway?"

"I was going to my crochet class."

"Your what?"

"Crochet. It's like knitting."

She goes to a class *to knit?* I really don't understand this woman at all. "Is this a regular thing?" *Is it fun?*

"Every Friday, from seven to eight. And then I have my art classes on Mondays, around the same time, though I teach there."

"You teach somewhere else?"

"Near the community center. I teach art to adults with learning difficulties."

Whoa.

Crochet classes? I don't even know what the hell crochet is. And she also teaches art to adults with learning difficulties?

Why am I not surprised? "I bet your life is nice and neat and scheduled right down to every single square in your monthly and weekly planner."

She looks pissed off. "I bet you don't," she throws back. "I bet you live your life not knowing what you're doing from one moment to the next."

We stare at one another. It's not what she's said, but the tone with which she's said it. I can't figure out why she's angry. I'm the one who's given up his time—and guaranteed sex—to come to her aid. "You should get going," I say.

She looks sheepish. "Thanks. Thanks for coming to help me. You didn't have to and ..." I don't hear the rest of the sentence because I've walked away. I don't want to listen to her apology.

Sadie's waiting.

I get on my bike and slip on my helmet then rev the engine waiting for Trinity to get going. I won't leave until I know she's on her way.

I follow her along the length of the street, and then when she's back on the main road, I go my own way.

I return to Sadie's place and we finish off what we started. It's great in the moment. We have sex for hours, and it feels amazing. I love that connection when I'm inside a woman and she's so out of control, all she can do is moan in ecstasy. I love how she makes me feel.

But when it's over, it's over.

I leave, even though Sadie begs me to stay, and she always begs me to stay, but I never do because I don't want her to get the wrong idea about us.

Outside of the sex, we don't have much in common. It's awkward, and I prefer my own space.

As strange as it might seem, friends-with-benefits have rules and boundaries, and I'm always careful to stay within mine, although I'm slightly more easygoing around Hot Gina. That's because what she and I have is a sex marathon. I'm entitled to stay at her place for the duration of the weekend.

I go home and decide to stay in and watch TV. I'm about to pour hot boiling water into my plastic cup of noodles when my cell phone rings again, and Trinity's name appears.

Fuck, no, I groan. *Not again.* I'm starting to regret being a knight and rescuing her, and I hope this isn't going to become a habit. Women find it hard to resist me, and while I'm secretly pleased that this reserved schoolteacher is finding the same thing, I don't want her to use me to fix all her car problems. What she needs is to change that piece of crap she's driving.

I answer her call and decide that I need to tell her.

"I'm sorry about what I said earlier," she says.

For a second I wonder if she's called me by mistake. "What now?"

"When I said you lived your life not knowing what you were doing from one moment to the next."

My heart swells a little at her apology and my initial anger—when she spat those words out earlier—melts away. "It's not a problem," I tell her. "You're right. My life isn't as ordered and as organized as yours." I'm curious to know why she's called me at this time of night, and what propelled her to apologize.

"That's not such a bad thing, you being spontaneous," she answers.

"You think I'm spontaneous?"

"Yes, I do."

Are we really having this conversation? Not that I mind. I quite like having her on the phone, talking to me.

I pour the water in my noodles and let them soften, then hold the phone closer to my ear.

Her words are different; unexpected and pleasing, and I let them wash over me like cool refreshing spring water.

I'm so used to talking dirty to girls, to have it always be about the sex, that a conversation like this—from a person I least expect—is sweet music to my ears.

"I think you're the complete opposite of me, as a matter of fact," she says.

I laugh easily. If only she knew how disorganized my

life is. "I live in chaos. I can't even balance my books, which is why I had to ask you to pay for your repairs."

"I suppose that would be a downside to being spontaneous."

"I need to get better at balancing my finances," I confess. "I'm still blown away by the fact that you agreed to pay for me."

"Did you give me a choice?"

"There's always a choice," I tell her.

"If I hadn't paid, you would've been in trouble with your boss."

"And I'm grateful to you that you did." Many in her situation would have told me to fuck off.

"You saved me earlier, when I was stranded on Jefferson, so I guess we're even now."

"I didn't do anything. The car started by itself," I remind her.

"But you came because you were worried."

It's true. I did. But I don't acknowledge that with an answer.

Something hangs in the sudden silence. Is she lonely tonight? Bored? *Interested in me?* It's a possibility I have to consider, because experience has shown me this.

"Anyway, I called to apologize about what I said earlier. I didn't mean it."

"Were you thinking about me, Trinity?" I'm curious now. That apology didn't just flash into her head. She must have been thinking about me.

"Did I interrupt you earlier?" she asks, not answering my question. "When I first called you to ask you about the car, I'm sure I heard someone in the background telling you to get off the phone."

There's no question about it; she definitely heard Sadie, if she can recite her words. "Yeah," I reply. "It was a friend."

"Your girlfriend?"

I'm not sure how to answer that. I don't imagine that fuck-buddies is a word in Trinity's vocabulary. "Are you asking me if I have a girlfriend?"

"No. I asked if the person I heard on the phone was your girlfriend."

"It's the same thing," I point out.

"No, it isn't. One assumes I'm asking because I'm curious—and someone like you might potentially take that to mean that I'm interested—while the other is questioning whether the person I heard was your girlfriend or someone else."

Her statement confuses me. "Are you curious to know if I'm available or not?"

"No, of course not. Stop twisting my words."

I grin. "How am I twisting your words?"

"I'm not asking if you have a girlfriend. The woman I heard could have been your sister or your mother."

"I don't have a sister, and my mom died a long time ago."

I hear a gasp, and she doesn't say anything at first. Then, "I'm so sorry, Max. I... I didn't know."

"You couldn't know."

More silence follows. I imagine Trinity twisting herself up into knots at this news.

"It's okay," I say. "Don't worry about it." Now I want to know something. "You seemed annoyed when I showed up."

"Did I?"

She's fumbling, I can tell. "Yes, you did," I state calmly.

"I was... I was annoyed because the car broke down again."

"That stretch of road isn't a safe place to be in, let alone break down in."

"I'm really glad that you came. I didn't know about the drug addicts."

"You do now, so avoid that route next time." She still hasn't told me why she was annoyed to see me. I rest the phone between my jaw and my neck as I stir the noodles, holding the plastic cup so that it doesn't tip over.

"I will. My sheltered life means I'm not as streetwise as some people."

I stop stirring because she seems to want to talk. Our conversation has gone on longer than I expected, not that I'm complaining, and I don't mind listening. She seems less guarded now that we're talking on the phone, compared to when I'm around her. In person, she's more prickly and easy to rile up. "It's common knowledge. I'm surprised you didn't know."

"Do you take drugs?" She blurts out a sentence that I wasn't expecting. I snort out loudly in shock, incensed that she would think this of me.

"No." But it doesn't surprise me that this is her opinion. I've smoked the occasional joint, but who hasn't? Class-A drugs, though, no way. I find comfort in sex, not drink and drugs.

I realize why she's asking me. "I know about that place because it's a well-known fact, Trinity. Everyone knows to steer clear of that area."

"I didn't. I've been using that shortcut for years." She clears her throat. "So, tomorrow, I'll see you at the garage?" She seems eager to want to take a look at the car. At last, I finally managed to get her to see some sense.

"Yeah. I'll see you there."

She hangs up, and I feel a tingle of something pass up my spine. It's not excitement, exactly. Not anticipation either, because meeting Trinity isn't like meeting Hot Gina, or Sadie.

And yet I didn't imagine that flurry of shivers. I now find myself looking forward to this as much as I do to Hot Gina's visits.

And that clearly doesn't make any sense.

CHAPTER THIRTEEN

TRINITY

A wave of disappointment cascades over me when I arrive at the garage and don't see Max there.

I tell myself that it doesn't matter, that one of the other guys can show me the car, but Max is the one I was hoping to see. I feel he has my best interests at heart, and that he'll check the car out carefully if I decide to buy it.

My dad wasn't too pleased when I told him this morning that I was going to buy a car from a garage.

He, like most men, seems to think he knows better than I do about the type of car I need. He says I'm silly for not getting it from a car lot. I understand his concern, but I don't believe that Max would tell me about a car that isn't up to spec.

He came out to take a look at my car when I broke down yesterday, and he didn't have to. I was annoyed when he showed up, but that's because I'm trying my hardest to get him out of my system and he's making it impossible for me by showing up when I least expect him to. But I can't tell him that's the reason I didn't look too happy to see him.

And now here I am this morning, at his garage, looking at a car he recommended to me. So much for me trying to get him out of my system.

This behavior isn't normal for me. I don't get reeled into situations like this, especially with guys like Max, total strangers. But the more I try to stay away, the more it seems that fate wants to put us together.

"Can I help you?" I turn around to face a guy I don't recognize.

My eyes take in his dirty coveralls. "I'm interested in one of your cars for sale," I reply, feeling foolish because I have no idea which car it is, or what make or model. I've completely relied on Max.

He frowns at me. "We don't sell cars much. Only the occasional one. Did you speak to Enzo about it?"

"Uh…" I look around for Enzo, thinking he might be able to help me because this kid seems to have no idea. "I'm not sure."

The guy shrugs. "You'd be better off going to a car lot."

"There is a car here. One of your—"

"I've got this." A hand rests on my shoulder. I turn to find Max beside me, and it's a little familiar the way he has his arm around me, but I don't flinch away. "There you are," I say to him.

"Sorry. I'm running late," he replies, then spins me around and starts walking in the opposite direction with me.

"What are you doing?" I ask. He takes his hand off my shoulder and walks away towards a corner of the garage. "Getting dressed," he says, then takes off his leather jacket and slips into his coveralls.

"Where's the car?" I ask, looking around. There's an

assortment of cars scattered in and around the garage, with some in the parking lot, but none of them appeal to me. Also, none of them have a 'For Sale' sign on them.

"Follow me and I'll show you," says Max. He leads me out of the garage, and around the back where a couple of cars are parked. These have prices on the windshield in huge, yellow colors.

"This is the one," he says, slapping his hand on the hood of what looks like a gray Nissan.

I don't like that they're hidden around at the back, out of sight of the garage. "Why are they here?"

"There's not a lot of room here, and Enzo's business is not to sell cars. Only the people who are interested are shown them."

It makes sense, but maybe I should go to a car lot, just in case?

"This one's sold," he says, tapping his fingers on the nice-looking dark blue Ford next to the car he has in mind for me. I like it better than the Nissan he has in mind for me.

"What do you think?" he asks.

I look at both of them, parked side-by-side and why is it that I prefer the one that's not available? "I like that one more," I say, nodding at the one that's been sold.

"Sorry. That's not for sale. Enzo bought it for his daughter." He whips off the huge price tag.

"And this one?" He slides his hand across the hood of the unsold car.

I walk around it slowly. It's priced at fifteen hundred dollars, and it looks to be in good shape. I don't know what to check for though. If I walked into a normal car lot, the salesmen would try to pull the wool over my eyes. I'd probably have to bring my dad along with me and he would want to check everything.

I feel that this way is easier. Max knows about cars and I trust his judgment.

"It's had two owners, it's nine years old, but it's got a low mileage and it's in great working order. I checked it out and it's legit. Do you like it?"

I like it. It's a nice gray color, and it looks shiny and new given that it's quite old. "Any problems in the past that I should be aware of?"

He shakes his head, watching me.

"Can I take it for a test drive?"

He looks dubious. "I can't let you do that. This isn't a car lot, remember. We don't have insurance coverage."

My face drops. I can't buy a car unless I've taken it for a test drive. I need to know how it drives, and how it feels in my hands. I wouldn't buy a bread-making machine without a recommendation from a bread-baking friend whose bread I had tasted, and similarly, I'm not about to buy a car just based on how it looks.

Appearances can be deceptive.

"How about you just drive it here around the parking lot?" Max suggests.

"Where?" There's hardly any space.

"You just want to get a feel for it, don't you? Sit inside and see if it's comfy, and get a feel for the controls, that sort of thing?"

"I want to see what it's like on the road, I want to hear the engine when it drives. I want to see if it's a smooth ride; that sort of thing." I can't believe he expects me to buy it just like that.

He lets out a sigh. "I understand, but we're not a car lot,

Trinity. I can break some rules, but not this one. Enzo would kill me if you crashed the car."

"Then at least let me sit inside and get a feel for it." But this isn't the type of thing I do. My father would think I'd gone crazy if I bought a car I hadn't driven, and yet this is exactly what I'm now considering to do. I haven't known this guy long, and I'm trusting his opinion. But my rational side kicks in and reminds me that Max has come through for me when it mattered. That my risks with him have paid off. That he hasn't hurt me. That I can trust him.

He runs over to the office and then reappears with the keys which he tosses to me. I get inside, and he gets into the passenger side.

"Start the engine, if you want."

"You sure?"

He nods. "Just don't drive off anywhere."

I do as he suggests, then adjust the mirrors before starting the engine and revving it lightly.

"Like it?"

"It feels okay."

"You still want to test drive it?" he asks.

I nod. "It would help, but you said I couldn't, so... anyway, I don't know much about cars, that's why I'm relying on you."

"You're relying on me?" he asks, surprised.

"A car salesman would pull the wool over my eyes, and bump the price up. You won't."

"It's not my car. I can't be flexible on the price, because Enzo has a set price for it depending on what he paid for it. But I can tell you the truth about the condition of it."

"And the truth is?"

"It's a good car, and well worth the price."

"Then I'll take it."

He coughs out a laugh. "You'll *take* it? Just like that?"

"What am I supposed to do? If I can't test drive it, I have to go on your recommendation," I protest.

"We're not supposed to recommend cars to customers."

"Then why are you recommending it to me?"

His eyes linger on my face, and I feel as if he's doing that thing again, staring at me until I burn inside. I look away because it gets to be too much. Just sitting with him inside this car is too much.

"I figured you needed a good car at a good price. This came up and I thought, why not tell her?"

"I appreciate your concern."

"It's the least I can do," he says. Even though I'm staring directly in front of me, I can tell from my peripheral vision that he's staring at me again but I don't dare to turn my face towards him. I can't get hot and flustered all over again.

"Fuck it," he says.

My head snaps to him. "Don't use that language."

"Buckle up."

"What? Why?"

"We're taking it for a test drive."

"We can't. You said I'm not insured—"

"Just do it. We can go around a few blocks—"

"But I'm not insured," I insist.

"Do you want to see how this drives or not?"

"Ideally, yes."

"You can't go crazy and do a hundred miles an hour."

"What?"

"You heard me."

"You're letting me drive this thing?"

"Yes. Just don't drive like a maniac and crash into something."

"That's more your style." We stare at one another, and I

can't help but grin at my easy put-down, which he seems to take gracefully. I suppose he's too worried to joke right now.

"Ease around the corner slowly, then pull out carefully. There are a lot of cars around."

"You're serious?"

"Yes. You can go around a few blocks. Enzo isn't around."

"What about the other guy?"

"Don't worry about him."

I hesitate, because I don't do things like this. I am a careful person.

"Don't you want to be spontaneous, Trinity?" His voice is husky all of a sudden, or I'm imagining it. I look at him, and see his eyes examine my face slowly. "You told me your life was orderly. You said you never do anything crazy but I reckon you've wished you could, am I right, Trinity?"

With Max beside me, my heart begins to race. I've never done anything illegal and now I find myself getting a thrill out of it.

It's only a few blocks, and I'm not about to do anything silly. I would be careful.

"Here's your chance. Let your wild side come out."

I swallow, because that sounds like a double entendre. "Okay..." I say, in what I hope passes for a normal voice.

Does he have any idea how he affects me? That I wasn't even aware of my wild side until I met him?

I cough, more to signal to myself to concentrate. I'm not doing anything big, no grand auto theft, nothing dangerous. I'm just taking a car around the block.

"Live a little." Why does his voice sound so much softer than usual? A breath escapes my mouth and I press my lips together. My heart hammers so fast inside my ribcage that I'm scared it might shoot out of my mouth.

All this because I'm taking a car around the block.

Or because Max and I are in a confined space, and he's coaxing me into doing something I shouldn't. I'm not insured on this vehicle, but for some reason, it doesn't seem to matter.

"Let's do it," I say, with a conviction I don't feel.

"Easy does it," he says. "Once you drive out, take a right, and then another immediate right, and we'll go around the block."

"Are you sure you won't get in trouble because of me?" Because that's the last thing I want.

"Don't worry about me."

I ease my foot off the gas and the car slowly moves forward. I drive out of the parking lot. "It's a smooth ride."

"Uh-huh."

I don't dare turn my head to look at him, even though my breathing suddenly turns shallow.

Keep your eyes on the road, I tell myself.

Soon enough, the car is cruising easily around the block. The steering wheel is light and easy to turn, and the brakes are good. The gas pedal is responsive. This car has more power than the one I currently have.

"I like it," I say, my voice all excited. I'm not sure if I'm excited about the car, or because I've done something daring. I don't want to think about that part.

"I told you it's a good car."

I'm focused on the road and I can't believe when we're soon back at the garage again. "Can I go around again?" I ask. I was only just starting to get used to it.

"Look at you," he chortles. "For someone who likes to stay within the law, I'd say you have a daring streak underneath all that schoolteacherish façade."

"Schoolteacherish façade?" I turn to him and raise an eyebrow. "It could just be that you bring out my wild side."

That seems to leave him speechless.

"Can I go again?" I ask, before he can say anything.

"Go on, then," he says, his voice sounding a little odd. "One last time."

I smile so widely, you'd think he'd told me a joke. I go around the block one more time, and then drive back, returning to where we started.

I stop the engine and take out the key. "I like it."

"Good."

"I want it."

"You *want* it?" he asks, his eyes sparkling with mischief as he makes my words mean something else.

"The car, I mean." There's a wobble in my voice.

"I know what you mean, Trinity. Let's get the paperwork done then." He opens the car door, and puts an end to our conversation. A part of me hoped he might say something else mildly inappropriate.

"What the hell do you think you're doing?" The voice is like a clap of thunder on a balmy summer evening. Unexpected and shocking, it yanks me right out of the moment and thrusts me into the cold light of day.

I find myself looking up at Max's boss who has a face like thunder.

CHAPTER FOURTEEN

MAX

What the hell is Enzo doing here?

I'm in deep shit, and now I'm scrambling to figure out how to explain myself. "Sorry." I raise my hands and shrug. I have no reasonable explanation and no good excuse.

Enzo smiles at Trinity behind me, and I'm relieved she's here, because Enzo will wait for her to leave before he gives me hell. "She wants the car," I say. "She likes it."

"I wanted to test drive it and Max said I couldn't, but I insisted."

I look at her lying so easily for me.

"He said that, did he?" Enzo looks as if he doesn't know whether to believe her or not, and behind his fake smile lies menace, I know that, but Trinity doesn't.

I'm touched that she's standing up for me, but I hope she won't say anything else.

"This was your idea, eh?" Enzo asks her. She offers him a sweet smile.

"Max told me you didn't have insurance on it, but I like the car. I *really* like the car, and I'm going to buy it."

"You look familiar," Enzo comments. "Have we fixed your car here lately?"

"Yes."

"She's my girlfriend," I pipe up, knowing that we're not allowed to sell or recommend cars to anyone other than family or friends. I slide my arm around her waist. This time, I expect her to flinch, but she doesn't, which surprises me.

"Your girlfriend?" Enzo asks, his voice full of suspicion.

Trinity turns her head towards me, but I stare directly ahead at Enzo.

He looks to Trinity for verification and she moves a tad closer to me. "I really like the car," she says.

"I'll take care of the paperwork," I volunteer.

"And I'll take care of you later," Enzo threatens. What's he going to do? Dock my wages for being careless? He's done that before, and it won't surprise me if he does it again now.

Jackass.

He walks over to the car he's bought for his daughter. "I need this checked over and cleaned. My daughter's going to pick it up tomorrow."

"Sure thing."

As soon as he leaves, Trinity moves away from me. "Your girlfriend?"

"Sorry about that, but Enzo prefers us to sell these cars to friends and family. He doesn't want people coming back and complaining if they have any problems."

"Is there something wrong with this car?"

"No. We fix everything and check it carefully, but he doesn't want the headache of offering warranties and having people bring the vehicles back for any little fault. You're getting a cheap car. You get what you pay for, but the cars we sell are good. It's just the aftercare we don't offer. This is a garage, not a car—"

"I know, I know. You keep telling me."

"If you have doubts, you shouldn't go ahead. I was only trying to help, but maybe you should look around. You might get something fancier, something better, and with a warranty." It seems like too much hassle all of a sudden.

"Why didn't you say I was your friend?"

"Because I wanted an excuse to slide my hand around your waist." I wink back, enjoying her discomfort. She bites down on her teeth, because a muscle in her jaw twitches, but she doesn't say anything.

"Let's do the paperwork." I walk over to the office.

"Did I get you in trouble?" she asks, following me.

"The guy's a moron," I whisper under my breath. "But at least you got to test drive the car, huh?"

"Your boss didn't look too happy about it. I didn't mean to get you in trouble," she insists.

"It was my idea, and there's no harm done. You didn't crash the car, nobody died or got injured, so it's no big deal."

I get the appropriate form and fill it out, then hand it over to her. "It's reserved for you while you sort out your insurance, and how you're going to pay, credit card, or cash, or check. You can come and pick it up when you want. Monday's a good day."

She takes the paper, and reads it, then signs and hands it back. I take our copy and give her hers.

"Congratulations," I say, holding out my hand. "You're

the proud owner of a fully working car that doesn't stall and won't let you down."

She flashes me a smile that's brighter than the sun. "See you on Monday," she says.

"Got any plans for tonight?" I ask, just as she's about to leave. She stops and looks at me, then hesitates.

"I'm just seeing friends."

"Yeah?" I want to know more. I'm curious about where she's going, and who with, and whether she has a boyfriend or not.

"It's just pizza."

"With some friends, or *a* friend?"

She opens her mouth, and instead of answering my question, she says, "I'm sorry to bring it up, but I wanted to say, again, that I was sorry to hear about your mom."

I grind my teeth together and inhale, but I have nothing to say to that.

"I just... I don't know why I brought that up..." She pauses, probably because she feels awkward for bringing it up, and because I'm still silent.

Women have a soft spot. A huge big fucking soft spot. Their hearts.

They feel sorry for me when they see my scars, and then they half-wince and half-stare at me in admiration. And also when I tell them my mom died. I've only told Hot Gina that, because it came up once. We were lying in bed one time, joking about meeting one another's families—it's never going to happen—but we got carried away, and I told her about my adoptive mom dying when I was a teenager. She felt sorry for me. Wanted to hug me and hold me.

Women and their hearts.

"It's okay," I tell her. "I better get going. Get some work done before Enzo fries my balls."

This elicits a giggle from her, and the awkwardness disappears in a flash.

"Do you have any plans?" She doesn't seem too eager to leave.

"Uh..." I did have plans to meet Sadie after I've been to the birthday drinks that Al invited me to. "Birthday drinks for Al's girlfriend."

"Oh, nice."

"Yeah."

"Well, I'd better go," she says.

"See ya."

Not ten seconds have passed before Al comes over.

"You told Enzo that Trinity was your girlfriend?" He wipes his hand across his forehead and spreads some grease on it in the process.

"Had to, she's not, *obviously*. She needs a car and you know what he's like."

"I saw her drive off."

I scratch my jaw. "She wanted to test drive it."

Al gives me a peculiar look. "Don't be late tonight."

"I won't, but are you sure you want me there?" I've met Sammy a few times, and only in social situations. I don't know her well enough to be invited to her birthday party. It's at their apartment. Nothing fancy, he told me, but still, he seems eager for me to be there. I think I'll feel out of place.

"I wouldn't have invited you otherwise. Make sure you come," Al says.

I don't know why he's so adamant. But since I'm the only work colleague he's invited, I feel as if I have to go along.

"I'll be there," I tell him.

CHAPTER FIFTEEN

TRINITY

It's the day of my 'just pizza and nothing else dinner date' with Ed.

If I hadn't seen Max earlier today, having pizza with Ed wouldn't feel like something I had to endure. I feel awful for thinking this, but I wish it was Max I was meeting tonight instead. I wish I hadn't pushed for this, but it's too late to back out now.

We meet at Nino's as planned, and Ed is already there when I arrive. He gets up when he sees me. We kiss on the cheek, because we're meeting outside of school, even though I only saw him yesterday.

A wave of overpowering musk hits my nostrils, and I force myself not to make a face. He overdid it with his cologne, but he looks quite handsome in a nice pair of jeans and a shirt.

I feel a little dressed down in my jeans and formal blouse. It's one I've worn to school before. I didn't bother with makeup much, because in my head I'm adamant that this isn't a date. I did put on a pair of hoop earrings, though.

"Nice earrings," he notices.

"Thank you." My gut twists because I didn't want a compliment, and having Ed give me one so early on gives me the jitters. "You look nice," I say, sliding into the booth and sitting opposite him.

"Thanks." He flashes me a smile, as if he's taken that as a compliment.

Oh, god. Did he dress up for me? My stomach sinks. Ed thinks this is a date even though I stressed it wasn't. What am I doing here with him?

This is a huge mistake, I tell myself, and then I hate myself for thinking these thoughts. I'm an evil person, nasty and selfish. I commandeered this get-together because of Max, when he was *just that mechanic* to me. A *hot* mechanic, but someone who's effect on me I couldn't understand. Because he made me feel things I shouldn't have been feeling.

Now he's *Max*. Still that hot mechanic, and the effect on me still persists, only I'm not so sure I want to forget about him.

"I asked Christina if she wanted to come along," I announce.

Ed's smile fades. "You did?" A silence hangs between us, like a gray cloud on a summer's day. He seems intent on making this be a date, and I'm intent on pointing out that it's not.

But in hindsight, what else is he supposed to take away from this? It's my fault, for using him as an excuse to stop thinking about Max. Never in all my adult years have I been so completely enraptured by a guy I don't even know.

It's insane. It feels almost as if my brain has been

invaded by a bacterial infection. "She's busy and said she couldn't make it."

He seems relieved with my answer. "Oh well, never mind. I'm surprised you asked her."

"Why?"

"Well, because... because..." He frowns at me, as if I'm forcing him to do something against his will.

"It's only dinner, Ed. I didn't want Christina sitting at home all alone on a Saturday evening."

"At least you and I aren't sitting at home all alone on a Saturday evening," he replies easily.

I hate that he keeps bringing the conversation back to me and him. "Have you decided what you want?" I ask, picking up the menu even though I always end up ordering the same thing whenever we come here.

"I have and I'm ready to order whenever you're ready."

"Let me have a quick look. I'll probably end up with the calzone as usual." I look through the menu. From my peripheral vision I can tell that Ed's staring at me. It's not a *Max-stare*. I don't *feel* it, I just know it. A Max-stare makes my skin prickle.

I scratch my neck, because I've been thinking of him ever since I left the garage. I thought about him all afternoon. I thought about him when I got dressed to meet Ed, and I'm thinking about him now. Max is nothing to me; he's a complete stranger, but I've somehow conjured him up into being someone sexy, and mysterious, and dangerous and by buying the car and having contact with him earlier, I've made him into some sort of fantasy figure in my head. He's real, but he has no idea of the things I'm thinking and feeling.

I'm the one who's changed by being around him. I did

something today that I never thought I'd do; I drove a car without insurance.

Worse, I did it twice.

That's the sort of effect Max has on me. I don't even know the guy that well, and yet I turn into a reckless floozy when I'm around him.

"Have you decided?" Ed asks, interrupting my thoughts. "It'll be closing time at this rate."

I look up sheepishly. "Sorry." I got carried away in my own head. "I'm having the calzone." I love pizza, and my hips are a testament to that. Folded-over pizza always tastes amazing.

"It's always the calzone with you."

"You know me so well," I say, then regret my words.

"I do, don't I?"

I avoid looking at him and pretend to fish through my purse for something. Luckily, the server comes over and we order our food and drink, and then we talk about the week at work.

Our drinks arrive a short while later and a couple of times our hands knock together as we reach for our glasses. I pull my hand away as if it's been touched by a live wire. I can't figure out if Ed is doing that intentionally or not, and this makes me even more uneasy.

"How's your car?"

"Funny that you should ask." If there was one topic I didn't want to discuss this evening, it's this. Without him knowing, Ed has taken me into Max territory.

"Why? Not another accident, I hope?" He looks at me as if he's worried.

"Nothing like that," I say, dismissing his concern with a wave of my hand. "I bought a new car," I announce proudly.

"You did?"

"Not *new*, new, but a used car. It's in really good condition, and affordable."

"Congrats!" He raises his glass of orange juice and I raise my lemonade. "What did you buy?"

I tell him about my second-hand Nissan.

"About time too. At least it won't have any problems. No more getting hit by some guy on a bike."

I almost choke as I sip my lemonade. "I—uh, I bought the car from his garage." There's no point hiding it because it would have come up at some point.

He sets down his glass slowly. "You did what?"

"I bought the car from the garage where that mechanic works."

Ed looks at me as if I've just announced that I'm pregnant. "You bought a car from a *garage*?"

I'm already on the defensive. "They sometimes sell good cars on from people who've brought cars in for repair, and then decide they want to sell them instead." I sound like a salesperson for Max's garage.

"But why not buy it from a car lot, like everyone else?"

The way he looks at me makes me feel guilty, as if I have something to hide. The truth is I bought the car because I trust Max and it was a convenient way to get a good car quickly—at least, I *think* that's the reason why I bought it.

Judging by Ed's frown, he thinks I've gone crazy.

"It's better to buy a car off of a mechanic than a car salesman," I reply. "It makes perfect sense. A mechanic knows all about the inner workings of a car, and the car salesman is only concerned about making his commission."

"I was worried that that mechanic would try to fleece more money out of you, and it doesn't look like I'm wrong."

I sense there's more to his tone than his suspicion that

Max is making money off me. "I'm not sure how you can come to that conclusion, Ed."

"I'm really surprised that you bought the car from that place."

"There was one available, and it seemed like a good deal." I don't like having to explain myself. "He checked it out properly."

"Who?"

"The...guy...that mechanic. *Max.*" It seems odd saying his name out loud, and trying to make it sound as if it doesn't sound weird on my tongue. Can Ed tell I'm being weird?

Thankfully, the server comes over with our food, and even though the food is hot, I sense a slight chill in the air. I detect that Ed doesn't like hearing about Max, so I change the topic to school, and the goings-on there. This is safer territory, and we soon end up talking about other things; our classes, our plans for the children for Halloween and Christmas, and just generally having conversation that is less than riveting.

Then, our conversation turns to the recent hot topic about the affair that Mr. Lefferty, a teacher who Ed knows well, is having with a new teacher who was recently hired. I'm surprised we didn't discuss this earlier.

"Doug should know better," Ed says.

"So should she." Getting involved with a married man is wrong. "It takes two to get involved."

"He told me he's been having problems."

I put down my glass. There's nothing like good old gossip to get the evening going a little. "He actually told you that?"

Ed nods. "He said he's been having problems for over a year now, ever since they had the baby."

The baby. I'd forgotten that Doug's wife had had a baby. He'd brought the little one into work with his wife, when the baby was a few months old. Cute little thing, she was. Doug and his wife looked happy, from what I recall.

"Does his wife know?" I ask.

Ed shakes his head, looking glum. "Terrible situation. I don't know what to do, I don't know if I should tell her."

"Do you know her?"

"No."

"Then there's nothing you can do," I tell him. "It's not your place."

"And when we see her at the Christmas party, what then?" It's going to be weird. It *is* weird, and horrible, that we know that this woman's husband is cheating on her, and not only does his poor wife have no clue what her husband is up to, she has no idea that we know about something that is so private and personal, and awful about her life. She's completely ignorant of it.

It's horrible, and unfair, and it sucks.

Ed makes a low sound in his throat. "You're probably right. I can't say anything."

We eat in silence then, and after the server has cleared our plates, we talk about my art and crochet classes. I even tell Ed about the blanket I'm crocheting, and he actually pays attention as if he's interested.

"Thanks for tonight," I say, right after we've had dessert.

"Don't you want coffee, or something else?"

I shake my head. "I won't be able to sleep."

He looks at his watch. "It's only nine. You don't have to go to sleep anytime soon."

"But coffee stays in your system for hours. If I have a cup now, it won't wear off until around four in the morning."

"You've obviously done your research. How about a mint tea?"

It sounds like he's begging me to stay. God, I hate that he's doing this. Did he become more needy, or did I just turn this into something else? I don't want mint tea. I don't want something else.

I want to go home. I want to check if the money for the car has transferred from my account, and I want to check if my insurance has gone through. I did it all online as soon as I got back from the garage earlier, but I didn't get a chance to check. I want to confirm all these things and then tell Max.

"I'm ordering a coffee. I always need an after-dinner coffee," Ed informs me.

I smile to cover my disappointment. "In that case, I'll get a mint tea." I'll need something to sip, otherwise I'll have to sit and watch him drink his coffee.

He raises his hand to get the server's attention.

It seems rude of me, that I would prefer to go home now than to spend more time with Ed, but he's begun to bug me slightly with his insistence on dragging the evening out. I also hate myself for thinking like this.

"This is nice," Ed says, when our hot drinks arrive. "We should do this more often."

I sense a double meaning in that sentence. "I'll ask Christina to come along next time" I say cheekily.

He looks at me, then shrugs. "Sure. Why not?" Then, "Do you want to do something?"

My insides stiffen. *Do something?*

"Like watch a movie?" he suggests.

I hold my stomach, needing something to ground me.

Ed's getting the wrong idea, and I am to blame, and now

I need to fix it. "I... I didn't intend for this to mean anything, Ed." I try to say this as gently as I can.

"What do you mean?" he laughs, but it's forced, and then he straightens himself up so that he's sitting taller. "This is just pizza, two friends having pizza, nothing else. We could also be two friends watching a movie, Trinity. Get real."

It's the 'get real' which gives away his anger.

"I'm going to see if I can have a chat with Doug," he says, completely changing the subject. My reply has killed the moment, and any ideas he might have had. "I ought to at least try to get through to him," he continues.

"That might be better, since you're friends," I tell him. I'm relieved that he's not pursuing the idea of us going anywhere after the meal.

"I don't understand why people lose their morals so easily and turn to sin."

I swallow and say nothing.

"I'll talk some sense into him."

"Good luck." I take a final sip of my mint tea. "Shall we get the bill?"

A few moments later, he gets the bill. We split it and pay, and then leave the restaurant.

Outside, there's an awkward moment in the parking lot as he stands near my car. I don't know whether to shake his hand, or to kiss him on the cheek. We kissed on the cheek when we met, but now that we've had this exchange, the air between us seems a little colder.

I place my hand on his arm, in what I'm sure looks like a pathetic and strange gesture. "Thanks for a lovely evening." I move my hand away and I'm about to get into my car.

"Wait."

I stop and face him again. "I'm sorry, if it seemed like I was snapping at you."

He's caught me unawares. I didn't expect this from him. "Snapping at me?" I'm confused, and a little surprised.

"I like you, Trinity. I thought you kind of liked me, too."

My heart seems to stop. My brain stops too, as I find myself caught in this ugly, awkward moment. "I do like you, Ed," I say slowly.

"You seemed different tonight, disconnected somehow."

I give a tiny laugh, one that's supposed to indicate that I don't know what he's talking about. "Different how?"

"Like you didn't really want to be here."

That's like a slap across my cheek. He figured me out. Saw right through me. I blink a few times, wondering how transparent I must have seemed?

"That's what you thought?" I ask in surprise. "That's not true. It was good to catch up."

"Really?" His tone indicates that he doesn't believe me, and I don't blame him. I've pushed him away at every turn.

"It's..." It's Max. "It's just one of those days." This is a vague get-out card. I'm hoping he might attribute this to being my time of the month, rather than my fixation with Max, which he obviously knows nothing about. "It's been a long day, what with getting the car and everything. I'm sorry if I gave you that impression." It's a lame answer, but I hope he'll buy it.

"I almost started to think you didn't want to be here."

I gulp. What if he can read my mind? Now I feel like a witch, no, worse, a bitch. The whole time I was with Ed, I couldn't stop thinking about Max. It didn't help that we'd seen each other only hours earlier.

Each time I try to get that man out of my head, he comes back into my life.

"Nonsense," I say, not wanting to discuss this anymore. My mood is none of his business.

The evening has backfired on me. Between me suggesting it to Ed and us going out, a lot has happened between me and Max. None of it is ever going to lead to anything, but I can't help feel my stupid, shallow crush on him. I'm not a teenager. I'm supposed to be a sensible, grown-up woman. A schoolteacher who should know better.

"It's just that I thought we were slowly getting to know one another."

I need to get into my car and drive away. "We are... slowly getting to know one another... as friends, Ed."

He looks at me silently, and I give him a hug. I initiate that in order to get the awkward goodbye out of the way. I even smile at his, 'We should do this again next time,' suggestion, and promise him that we will.

Anything to take my leave and go home.

Once I'm home, I change into my PJs and settle down on the sofa, happy to be back in the comfort of my own home.

Because I can't sit still, I check my bank account and see that the payment for the car has transferred. I've also sorted out my insurance, so I text Max to let him know. I'm half tempted to call and tell him, but this isn't important news. I don't think he'd be too pleased to hear from me on a Saturday night.

I try not to think about what he might be doing right now, and I send the text, then sit expectantly waiting for him to acknowledge it.

He doesn't.

A few minutes pass painfully before I check to see if he's read my message.

He hasn't.

He's probably with his girlfriend. He never denied he had a girlfriend, but he said he didn't have a mom or a sister. I want to ask him what happened with his mom, but he doesn't seem to want to talk about it. So now I'm not only lusting over him, I also want to put my arms around him and hug some love into him.

Feeling irritable, I get out my crochet basket. Crocheting always calms me down. It's therapeutic in the way that shopping for clothes and makeup, or having sex might be for some women.

I switch the TV on and crochet with Benji lying on the couch next to me, stretched out regally, as if this is his own cushioned throne.

From time to time, I check to see if Max has read my message, but he still hasn't.

He probably has better things to do on a Saturday night.

CHAPTER SIXTEEN

MAX

"Thanks for coming, and thank you for this," says Sammy, giving me a kiss on the cheek as I hand her the present I bought for her; chocolates and flowers. I didn't know what else to get.

"Happy birthday," I say.

"Come in, and make yourself at home," she says, looking pretty and all dolled up in a bright red dress with her hair up. She's all smiles and excitement. "I'll go and put these in water. Help yourself to the food."

"Thank you."

Al pats me on the back and leads me into his living room. It's crammed full of people. Music is playing, and there is a table full of food. "Come inside, let me introduce you to a few people."

"I hope she likes the flowers and chocolates. I wasn't sure what she would like." I'm not good at buying gifts. I've never really had to buy them for Hot Gina and the others.

"Sammy likes everything," Al chortles. "She especially likes chocolate. Thanks for coming. I wasn't sure if you would."

I frown. "To help you celebrate Sammy's birthday? I wasn't going to miss that." I wasn't sure about coming, but there was no way I wouldn't have, especially since he invited me. Now that I'm here, I'm kind of glad I did come.

He leans closer. "Can I let you in on a secret?"

I nod, then wait for him to speak.

"I'm going to do the deed tonight," he whispers.

I pull away. "Dude, I don't need to know about your business."

He leans in again. "I'm going to propose to Sammy." This throws me completely, but I shouldn't really be surprised, because Al has been going out with Sammy for years. Despite all his comments about wanting to hook up with one of Hot Gina's friends, I know he's only joking because he's completely besotted by his girlfriend, who is possibly his soon-to-be- fiancée.

I feel a pinch of envy. "Wow. I didn't see that coming."

He shrugs. "We've been dating for years and I want to make it permanent. It's time to put a ring on her finger."

I give him a congratulatory pat on the back. "Hey, congrats, dude. I'm really happy for you." I glance over at Sammy who is surrounded by her friends. She's a nice girl, and she's good for him. Al's happy, and his life is swimming on by just fine.

That's what happens when you don't have the kind of baggage people like me have. I wouldn't have known any better, if I didn't have the marks to remind me daily of what my dad did to me. But they're there, hard to miss, and hard for me to forget.

Al's good news leaves me feeling melancholy, and I

don't understand why. I perk up though when he introduces me to his family and some of his other friends, and I fill my plate up to the max with all that wonderful food.

Some of Sammy's sisters—I assume they're her sisters because of the resemblance—keep coming up to me with bowls of food, asking me if I need a refill. I tell them 'no, thanks,' but I get the impression they're less concerned about the food, and more interested in catching my eye. It's easy to tell when a woman is hitting on you.

I manage to be gracious and end up talking to a few people. Then, Al hushes everyone, and one of Sammy's sisters brings her birthday cake in. A great big chocolate-covered cake with sparklers going off on top.

Then Al grins and drops to his knees. A silence falls in the room, and girlie murmurings of delight soon erupt.

I stand back, watching him pop the question, and see her eyes fill with tears, and her 'yes,' at which point the room erupts in claps and cheers. I clap and cheer loudly too.

Soon, Al and Sammy are kissing, and everyone starts taking pictures with their phones.

I manage to make my way to both of them and congratulate them. It's hard to talk to them for long because they are surrounded by so many people, so I wish them both good luck and decide to leave. I hadn't intended on staying for this long anyway, because I kind of had plans to stop by Sadie's place on the way out, but I'm glad I stayed around to see this.

As I move towards the exit, I pull out my phone to call Sadie. And then I hesitate. Suddenly, I'm not sure that I want to see her tonight.

The sex is always great, but I still feel empty afterwards.

I glance back at the room and see Al and Sammy with

their arms around one another. I don't feel as if I belong in the midst of such happiness, and that is the wrong way to be, especially about a guy who's a great friend.

Of course, I'm super thrilled for him. Some happy-ever-afters are predetermined. Some are never meant to be.

Maybe I should go see Sadie. She, like Hot Gina, makes me feel good, she makes me feel wanted, and that's what I want to feel tonight.

I hit the button to call her, but my phone dies and I'm strangely pleased. I *could* surprise her by showing up at her door, but that doesn't appeal to me, either.

I've become more aware, the older I get, that having sex for the sake of it doesn't make me feel better.

That's the problem with lust. It satisfies a primal urge, but it doesn't last. It doesn't fill that gaping big hole inside because it's a short high, and I don't want that anymore.

I want something longer, something lasting, something like Al has. What I want isn't something that Sadie, or even Hot Gina, can give me.

So I go straight home and flop in front of the TV.

I wake up late the next day to discover that I've fallen asleep on the couch. It's a pain in the ass, because I'm supposed to be at the garage, fixing a couple of cars, and doing overtime.

I get ready quickly and rush to work. Once I'm in my coveralls, I plug in my phone to charge up, and then I get to work.

Sometime later, I check my phone to see a whole heap of messages have come in.

But it's the text from Trinity that I read first.

She sent it late last night. She texted to let me know that the money's been paid into Enzo's account and she's ready to pick up the car.

I call Enzo and tell him the news, and he confirms that Trinity can come and collect her car.

I call Trinity but when she doesn't answer, I leave her a message and tell her that I'll be here for the next hour if she wants to come now, or she can come during the weekday. Then I get back to fixing the car.

It's because I need this job, because I want to stay on Enzo's good side, that I offered to come in and fix this car for a good friend of his. I need to do a good job because Enzo didn't dock my wages for letting Trinity go around the block a few times in the car.

He would have, if she'd crashed it. He'd have fired me as well. I'm lucky she's a safe driver and didn't do anything stupid, otherwise that could have been the end of me working here.

It was a silly thing to do even for someone like me who likes to ride on the wild side. Trinity isn't as restrained as she makes out. There's another side to her. I'm sure it's been there all along, but she either hides it, or she's not aware of it.

I seem to bring out that side in her, not that I want to take credit for it, but she starts to falter whenever I'm around. I can sniff that type of vulnerability.

She wants me, and she's fighting it. She plays it safe, but I reckon she sometimes wants to let her hair down, and the only reason she hasn't so far is because she hasn't met the type of guy who can help her to do that.

I'm not that guy, because I would be so, so wrong for her, but there's definitely something going on between us; a sizzle that I don't get from the others. Even Hot Gina naked with pizza slices all over her body doesn't do it for me as much as Trinity does, and that is how weird our entanglement has become.

An hour later, I've finished working on the car. I glance at my watch because it doesn't look as if Trinity is coming today. I'm ready to pack up and go home, so I go into the office and climb out of my coveralls. I whip off my T-shirt and pull out a fresh one when I hear the sound of someone coughing. I spin around with my arms in the arm holes of the T-shirt.

It's her.

Trinity stares at me with her mouth open, but her gaze isn't one of admiration.

"Sorry, I didn't realize you were getting changed..." she says, but she's not checking out my abs, or my muscles, she's staring at my scars.

"You should knock," I tell her, quickly slipping my head through the T-shirt and pulling it down. I try to gauge her reaction. She looks as if she has questions, but I'm not giving her any answers.

"I thought everyone had gone home."

"The shutters would be down if that was the case. You're here for the car, right?" I ask, more harshly than I intended.

"I got your message, that's why I came."

"Let me get you the keys. Enzo has some more paperwork he wants you to sign. Goddamn paperwork," I mutter under my breath as I head towards his office. Trinity trots after me.

"If this is a bad time, I can pick it up during the week, if you need to be someplace else." That's the thing about her. She's always so polite, so accommodating even when she doesn't need to be, and she doesn't need to be because she's the customer.

I smooth back my hair and leave my T-shirt out of my

jeans. She probably thinks I'm going on a date, but I'm not. I'm going to shoot some pool with my friends.

"You should have come earlier." I don't want her making me too late.

"Sorry. I was having lunch with my parents. It's a Sunday thing."

Lunch with her parents. Well, isn't that all peachy-keen?

"Would you rather I came during the week? I don't want to put you out."

I huff out a breath. "You're here now, but didn't you want to ..." I stop, because what I'm about to say might come across as patronizing.

She peers at me. "What?"

"Didn't you want to get a second opinion about the car?" Maybe she should show it to someone, like her dad, or a guy friend, even that weird guy Ed.

"You've already told me it's a good deal."

"You shouldn't take my advice so willingly."

"Did you lie to me about the car?"

"No."

"Then, why are you asking me these questions?"

"Just wanted to make sure you did your due diligence."

"I took your word for it. You're a mechanic, aren't you? You'd be the best person to give me advice."

That's what I was worried about, that she took my advice, and based solely on that, and the test drive, she bought the car. It *is* a good car, and I haven't lied or tried to sell it to her like a snake oil salesman, but even so, I'd feel better knowing she'd gotten a second opinion. "I was only making a suggestion," I mutter.

"You seem annoyed." Her voice has a hint of accusation in it, enough for me to take note.

"Do I?" I say that in a tone which is supposed to indicate surprise. But I am annoyed, and I can't put my finger on why. Maybe, it's because I don't usually meet a woman then have to forget about her, especially if there's something about her that catches my eye.

I'd usually end up in bed with her.

I don't understand what it is about Trinity that I find appealing, but I do know that getting her into my bed is out of the question.

She's forbidden fruit. She's a goddamn elementary schoolteacher, kind, and friendly and nicer than nice. She knits, or something, and has a goddamn cat. She's not a friends-with-benefits type of woman.

Her life is simple and uncomplicated.

She's someone whose heart I would break.

"I texted you last night," she continues, surprising me again.

"I was busy." I scratch my chin, and my eyes take in her linen pants and her loose top. She dresses way older than she should, in my opinion.

"I bet you were."

Something about the way she said that makes me tilt my head. "My friend Al, you've met him, he's the guy who towed your car. It was his girlfriend's birthday."

"I know Al," she cries.

"He proposed to his girlfriend right before she cut the cake."

Trinity's eyes ooze as if I've made her day. "He proposed?" she asks, on a sigh.

"Cheesy, huh?" In fact it wasn't cheesy at all, so I'm not sure why I said this.

"Romantic."

I cock my head. "Yeah, maybe."

"Truly romantic," sighs Trinity. "Was she surprised?"

"I think so. She said 'yes.'"

"Awww," she coos as if they're her best friends and she's over-the-moon ecstatic about their news.

"It was great. I didn't stick around too late though."

"Why not?"

"I didn't want to."

She looks puzzled.

"I had other plans."

"Other plans?" She looks at me with fearful eyes, as if she thinks I've done something illegal. I can't figure out if she's judgmental or curious.

"Do you want to know what I almost did last night, Trinity?" I take a step towards her. To my surprise, she doesn't step back. Her lips are still parted, and I imagine what it would be like to take her face in my hands and press my lips against hers. Then I think of a hundred reasons why I shouldn't.

"What did you almost do?" she whispers.

Christ. There's a hungry look in her eyes that I'm familiar with. With only me and her in this office, I could so easily kiss her.

"You'll judge me if I tell you."

"I won't," she insists.

My lips curl up slightly. "I'm pretty sure you will." I'm half-tempted to tell her about Sadie, because I don't want to lie, and because I want to see how easily she shocks.

"What did you almost do?" she asks.

I swallow, because it's on the tip of my tongue. I'm debating whether to lie, or tell the truth. If I lie, she'll think I'm a good guy, if I tell the truth, she'll see me for the loser that I am.

"I almost called my friend for sex."

She takes a step back, and disappointment colors her eyes.

She looks at me as if she doesn't know whether I'm joking or not. The look of disgust on her face stings me. "I bet you think badly of me now, huh?"

She shrugs. "What you do is none of my business."

"You did ask," I say.

"I didn't know you were going to say *that*." She believes me, and all of a sudden I don't want her to. Her words cut deep and she would hate me if she ever found out the truth.

"I'm kidding," I say, rushing to contain the damage.

I want her to think I'm a good guy.

Good enough for her.

She lets out a short huff. "You joked about something like *that?*"

I pretend-laugh. "Yeah."

"Why?"

"To see what you'd say."

"Sick." She shakes her head as if this doesn't make sense and walks towards the door.

"My phone died, and I didn't charge it up until just now," I say, in an attempt to explain. "That's why I didn't get your text last night. And if you were in such a hurry to pick up the car, you should have called the garage. You don't have to call me direct."

A flash of disappointment crosses her face. "It was late, I figured the garage would be closed, but I wanted you to get the commission for the sale."

"Why?" Why does she always want to do nice stuff for me? She doesn't owe me a thing.

"I was only trying to do you a favor. You've asked me to do you a favor before, remember?"

I'm not in a great mood, and neither, it appears, is she.

I'm not sure why that's the case when yesterday we were just fine together.

"I don't get a commission since this isn't a car lot."

She holds her hand to her forehead, "Don't you start."

"Start what?" I shrug when she doesn't say anything. "Let's get this over and done with quickly. I need to be somewhere."

"Another date?" she asks, her voice cool and collected.

"I'm going to shoot pool with some friends."

"Oh." She sounds as if I surprised her. But I'm now having second thoughts about that. Seeing Al surrounded by his family last night, and Trinity telling me she's just had lunch with her parents convinces me I need to go see my adoptive dad. He would love it if I brought Trinity home to meet him. I've never introduced any of my girlfriends to him before. Never felt the need to.

I push that thought right out of my head and call her over to the desk to sign the relevant paperwork.

While she's doing that, I remember that Enzo told me to hand her the car's logbook which he'd checked. I search the desk, find it and hand that to her. "There's the car's logbook. You should look through it. I should have shown you yesterday, before you bought the car."

She flicks through it quickly. "It looks fine. I'm not sure what I should be looking for. It says one owner."

From the envelope Enzo left behind, I fish out the two sets of car keys for the car. "Here you go." I dangle them in front of her.

"Thanks." She takes them from me, and we stare at one another.

"Do I just drive off? No more paperwork to sign?"

"No more paperwork," I force myself to say. "You just get in and drive that baby away."

But I don't want her to leave. The atmosphere is suddenly heavy, and that's my fault. "You didn't tell me what you did last night," I say, in a bid to stop her from rushing off, in a bid to try to salvage myself.

It works, because she stops, and seems to hesitate.

"What about you? What were you up to last night?" I ask, wanting to get a sneak preview of her life.

"I went out for dinner," she states calmly.

My eyes widen in surprise. "With who?"

"With a friend."

"I didn't expect you to go out alone. Who was it?" A smile curls onto my lips, because I sense her reluctance in sharing. "Was it Ed?"

"Yes, it was, if you must know."

"When are you going to admit to him being your boyfriend, Trinity?"

"He's not my boyfriend," she insists and she's doing it again, setting off those anxious vibes.

"He must be pretty special for you to want to spend your Saturday night with."

She blinks at me, a few times. "It was a friendly pizza."

"*Friendly* pizza?" I probe, taking enjoyment in her uneasiness. "Not a ham and cheese pizza, or a Texan BBQ, but a friendly one. That's new."

She gives me a look that could freeze the blood in my veins.

"That's right, a friendly pizza. It's a new topping."

The sarcasm in her voice is hard to miss, but all this talk of pizza reminds me of Hot Gina and her pizza. "He's a lucky guy," I say, lowering my voice an octave.

"He's a good friend."

"Whatever." I clear some things away on the desk, wanting to leave it neat in case Enzo complains.

"It was just pizza," she says.

"Probably not for Ed," I toss back. "I'm sure he thinks it was much more."

The tightness around her mouth tells me she doesn't like this. "How about you and me go out for a pizza one evening, as just friends?" I suggest, feeling cheeky, and daring.

The muscles of her throat inch up and down a little. "We could have *just* pizza, too, couldn't we?" And then, because I can't resist it, I reach for her wrist and run my thumb across it. She swallows again, the telltale motion of her throat giving it away.

"What are you doing?" she asks, but she doesn't move her wrist away.

"I'm reacting to you."

She opens her mouth as if she's about to say something, but doesn't.

I can smell her vanilla perfume, and my mind's eyes pictures her daily getting-ready routine. I wonder what she showers with, and what moisturizer she slathers all over her body. I wonder how she does her bra up. From the front, or the back?

And then I realize I can't be near her. She would be shocked if she knew what I was thinking. Just like she would be shocked if she knew the type of girlfriends I have.

I stop stroking her wrist, and the moment I do, she lifts her hand up, and presses the thumb of her other hand on the part I touched. She rubs it lightly, as if I've left a mark she needs to erase.

"I'd better go," she says, and moves towards the door.

"Good idea." I don't know what I was thinking when I pulled that move just now. I know only that I needed to touch her.

Trinity isn't the type of girl to get involved with a guy like me, but she interests me, and it's not often that a woman interests me the way she has. She hasn't done it by flirting, she hasn't caught my attention by showing any flesh.

But caught my attention she has.

How can I look away now? Pretend I haven't met her? I'd like to kiss that sweet little mouth of hers, but I say, "You'd better get going, before you get into trouble."

She raises an eyebrow, as if she wants to question what I mean, but decides not to. I can read it in her eyes. There's been a flirty tone to our conversations lately, and she doesn't quite know what to make of it.

She obviously thinks it's safer for her to leave than to stay here with me.

She's not wrong.

CHAPTER SEVENTEEN

TRINITY

Over lunch I'd told my dad that I'd bought the car I'd mentioned to him the last time we spoke but, like Ed, he wasn't pleased to hear that I bought it from the guy who crashed into the back of my car.

So now, because he's concerned that I've been bamboozled, and I want to prove that I haven't, I drive back to my parents' house.

I get there and proudly show it to my parents. My dad looks it over but doesn't say anything much, aside from examining the wheels and the body carefully. "Not bad. Let's see how it drives."

He wants me to take them for a drive in it, so I do.

When we return to their house, he begrudgingly accepts that it isn't so bad.

"See, Dad," I say proudly, as we all get out of the car, "I didn't get tricked. I *do* know a thing or two when it comes to buying a car."

Or rather, I know a friend who does, but my dad doesn't need to know that.

"Let me have a quick look at the logbook," my dad says. I open the glove compartment and look for it but I can't find it. Then I remember that I left it on the desk in the garage office.

"Uh... it's not there."

"What do you mean it's not there?" My dad eyes me as if I've committed a felony. "Please tell me that you checked the logbook thoroughly before you bought it?"

"I did!" I might not have looked through it *thoroughly,* but I did flick through it.

"Really?" my dad asks, as if he doesn't believe me.

"Trinity," my mother chimes in before I can answer. "You really should have taken your father along to look at the car. And if you were going to pick it up after lunch, why didn't you ask us to drive you there?"

"I wanted to surprise you."

"You *have* surprised us," my father retorts. Displeasure is written all over his face. "Is it a reputable garage?"

"Yes, Dad, and I checked the logbook. I left it at the garage because I was in a rush."

"In a rush to buy a car?"

"I'll get it back, Dad. It's no big deal."

"It *is* a big deal, Trinity. You wouldn't take on a new job without looking at the contract, would you?"

"This isn't like that, Dad. I checked the logbook. I really did." I'm now beginning to wish I hadn't been so eager to drive over and show them my latest purchase. "Do you like it?" I ask them both.

"It drives really nice," my mom says.

"It seems like a good car," my dad acknowledges, if somewhat begrudgingly.

"Then what's the problem?"

"That you bought it from a garage and not a car lot. And there isn't even a logbook."

"There is a logbook," I cry. "I'm trying to save up money, Dad. I don't see the point in getting a brand-new car."

"We could have helped you with the financing."

"You've already helped me enough."

"There are plenty of zero percent financing deals available."

"It's a good car, Dad. You said so yourself. I didn't walk in with my eyes closed. Max checked it out."

"Max? Who's Max?" my mother asks.

"He's...he's...he's the mechanic there." I hate that my face begins to flush, especially when both my parents are staring at me. There is nothing for me to feel heated about—well, not much. Nothing has happened between me and Max to warrant me feeling guilty.

Nothing real.

It's all been in my mind. But I feel strange talking to my parents about him.

I especially don't like the way my mother is staring at me. "Sometimes, Trinity, common sense flies right out of your head," my mother says.

I can't believe what a big deal my parents are making of this, but I shouldn't be surprised. They've always been a little overbearing, a little too involved. They've always looked out for me, always wanted to fix things for me. I love them to pieces, but it sometimes gets to be too much. Especially now that I'm in my mid-twenties.

"I'll get the logbook and you'll see that everything is fine," I say quickly. "But you like the car," I remind them.

Then I give them both a hug and tell them that I need to go home and prepare for school tomorrow.

I decide not to call Max and tell him about the missing logbook. After what happened between us at the garage earlier, I don't want him to think I'm calling him because of *him*. I liked him taking my wrist in his hand. I liked what he did. I was surprised by what he did, but not repulsed, and I wish he'd carried on doing more of it. I wish for many things each time I think of him.

I wait until the next day and call him during my lunch hour. A ripple of excitement shoots through me when he picks up.

When I tell him that I forgot the logbook on the desk, he says he'll come over and drop it off at the end of the day. But I tell him that I'm busy and have a meeting with the principal then, and that it's not a big deal and can wait. I'll pass by one day in the next week to get it.

He seems fine with that.

At the end of the school day, Ed doesn't drop by my classroom for his usual daily chat. I'm off to my art class and am eager to get home, so I'm kind of glad to not see him. Plus, Saturday night was awkward, and I'm scared he'll ask when we can go out again.

I don't want to go out again, for dinner with Ed, anytime soon. Not unless I can get Christina to come along.

I don't really think about Ed these days.

It's Max I can't get out of my head.

Going to my art class is a good distraction, and it makes me feel better.

But not long after I get home, someone rings my doorbell. I'm not expecting anyone, so I open the door warily. Max is standing there with the logbook in his hands.

"Here you go," he says, handing it to me.

The sight of him sucks the air out my lungs. I'm already starting to breathe faster.

"I was going to pick it up one day in the next week," I manage to say.

"I was in the area."

"You were?" I'm not sure whether to believe him or not, and a part of me is in shock because of his timing. He knocked on my door moments after I walked in. "Have you been waiting for me?"

"No, why?"

"I only just got back. Have you been spying on me?"

"Would you like me to spy on you?" he asks with amusement.

His gaze heats up my skin, warms my insides as if I've sipped velvety hot chocolate. Our conversation seems to be similar to that of people who know one another well—people who are dating, or are familiar with one another, not people like us, who are practically strangers.

There is no good answer to that question, so I avoid it, and in the next moment, he steps inside, even though I haven't invited him in. His boldness startles me. "You teach art to adults with learning difficulties," he states.

"Who told you that?"

"You did."

"I did?" I don't remember telling him but then I seem to forget a lot of things when Max is near me. My sanity vanishes into thin air. I close the door and watch him giving my place a once-over. His eyes scan around my dingy little living room, taking everything in.

I had a hard time falling asleep last night, and it wasn't because of my parents' displeasure over the logbook. As I watch him, I realize that the reason for my sleeplessness is standing right in front of me.

"Thanks for coming all this way," I say.

"Like I said, I was in the area."

"You have friends around here?"

"What's with the third degree, Trinity?"

This isn't about the logbook.

He knows it and so do I.

I wonder why he came when I said it could wait. "There was no rush."

"Why did you need it?"

"I didn't." I push a lock of hair back behind my ear. "My dad wanted to take a look at it."

"What did your parents think of the car?"

"The truth?" I wince, remembering my dad's comments.

"Do you ever lie?"

"No. Do you?"

He doesn't answer as quickly as I did. "If I have to."

I raise my eyebrow, curious. "Have you ever lied to me?"

"We don't have that kind of relationship." His eyes burn into mine. And then he seems to catch himself. "And no. I've never lied to you, about the car or the repairs or anything like that."

I tell him what my dad said and how my parents weren't too happy that I bought the car from the garage.

"I don't blame them," he replies, good-naturedly. "Most parents wouldn't trust a mechanic to sell their daughter a wrench, let alone a car."

I laugh inwardly, because he has no idea that my dad is just as wary. My parents wouldn't trust this man, but I do, even when everything about him tells me I shouldn't.

I shouldn't even be talking to him, let alone have him here in my place. But it's hard to resist when he's staring at me as if he wants to kiss me. His gaze keep lowering to my lips, just like mine keep falling to his.

He was bold yesterday, when he did that thing to my wrist.

It felt good.

Until he stopped.

He arouses emotions in me that Ed has never been able to, and Ed is more my type.

Or maybe Ed *was* my type.

Ed is safe, and consistent, and normal. And boring and mundane.

Max is everything I should avoid. He's dangerous, and sexy, and flirty. He looks at me as if he's undressing me, and a part of me wishes he would.

He is everything I should run from, and yet here I am, rooted to the carpeted floor.

You're saving yourself for marriage.

He's standing a good couple of feet away from me, but his gaze heats up my body like a blowtorch.

I want more of what he did to me yesterday at the garage.

I want to know what it's like when he doesn't stop. I want to know what his lips will feel like on mine.

I want to start *feeling*, instead of imagining.

"I should go," he says, but his voice sounds odd. Gravelly. I don't want him to go.

"Already?" I ask, my voice weak. He takes a step towards me, and my knees go weak. "I couldn't stop thinking about..."

"Couldn't stop thinking about what?" he asks.

"About what you did yesterday, when you grabbed my wrist."

He laughs, and I immediately feel silly because that's not the reaction I wanted. I breathe out slowly.

"Really?" he asks, his expression turning serious, his eyes turning soft. "You liked that?"

I nod. My armpits suddenly feel hot and sweaty and I wished I'd gotten out of my school clothes and put on my loungewear. I'm suddenly conscious of my appearance and I wish I'd freshened up. I wish I had the type of figure that could slip into sexy, slinky, dinky lingerie that those gazelle-like models wear.

"What are you thinking, Trinity?"

I swallow. "Nothing." Only me in a sexy item of lingerie. About fifteen pounds thinner.

"I should go," he says again, this time heading for the door as if he means it.

"I liked it," I blurt out. "I liked it a lot; you touching my wrist like that."

He turns around, his eyes twinkling. "Did you know that inside of your wrist is an erogenous zone?" he says slowly. I squirm under the weight of his words.

He comes towards me, and I forget to breathe. "Want me to touch you like that again?"

I dare not breathe, nor speak, nor move my head.

I am not supposed to like this. I'm not supposed to invite such presumptuous behavior. I'm not supposed to want him to do things like that. Not to me.

And yet my heart and soul yearn for it.

He takes both of my wrists in his warm, hard hands, and goose bumps rise like magnetized hairs along my arms.

I'm not cold. I'm caught in Max's spell once more. He watches me closely, as if he's reading my face, trying to figure out what I'm thinking.

His thumbs circle gently around, and my heart rate

starts to climb. Shooting stars zig-zag across my belly. "Like this?" he asks, his voice dropping to a whisper.

I manage to nod.

He indulges me for the longest time, and we stand facing one another, caught in a hypnotic time-freeze. I don't know how it is possible, but whatever he's doing to my wrists sends a signal straight to that place between my legs.

I shudder out a breath, because every point in my body is on fire.

"Want me to try elsewhere?" he asks. "Not the obvious places," he says quickly, "but other parts; safer parts... like the back of your neck, or your ears."

I consider all these other parts as he names them; even the parts he said were off limits.

"Tell me what you want, Trinity."

"Can't you tell?" The words slip out easily.

"I don't want to take advantage of you," he murmurs.

A fire rages inside me, and every cell in my body wants him to take advantage of me.

With his thumbs still on my skin, he moves closer. "Tell me where you want me to touch you, and kiss you...tell me what you want me to do." His breath is warm and sweet, and his words are like long, slow wet kisses on my body. Every move he's made has been unexpected and full of surprises.

He knows how to shock me, and make my heart run wild. My breath speeds up. "I want you to not stop." I know that's a cop-out, because instead of telling him what I want him to do, I tell him what I don't want.

"What do *you* want?" I ask him. My voice sounds strangely hoarse and husky.

"I want to kiss you," he whispers.

CHAPTER EIGHTEEN

MAX

Some men ask for permission to kiss or touch a woman, but I don't ask. I never force myself on a woman, but I can tell if she's interested.

Yet with Trinity, I'm unsure, and this is something rare for me. I don't want to make a move, unless she wants me to. I know she wants me, but she won't admit to it. I can't even get a straight answer out of her.

So when she turns the tables and asks me what I want, I tell her.

"I want to kiss you," I tell her, and I watch her dark eyes glisten in surprise.

Hell. I could do so much more than kiss her right now. I want to skate my fingers across her skin, I want to trace each and every contour of her body. I want to leave a trail of kisses from her head to her toes.

Her mouth falls open and she lets out a sigh. I move even closer and my hand skims her stomach. She wasn't expecting that, and when she lifts her face to me, wondering what the hell I'm doing, I take her mouth

I press my lips over hers and kiss her. A soft moan escapes her lips just as my hands slip around her waist. She's soft and fleshy, and my fingers skate over her waist and bottom. I love the feel of her, the softness of her, and I'm so turned on that I tilt her face up and my tongue sinks deeper into her mouth.

We press against one another, I can actually feel her press her body against mine. She arouses me, and I can't help but grind my hips instinctively into her.

She gasps so loudly that I'm scared I've hurt her. "What's the matter?" I stare into her eyes but it's her big beautiful breasts I want to bury my face in. I raise my hand to cup a breast then stop myself.

Too much, too soon.

I'm aware of her hands on my shoulders, and as I pull away to take a breath, she exhales slowly. Her lips are red and moist.

Tempting.

She doesn't say a word, but looks at me with hunger in her eyes, as if she hasn't been kissed like this in a while, or ever. I don't need her to tell me, I *know* it.

Her gaze drops to my lips again, and she doesn't need to beg. I kiss her again. This feels different. It's not like being with Hot Gina or Sadie, or any of the others. Kissing Trinity is like the slowest slow dance. Her hands slide up around my neck, and she pulls me closer.

This girl wants more.

But I'm not sure getting involved with Trinity is the right thing for her.

For now, I have to go slow. I kiss her slowly, not too

deeply, just slow getting-to-know-you kisses now, as I start to become familiar with her taste and scent.

"I love your kisses," she whispers, in between our kissing and rest phases.

"Yeah?"

She nods.

So I oblige.

Somehow, like drunkards back from a late-night party, we flail and make our way towards her bedroom. I almost trip over the endless piles of books lying on the floor. We end up on her bed, her lying beneath me as we make out like curious teenagers.

I have a boner that pokes into her but she hasn't said a word. We're not going there, although I intend to keep this going for as long as I can. For weeks, this woman has been around me, in my head, if not always physically near me, and I finally get to have her this close, in my arms, like this. And now that we are finally together, it's a process of discovery, every moment yields something new.

She likes deep kisses, she likes when I squeeze her buttocks, she likes when I cup her breasts. She doesn't like so much when I grind against her.

All we've done is make out. There is no conversation, just kissing sounds, contented sighs, and moans. "You're a great kisser," she tells me again.

"Thank you," I manage to reply. It sounds as if she's experienced a little drought, or had some lame-ass lovers in her line of boyfriends. She has the most gorgeous lips, I notice. Lips that demand to be kissed. Lips that I enjoy kissing over and over and over again.

I'm not lying completely on top of her, but on the side so that my weight doesn't squash her. My fingers trace a line around her mouth then my hand lowers to her chest.

She's hard to resist, lying as she does on her back, with the top button of her blouse open. I can't see much, and I need to see more, because the cotton blouse she's wearing doesn't conceal the pebbled peaks of her hard nipples.

My fingers skim over one of them, causing her to let out a sigh. Our gazes lock. Her eyes are dark, as black as the night, and when I tweak her breast over the fabric, making the peak sharper, more pronounced, she wriggles to my touch. Her mouth falls open and I can't resist licking her lower lip. When she shifts under me, I place my entire hand over her breast but even then I can't cup all of it.

I take a sharp inhale because I should stop, but I can't. I want to rip her clothes off, but I brace myself, because this woman isn't like all the others.

"What?" I ask, when she doesn't say anything, but her flushed face tells me she's turned on.

"The way you kiss," she murmurs, biting her lip, her hooded bedroom eyes gazing at me.

"What about it?" I ask, knowing full well that she has enjoyed every second.

"I've never been kissed like that before."

Oh, boy, is she in for a treat, then.

"It's a tragedy," I remark, tracing the outline of her wet lips with my fingers. She smiles again, and lets out a little breath.

It turns me on even more to know that I can draw this truth out of her. It's like peeling a fruit, bit by bit. You can only get to the sweet juicy segments after you've slowly peeled away the outer layer.

"I intend to keep kissing you, to make up for the loss." My voice sounds croaky, and I'm so hard that I can't think straight. Doesn't help that she's lying here, soft, and hot, and wants me.

She smiles.

I lower my head, and struggle to stop myself from doing what I am desperate to do—to unbutton her blouse and have her topless beneath me—so instead I kiss her softly, and for the longest time. She moans as if I've made her feel something deep, something passionate. It's a sound I love to hear. I lift my hand to her face and cup her soft cheek. She looks half-scared, half-excited.

My hard-on turns to steel.

I so desperately want to fuck her right now, but instead I kiss her again, claiming her mouth as if every inch of her body belongs to me.

My tongue sweeps inside her mouth and I savor her sweetness, not letting up.

"Wait, wait, wait," she sighs, breaking our kiss. Her chest rises and falls as I lift my head. "Too much?" I ask, my eyes pinned to her moist lips and it's almost impossible for me to do what she's asking.

She wraps her hand around mine, and the skin-on-skin contact sends shivers scurrying all over my body. It's strange, that all we're doing is holding hands and kissing, and yet my cock is throbbing like it's poised for entry.

"You're so damn gorgeous," I say, lifting her face with my finger under her chin, directing her to face me again.

"You're only saying that bec—" but before she can finish, I've claimed her lips again, and she sighs like she's floating in heaven. She will be soon enough, and she'll be screaming when I make her come over and over again.

I'm so hard now that I can't stop my hand from sliding inside her blouse, and into her bra.

Her warm breast greets my palm and I squeeze gently, loving the feel of her softness. Instinctively, I deepen our kiss, and move my thumb over her nipple again, it's hard, and grows harder still when I rub it gently.

Her moans grow louder, and I'm desperate to slide my fingers into her panties and see how ready she is, but I resist. Exploration is going to have to wait a while.

I usually end up in bed with whoever I'm kissing on the first date. I haven't had a first date in a while, and while this isn't technically a date—I don't know what this is—I'm pretty sure that Trinity doesn't give up anything even on the tenth date.

I start to unbutton her shirt, pulling back so that I can read her face and stop if she wants me to. She watches me, and her parted lips and her shiny eyes tell me all I need to know. My fingers move gently and quickly, and even though I'm desperate to bury myself inside her, I won't. She lets out a sexy sigh, and I can't think straight, because arousal has fogged the thinking part of my brain, but I know not to do *that*. I can't have sex with her on this first time, not with Trinity.

We've been making out for the longest time, and my boner is so hard, I'm going to have a bad stomachache.

Hot Gina would have had her mouth around me by now, or her legs wrapped around my waist. We'd go at it for hours, in all sorts of positions.

I've never had to wait so long to get my release.

Trinity giggles lightly as I peel her shirt away and expose her great big white bra. I'm used to seeing pretty, flimsy, lacy numbers, not an ugly contraption like the one she's wearing. It looks like it's from the Victorian era, and has all the sexiness of a praying nun.

The sight of it clogs my thinking for a brief second, but I quickly move past it. I don't undo her bra clasp, but my breathing speeds up, and I torture myself with holding back.

Trinity's face is everything I'm not used to seeing. She's shy, and vulnerable, and unsure, and it's like she's let me open a treasure chest and given me access to all the loot.

I could strip all her clothes off and have sex with her, but I don't.

My cock says yes, but my head says no.

She's a nice girl.

A *good* girl.

But I have a lot of baggage.

I'm the wrong guy for her.

What she needs is someone slow and safe and boring. Like that schoolteacher friend of hers.

"Why did you stop?" she asks, as if she can read my mind.

"You're fucking beautiful, Trinity," I say, staring into her eyes and feeling my heart float away in them. "I don't want to stop, but I have to, otherwise we'll go too far."

"Don't you want me?"

I blink. Oh, sweet Jesus. Of course I want her. But she doesn't know the real me, and for some reason, I don't want to be that guy to her.

"I've never had sex before," she says, shattering the warm, intimate bubble we've been floating in.

"What?" It's like she dropped a glass boulder straight onto a concrete floor.

"You heard." Her face flushes, only this time I suspect it's not from her arousal.

"You're a *virgin?*" I let out a gasp, one that sounds more like disappointment or maybe it's shock, I can't tell. I'm not sure what I feel, but it's not overjoyed.

I should be ecstatic—because she won't know what to do and everything will be new. This is so rare, so unheard of, I should be happy.

I should feel pleased.

I should be honored, but I don't feel any of those emotions because she thinks I'm the best thing to happen to her and I know what a bastard I can be.

I roll away and sit up, trying to make sense of what she's told me.

"Is it a problem?" she asks, sensing the chill as the moment flattens and shatters to the ground like a dropped icicle. She covers her chest again with the blouse, and folds her arms over it. I notice that she doesn't start buttoning it up, though.

"No," I say, turning away, wanting her not to feel bad about this because it's a good thing, only I'm not a good thing for her, and I don't want to be the one who takes this precious thing from her.

She's been holding onto it like a Golden Ticket out of Charlie's Chocolate Factory, but I'm no Willy Wonka. I won't do the right thing by her in the end.

I'm not a guy who does long-term. I do Hot Gina, and other easy girls like her; girls who know the score and like it that way.

"It's not a bad thing, No. It's not," I tell her, though who I'm trying to convince here, I'm not sure. I don't get involved with women like Trinity, and I don't know why I let myself this time.

"Then, why don't you look happy?"

"How come you've never had sex?" I ask, because that's got to be the million-dollar question.

"I never met anyone I cared enough about."

Oh, shit. I really don't want to be the guy who pops her cherry, and this just confirms it a million times over.

"I was saving myself," she continues.

Saving yourself? For what? I want to scream. "How old are you?"

"Twenty-five."

Twenty-fucking-five. "Huh," is the only word I can muster in response. How the hell do you reach the ripe old age of a quarter of a century without having had sex?

She has no idea what she's missing.

I stare at her downcast face. "What's wrong?" she asks.

How can she not know? "I can't...I can't ..." I'm out of words, and instead I jump up off the bed and stare down at her. She's sitting up now, and slowly buttons her blouse again.

"What did you think was going to happen just now?" I ask her.

"We were kissing. I liked it, didn't you?"

"Yes." A bit *too* much. She must have known exactly how much I liked it with the way my hard-on must have dug into her belly. "Where did you think we were going to end up?"

"I don't know. I've never been kissed like that, for that long before."

I rake a hand through my hair. I'm still in shock. I can't believe a human being can reach this age and still be a virgin.

"Are you laughing at me?" Her eyes narrow.

I reach down and cup her face. "I'm not laughing at you. I find it hard to believe that someone ... that you're still a virgin." Now it makes sense, her telling me how much she likes my kisses.

"How many boyfriends have you had?" My curiosity gets the better of me.

"Why do you need to know?" she asks. I'm intrigued. She's like a specimen to me, and I don't mean that in a bad way, but for someone like me, who is addicted to sex, Trinity is an anomaly. I want to understand how she could reach this age without ever having had sex. No wonder she liked me stroking her wrist so much. "No touching, and stroking?" I ask her.

"Why did you move away? I'm not a leper."

I sit back down quickly again. "No, you're not. I moved away because I don't want to do something you're not ready for."

"You make me feel like a freak."

I turn to her, and brush my thumb over her lower lip. "You're not, and I apologize if I've made you feel like that."

"If you're going to ask me about my lack of sex, I want to know all about your sexual exploits."

My stomach hardens as I lie down.

"You didn't like that, did you?" she asks. She's resting her head on her hand, and her elbow digs into her pillow. I don't say anything. How will she ever understand the concept of fuck-buddies, someone like her who has waited so long before having sex?

I can't answer her question, but I try to. "There's nothing to know. I love sex. That's it. That's why you're the last person who should be around a guy like me."

"Who was your last girlfriend, how long ago?" she asks, not heeding my warning.

What am I supposed to say to that?

I push the thought of Hot Gina away. And because I have no answer, I pull Trinity towards me and kiss her again. This sets off another round of getting-ready-to-fuck type of kissing. I can't resist her. I can't keep my mouth away from her even though I know I should. "You're so sexy, so goddamn irresistible. You're enough to drive a man delirious."

"Am I?" The way she asks me, it's like this is a completely new revelation to her.

"Yes, you are."

"You're just saying that because I haven't had sex before."

I run my hands through my hair. She is a bigger prize than Hot Gina. I could be all her firsts, and I'm pushing her away. It's the right thing to do, even though my cock doesn't agree with me. "I'm saying that because it's true. I find you sexy beyond belief, but I didn't know you were a virgin until a few seconds ago, so no, it's not because of that. It just makes you unique. You're gorgeous and sexy because that's the truth, not because I have any ulterior motives to get inside your panties."

She props her knees up on the bed. "I didn't want you to stop."

She's making it impossible for me to abstain. "I shouldn't have done that. *We* shouldn't have done that."

"But we did," she replies.

"What do you want from me, Trinity?"

She shrugs.

"I'm not the type of guy you should be interested in, Trinity."

"I didn't come looking for you. You're the one who came crashing into me."

When she puts it like that, I can't help but smile, even though this is serious. It's serious in that I need to step away from her.

She was disgusted when I told her that I phoned my friend to have sex. I had to lie to save myself, because Trinity couldn't stomach the truth.

And now she thinks I'm something I'm not.

There's no way we can be together.

"I have to go," I say, getting up. Sometimes tough love is the right thing. "I was only supposed to give you the logbook."

She stares up at me with her big Bambi eyes, and makes my heart melt. I have never walked away from a woman who tells me she wants me.

But I do, because this time it's the right thing to do.

CHAPTER NINETEEN

TRINITY

The throbbing between my legs continues even after Max leaves.

What just happened?

Every shred of common sense disintegrates when he's around me. I should know better by now. I should know that every interaction with him leaves me feeling as if I've been sucked into a twister. He's bad for me, but he always sucks me in, no matter how hard I try to stay away.

I want to be with him, even though being with someone like him probably won't make for lasting happiness. I want romance, and dating, and marriage; all of it, but I don't think Max is the type of guy to offer that.

Yet I still want him.

This can't continue. What we did, it can't carry on. I need to wean myself off the drug that he is.

I am determined to get over this temporary flash of insanity with which I've become inflicted, and during the following week I do my best to block all further thought of him from my mind, which is easier said than done. I try to concentrate on the things at hand, grading workbooks, preparing lessons, being present as much as I can.

It isn't easy, it wasn't easy especially after our last meeting; I can't forget about the taste of him, the feel of his lips, and the giddying sensation of his hands over me. All of these things are imprinted on my mind and body.

I make it to the end of the week and on Friday, after our crochet class, Christina and I go to dinner together as usual.

I want to tell her about Max, even though I don't think she'll approve. If she met him, saw his sexy swagger and his mannerisms, and that too-handsome-to-be-trusted face, she would ask me what I'm doing with someone like that.

The urge to talk about him becomes ever more potent the more I try to suppress all thought of him. What I have for him feels like a stupid schoolgirl crush, but at this age I'm supposed to know better.

To stop myself from talking about Max, I tell her about Dylan and my latest concerns. His recent drawings have been a slight cause of concern for me. In one, his mother was lying on the floor while his dad stood over her. When I asked Dylan what was going on, he looked away.

"You've either got to report him to child services, or tell Marshall about your concerns," Christina says.

"But what if I'm wrong?" It's a fine line, being concerned, and reading too much into a situation. Dylan's drawings have only now become worrisome. Previously, it was the state of his clothes, or the fact that he looked so undernourished and gaunt, that worried me. I can't go to the principal with my concerns based on these things alone. And Dylan's mom seems to be trying so hard. I've spoken to her on a few occasions when I've been outside at the end of the school day. She seems normal. A doting mother.

"Are you still giving him pieces of fruit after school?" Christina asks.

"Sometimes."

"You're going to get into trouble, Trin."

"For giving him an apple?"

"You know what I mean."

"I'm just being a human."

"If you're that worried, you need to tell someone."

"But I don't want to cause more problems at home. His mother is nice. Maybe she's struggling a little, and she's trying to do her best, but most moms are, aren't they?" The wisp of a woman, with sunken eyes and bad skin, was pleasant enough. She was interested in finding out how Dylan was getting along at school. She told me she worked as a cleaning lady at one of the schools nearby, and that her husband was out of work, which was why I never saw her do many of the school pickups.

"You're being an overly interfering teacher."

"I'm concerned."

"Then tell the principal."

"He might get child protective services involved."

"Isn't that what you want?"

"I don't see any *evidence*." I haven't seen any bruises, or cuts, or cigarette burns. I know Max had them, I know what they look like. In my earlier training, I saw a child with the most horrific burns on her. I still can't forget them.

"Then don't get involved."

I honestly don't know what to do. I would hate myself if something happened to Dylan that I could have prevented, but I also know that I might be imagining the worst, that his mother is doing her best to get by, and maybe his father isn't a tyrant, but just a man trying to juggle life.

Being out of work causes pressure. Maybe the man has debts, and low self-esteem, and is trying to find work. Maybe Dylan's parents, like many parents, are dealing with the usual life stuff that many of us deal with and some can handle better than others.

Me reporting Dylan as a potential neglected child could make things worse for a family who are already on the brink.

To think that when I went into teaching, I had naively assumed it would be all about inspiring and motivating young minds. I didn't know I'd be on watch looking out for signs of neglect and abuse.

"When are you going out with Ed?" she asks, pulling me out of my burdened thoughts.

"I've been. It was last weekend."

Christina throws down her fork in surprise or annoyance, I can't tell.

"And you never thought to mention it?"

"I was going to get to that," I reply, calmly.

"I'm beginning to think you're keeping things from me."

"I would have told you. I was going to get to that. It was fine. The calzone was—"

"I'm not interested in the calzone. Ed, date, chemistry. Tell me about those things."

"He'd made an effort, he looked quite nice, I thought. It wasn't a date, and we had no chemistry."

"You didn't like him even a teeny-weeny bit?"

"I like him, I'm just not attracted to him."

"But you've been talking to him for ever. You said he seemed nice, and decent, and you both wanted the same things." She's alluding to the no-sex clause, and that it's easier to date guys who have the same mindset, otherwise things can get tricky.

"I know." I rearrange the cutlery on my plate. "I just didn't want anything to happen."

"And what about him?"

"He wanted to do something."

"Do what?"

I shrug. "Go to the movies, not go home so early."

"And you?"

"I wanted to go home." I prop my elbow on the table and rest my cheek on my hand, pondering my options. "He's interested, but I'm not."

"I really thought seeing him outside of school might get things going with you and him."

In my pre-Max days, Ed might have had a chance.

"He's not bad looking, Trin. And he seems nice. That's a real shame." I sense that Christina really wanted us to hit it off. She likes Ed, even though she's only met him once in real life, and heard plenty about him from me. Things have changed though.

"I bought a new car," I tell her, since she's going to see it when we both leave.

"Oh? Which one?"

"It's not brand new, it's a used one but it was a bargain." I tell her.

"That was quick."

"When I broke down last week, I knew I had to do something."

"Shame, since you got it repaired recently."

I take a sip of my drink. It was easier to tell Ed where I got the car from than it is to tell Christina. She will judge me, and then if we start talking about Max, I'll end up telling her what's been going on between us.

She'll be offended that I've kept so much from her, but I'm equally hesitant to tell her everything because, with her being my friend, she'll try to steer me away from him.

So I say nothing more, and decide to keep the news about Max to myself for a little bit longer before I tell Christina everything.

CHAPTER TWENTY

MAX

"Your friend is here," Al announces, giving me a mischievous wink.

My heart drops. Hot Gina called me a few days ago, but I didn't take her call. It was the first time I hadn't, and now I'm not so thrilled about the prospect of seeing her. We have an agreement not to show up unannounced at each other's apartments, and now I'm suddenly worried that she's here, at my place of work.

But when Al moves out of the way, it's Trinity I see standing before me. My heart skips a beat. My cock twitches. Everything about our last meeting bursts into my mind.

"Hi," she says, even though it's one word, her voice sounding oddly wobbly.

"Hi," I try to downplay the happiness I'm feeling. I straighten up and put down my tools, then wipe my hand on my coveralls. Behind her back, Al gives me a thumbs-up.

I bring my gaze back to Trinity before she realizes what that jackass is doing.

"Something wrong with the car?" I ask, thinking that this is the reason for her visit.

"No." She hesitates a moment, and looks at me. It's been over a week since I last saw her. I can't get that time out of my head. I wake up and think about what she told me, about never having had sex, and it makes me want her even more.

I've missed her.

Been tempted to call her. I've wanted to see her again, but I somehow managed to respect her distance and silence.

And now, here she is; the cause of my hard-on every single morning when I wake up. I wonder if she has recalled our last meeting as much as I have.

"I, uh, I want to sell my old car."

I blink, because I have no idea what this has to do with me.

"Can you sell it here, maybe?" she asks. "I don't know what else to do with it."

"Uh-," I wipe my hand on my coveralls again. "You should have said something when you bought the other car. We could have maybe considered a parts exchange."

"You didn't mention anything about it."

"You didn't tell me you wanted to sell your old car," I reply defensively. "But I don't think you're going to have much success with it. It's only good for the dumpster. I can ask Enzo, if you want me to."

"Oh, okay. If you could. I thought that since you sell some cars here..."

"Cars in good working order, with nothing major wrong with them," I remind her.

"I'm not looking to get much for it. I just don't know what to do with it. I thought I'd ask you."

I swipe my hands on the back of my neck, thinking, and looking at her. Drinking in her image. She's in a loose-fitting blouse again, and tighter-fitting pants.

Just looking at her makes me want to touch her. I want to run my fingers over her again, and then some more.

"Uh—okay. Leave it with me. I'll ask Enzo, but don't hold your breath."

I'm curious to know why she didn't call and ask on the phone, or call anyone here at the garage, but the way she looks at me tells me that this isn't about the car.

That's just an excuse.

Maybe she needs to get rid of it, and I'm sure she's smart enough to know how to get rid of it herself, or to ask her dad or even that guy at her workplace.

I wonder if she's thought about me, because I've been thinking about her. It has me bone hard most of the time, and it hasn't helped that Sadie's called me a couple of times and I've ignored her calls, too. There have been moments when I've considered that it might be better to go to Sadie, just to get some release, but I haven't, out of a sense of duty to Trinity, and I don't even understand why.

I've ignored calls from my friends-with-benefits—the sure thing—because I feel as if I can't cheat on Trinity, even though she and I don't have anything permanent going on.

I want her more intensely than I've wanted anyone in a long time. I want her because she is so sweet and innocent, and she wants me.

"Thanks," she says, and turns to go.

I try to think of something to say to keep her here, and then I wonder if that is wise.

The thing with Trinity is that she plays too safe, whereas I'm too reckless. Her life is ordered, while I'm easy come, easy go. I love sex, she's never had it. These are a few of the million reasons why I should stay away from her.

But I can't, and I don't want to.

"It's good to see you again," I say, lowering my voice as I glance around the garage to see where everyone is. It's Al and Enzo specifically that I'm worried about. Trinity looks around, too.

It's fine, we're good. There's no one nearby, and only a stretch of cold stone floor that separates us. She nods her head at the car next to me. "Is that what you're working on now?"

I nod.

She's struggling to make conversation too. It seems awkward how we are now, compared to how we were the last time.

We seem awkward, and it feels as if we're back to square one. Make that minus square one.

"It's got a problem with the catalytic converter, but I don't suppose you know what that is, and you don't really care."

Her lips form into a smile that reaches into my belly. I want to close the distance between us. I want to cup her face and take her wrist again.

"I..." Her mouth opens and she stares at me as if she's unsure of what to say. "I was going to call and ask you, but I thought it would be better if I asked you in person."

I know why you're here in person, Trinity. But that's not what I say. "I understand," I tell her. "You were probably in the area."

She bites her lip at the lie I told her when I showed up on her doorstep with the logbook.

Fuck, what I wouldn't do to go back in time again. What I wouldn't give to have that hour with her all over again.

"I've been thinking about you," I tell her, because now that's she's here, she's undone all the good work I did in trying to push her out of my head.

Now that she's here, in the flesh, with her blouse hanging on her and swaying as she moves, it makes me want to feel her up all over again. I want to make out with her again, seeing her standing not so far away from me makes me want to claim her mouth, run my hands over her body. Feel her close to me.

She nods, and blushes, and even though she doesn't say the words, it's proof enough to me that she hasn't yet managed to get me out of her system. Her gaze keeps dropping to my lips and I wonder if we have unfinished business.

I deliberately didn't call her, or text her, but it doesn't mean I haven't thought about her.

"Let me know what your boss says, if you ask him about the car," she says, then starts to move away.

"I will."

"Bye, then." She presses her lips together and walks away.

I can still feel those lips on mine as I watch her all the way until she's out of sight. Then Al pokes me in the side.

"She can't keep away from you," he comments with a grin. "When you told Enzo she was your girlfriend, I thought you were joking."

"I was."

"Then how come I've seen more of Trinity than I have of any other customer we've ever had?"

I reach for the wrench, and walk back to the car I was working on. "She's had a repair, and she's bought a car, and now she wants to sell her old car. I'd say there have been plenty of reasons for her to come here lately."

"That's not it. I know the babe magnet that you are." Al winks at me. "But she's not like one of your usual babes." Al points a finger at me accusingly. "She's too nice for you, don't go messing around with her."

"Too late."

"Too late?" Al splutters in surprise. "Too late for what?"

"For me to stay away from her."

Al wipes his hand over his face as if he's just woken up. "You've been messing around with her?"

I huff out a breath. "I kissed her. Nothing more." But I've already decided. We have unfinished business, and I need to see her again. I'm *going* to see her again, no two ways about it.

"Does she know what you're like?" Al asks, as if he's suddenly Trinity's guardian.

Does anyone?

I shrug.

"Max, buddy," Al hangs his head in despair. "Why do you have to go sniffing around someone like that? She's not like Hot Gina."

"You say that as if you know Hot Gina."

"You've told me so much about her, I feel like I do."

"Aren't you now glad you never hooked up with her friend?" I ask, putting my arm around his shoulder. "Now that you're engaged to Sammy."

"You know I never meant it, right?"

"All the time. I know the type of guy you are, my friend. Plus, I've never met Hot Gina's friends. We didn't have that kind of relationship."

"*Didn't have?*" Al asks, stepping away. "Have I missed something? Did you dump her?"

I snort. "No, nothing like that."

I mean, I haven't called her up and told her anything like that, I just haven't answered her phone calls.

Now's not the time to tell him about what exactly has gone on between me and Trinity, especially because I don't think that's the last of it.

CHAPTER TWENTY-ONE

TRINITY

Dylan leaves and I hold my head in my hands. He had bruises on his arms. I saw them while he was getting changed for gym class. I gave him an apple just now and tried to get some information out of him but he didn't say much.

I need to speak to the principal.

"What's wrong?"

I look up, and in the split second that my ears mistakenly think it's Ed, I see Max.

My heart soars. I needed a pick-me-up, and what better person to do it than Max? I can't hide my smile, as a hundred thoughts fly through my head.

He's come about the car, I'm sure, but I don't care, I'm so happy to see him again, especially because he never got back to me about the car after I went to see him last week.

"Why are you sitting there looking like the world just

ended?" he asks, walking towards me with his sexy swagger. My eyes take in his hips, his movement, his eyes, his smile.

I feel a burst of happy anticipation, the way I do when I unravel the wrapper off a large bar of my favorite chocolate.

"I'm worried about someone," I manage to say, and try to stop looking him up and down too obviously.

"The kid with the apple? The one I saw last time, right?"

I vaguely recall Max meeting Dylan before. "Yes."

"Does he always hang around after class?"

"I have a feeling he doesn't like going home."

I get up and reach for the blackboard cleaner, then start wiping the chalk away. Because Max doesn't say anything, I glance over my shoulder to see what he's doing.

He's right behind me, perched on the edge of my desk, watching me.

I didn't expect him to leave, but I also didn't expect him to sit here silently. It unnerves me that he's this close to me. I wish he'd perched on the other end of the desk, not at this end, where my chair is.

The blackboard is clear now, and there's nothing else for me to busy myself with, so I turn around and set the blackboard cleaner down.

"You're worried about this kid?" he asks.

"I'm always worried about him."

"Why?"

"I can't tell you. It wouldn't be ethical."

"I don't recall you always being ethical, especially when I'm around."

He's gone right to it. I like his directness. I like that he doesn't hide behind vague words.

I can't help the smile on my face. Maybe it's because he's in my territory that I feel more relaxed.

"I don't know what you're talking about," I reply, trying to sound a little haughty.

"Really? 'Cause I can't stop thinking about the last time you and I were alone together."

"In the garage?" I ask, knowing full well that's not what he's talking about.

"You little tease, Miss Weldon," he says. "What I wouldn't give to turn you over on my knee and smack your gorgeous bottom."

My breath hitches in my throat, because this is too much, and yet it's also strangely exhilarating and dirty, too. Now I have an image of me splayed face down over his thigh.

"I'm joking," he says, when I'm too stunned to reply. I allow myself to breathe out. He did that on purpose. He said something that would shock me and get me all heated up.

And it has.

"Why are you here?" I ask, trying to force myself to move on from the visual he's put into my head. "You didn't come to discuss my students, and if you've come about the car, it's too late. My dad got rid of it for me."

"He did?"

"You didn't get back to me, so I asked my dad what to do, and he drove it to a junkyard."

"Sorry," he replies, shaking his head. "I should have called you back."

I was surprised when he didn't. "I thought you might be avoiding me," I reply, surprising myself with my directness.

"I might have been."

I really do like his directness. No lying, no deceit.

"Why?"

"Because," he shrugs. "Why do you think, Trinity?"

"I don't know. I want you to tell me." I fold my arms, one over the other, and wait expectantly.

We stare at one another. He's looking at my mouth, and I'm staring at his. We're not inches-close, but we're less than a yard apart, and I'm directly inside the danger zone; close enough to get drawn into his lair. I only have to step within a few inches of him, and I start to come apart.

Ethics and good reason desert me.

He gets up, as if he's going to walk away but instead, he steps towards me, then slides a hand to my jaw and presses his mouth down.

The unexpectedness and suddenness of it takes my breath away, and when his hand snakes around my waist, I move into him and fall deeper into the kiss.

His skin is warm, his body hard. He kisses me, and I kiss him back. A storm of emotions engulfs me. I have no control and I don't care.

I need him.

His tongue sweeps around my mouth as if it's doing a victory lap, and each cell in my body cheers him on.

I was afraid I would never see him again, especially when he didn't call. But maybe me turning up at the garage last week gave him a green light, and now here he is, in my classroom, kissing me as if it's the most natural thing in the world.

A cough interrupts us. It breaks our kiss, and we pull apart and look towards the door. It's Ed.

"I see you're busy." He looks worse than crestfallen. He looks as if someone blew a gust of air right into his face.

Guilt trickles over me each second that he's staring at us; his gaze darting from Max to me. I can almost hear Ed's brain clicking into overdrive as he tries to make sense of this.

Before I can say anything, he's gone, and I see some

older children from another class sniggering as they walk past.

"I think we pissed your friend off," says Max, turning to me with a wink.

I say nothing, and wonder how I'll explain this to him.

"He's got a thing for you," says Max.

I turn to him. "You're right, and that's what I was afraid of."

"Too late. You're mine." His fingers press gently into my waist and he stares at me with a new intensity. "That's if you want to be."

I chew my lip, because I'm not sure what he's asking. "If I want to be what?" I ask. Does he want sex?

"If you want to be with me."

Yes, that's exactly what I want, and I'll figure out what it means later, how much of me he wants. And whether I can abstain, because my past experience with him has shown me that I have no willpower when I'm around him.

I don't think a nun would have much willpower around a guy like Max.

"Shall we get out of here?" I say, knowing that it's a provocative line. I don't mean to get a hotel room by the hour, but I shouldn't be here, with him, with anyone, doing this. I also can't stop thinking about the last time we made out, on my bed. Despite me trying, I've failed miserably at forgetting him.

"What exactly did you have in mind?" he asks cheekily.

"Not what you're thinking." A guy like him wants more than kissing.

"How do you know what I'm thinking?" he asks, tipping his head down and kissing my neck softly. I shiver in excitement.

"I can *feel* it," I reply, hoping he doesn't notice the

wobble in my voice. It's hard not to feel something that hard against my belly. The thought of it makes my body burn.

Max paints pictures in my head with bright, vivid brushstrokes; things I've never entertained before. Each time I'm with him, even for harmless, innocent, normal things, like picking up the keys to my car, I walk away with my cells on fire.

He moves away slightly. "I can't help it. That's what you do to me."

I'm not that naïve to assume that I am the only woman on the planet to give this man an erection, but I take the compliment, for that's what this is, that I have the ability to excite this man in that way. We fall into another kiss as his tongue slides into my mouth and teases me.

Not long after, we end up at my place and no sooner have we walked into my apartment, than he kisses me up against the door.

I've barely had time to take off my jacket, or slide off my shoes, and my bookbag is almost falling off my shoulder when he presses against me. He kisses me tenderly at first, but the kiss quickly turns deeper, more passionate, rising like a crescendo.

My lungs are on the verge of collapse. His kiss sucks the air right out of me and renders my brain useless. I cease to think. I can only accept this assault on my mouth and my senses.

Max kisses like no one has ever kissed me before. He doesn't even kiss so much as plunder my mouth while taking my heart and soul.

I give in, because I want him and all he stands for; everything that he promises and threatens with his sexy ways.

His erection jabs me, and I let out a moan as I grind my

hip into him. With lips sealed together, we meander through the living room and I lead him to my bedroom. Once inside, we sidestep my books which are everywhere. I wish I'd tidied up a little.

We kiss for the longest time, until I fall onto the bed and scoot back towards the headboard.

I sense—or perhaps it's my naiveté that leads me to think this—that he's not going to expect anything more.

The question is, can I hold back?

He takes off his T-shirt, and I bite my lip. He stops and stares at me, bare-chested now but with the T-shirt in his hands. I see the scars, but it's his eyes I'm staring at. This feels fast.

He squeezes his eyes closed for a second longer than usual, then apologizes, and starts to put his T-shirt back on again.

"Sorry, I didn't mean to strip off," he says slowly. "It's just a habit."

"Habit?"

"I ... I didn't get a chance to change into another shirt," he starts to explain. "It's got grease marks all over it."

"Then take it off," I say, moving towards him on my knees. I place my hand on his to stop him from putting his head through the T-shirt.

"I'm not trying to trick you into anything, I swear."

I raise an eyebrow. My hand skims across his hard-as-steel stomach and stays there. I breathe out slowly.

"I believe you." I'm grateful to those grease marks for soiling his T-shirt.

"I didn't mean to move so fast," he says, "I didn't think we'd end up here." He holds my gaze and turns my head all fuzzy with his electric stare.

"Don't put your shirt on," I say, trying not to sound as if

I'm begging. He lets it fall to the floor, and I skim my fingers across the peaks and valleys of his abs. Now that I'm so close, I see his scars more clearly; raised splotches of pink skin, circular welts dotted across his chest and arms.

I know what they are.

Cigarette burns, and my heart crashes into pieces. The pattern is too familiar.

These aren't accidental burns.

I don't say anything, but my fingers skim over them, not purposely seeking them out, or avoiding them. I rise up from my knees, hook my arm around his neck to bring his head down, and kiss him.

This time it's my lips that claim his, my tongue that sweeps into his mouth and explores. I catch a whiff of oil, and sweat, and a hint of sea breeze from his cologne. My mind is overrun by his scent and the feel of him, and a fire rages through my body.

Our passionate kiss lingers, and we end up on the bed again, this time with him lying on his side, and me on my back. It's the first time I've had him this close and bare-chested, and I can't help myself. I stare into his eyes as my fingers graze over his skin. He's a muscular wall of hardness, and I slowly explore, touch and feel him all over.

"War wounds," he says quietly, even though I haven't asked. It's not the thing I'm focusing on, because my insides are on fire, and the ache between my legs deepens.

I say nothing in reply.

He kisses me again, and even though he's still in his jeans, and I'm fully dressed, I can feel his hardness.

This must be agony for him.

It's hard for me, the hardest it's ever been, but I've always abstained, so I don't know any better.

After a while, we stop kissing and he stares down at me. "What are you doing with me, Trinity?"

I look at him, trying to answer that and failing. I have no idea what we're doing together.

His hand rests on my hip. I wish he would do what he did last time. Instead, he seems to hold back, and I don't like it. I want more. I want his hands under my blouse and in my bra. I want him to touch me there again.

"What are you doing with me, when you can have any woman you want?"

"I asked first," he says.

"What am I doing with you?" I ask. "Hanging out."

The corners of his lips turn upwards. "Hanging out? You think what we're doing is hanging out?"

I nod. "And because it beats lying here and making out with someone like Ed." I catch myself too late, and cup a hand to my mouth, rather like the children I teach, who do this when they've said something they shouldn't have. "I sound awful." I hate that I just said that, but it's the truth.

Max hoots with laughter so hard that he has to lie on his back.

It's true, though. Given the choice, I'd rather be lying here with Max than with someone like Ed, who pales in comparison.

I can't think of anyone else now that I've met him.

"I didn't mean it in a nasty way," I say, shuffling up on my elbow, and trying to make myself not sound like a nasty person.

"Did you two ever...kiss?" he asks.

"No. We just went for a pizza."

"He wants to have more than pizza with you." He shifts onto his back and lifts his arm, motioning for me to lie down. I scoot towards him and snuggle up close.

I pinch his nipple gently, as a warning.

"Do that again," he asks, "that felt good." I wish he'd do that to me. But I comply. His nipple doesn't rise up as much as mine did, so I kiss it, then lick it, then suck it. It puckers up a little. "Like it?" I ask, turning on my side. His hand moves down my thigh, but unfortunately, still over my clothes.

I kiss him again, then move my hand down, lower, lower, lower, until it falls on his huge bulge.

This is daring, even for me. I have never gone there before. I don't tease guys like that, because I know what follows. Yet I can't stop myself with Max.

He squirms at my touch.

"Careful there, Miss Weldon," he says, his eyes shining. "You've already given me a boner. If you excite me too much, I'll have to leave."

"What will be too much?" I ask. I know perfectly well, and I don't know what I'm doing being around him, but all I know is that I can't resist him.

I move my hand away reluctantly. I want more with him. More than I've given any other man, but can I give him the very thing I've held onto all this time?

"What are you doing with someone like me?" I ask, needing to know what it is that draws him to me. He knows I don't put out, and I want to know if he sees me as a challenge to overcome, or if he really likes being with me.

"You excite me," he murmurs, his hand falling to my buttock and gently pressing. I jerk a little in response. I'm so amped up, so turned on by what we're doing, that I can't contain myself.

"You've never had a boyfriend?" he asks.

This is a regular question. I'm used to it. "I've had a few. I'm not a nun."

His lips find my collarbone and he sucks the skin gently, as if he's leaving a trail of hickeys, only he doesn't linger for long. Waves of arousal make me squirm to his touch, and I feel as if I'm sinking in a vat of honey.

"But you're single now?" he asks.

"Obviously. Otherwise we wouldn't be doing this."

"And you?" I ask sitting up abruptly. "Are you single?"

"Obviously. Otherwise we wouldn't be doing this." He smirks as he echoes my answer. "Your last boyfriend was when?"

I throw my head back, trying to think. "A year ago."

"A year ago?" he asks, as if I've told him that I haven't eaten for a year. The way he says this makes me suspicious. Despite the crazy things he makes me feel, I'm still on high alert. I still have to be careful despite it being almost impossible to be that around him. My guard slips down all the time around him.

"What about you? When did you last have a girlfriend? Because I can't imagine anyone like you being single for too long." He cups my breast, the movement so unexpected that it hitches my breath. I can't help but let out an appreciative moan.

"You're so responsive," he murmurs, rubbing his thumb over my nipple, making it shoot up to attention. I giggle. He has no idea what he's doing to me. I feel things, things I want to do, things I want him to do.

I don't care that he hasn't answered my question, because in this moment all that matters is the thing he's doing.

"Feel good?" he asks, tweaking and pulling. Exciting me.

"Mmmmm." He stops for a moment, his face turning

serious. "I'm not the right person for someone like you." His candor surprises me.

"I don't care." Because I don't, especially when he rubs me hard. I wish he would do that down below where I am a bundle of hot, throbbing nerves.

"You should care."

"Let me throw caution to the wind, for once." I turn and twist, then lower my head to him. I am so aroused and desperate that I need to kiss him again.

"That's what I like about you," he says.

"That I'm boring?" To a guy like Max, I must seem quite boring.

"I never said anything about boring." His lips brush against mine, raising my temperature a notch. "You're constant, and sweet, and beautiful."

I'm about to ask him what he means by constant, when he rewards me with another toe-curling kiss. As I squirm and sigh beneath him, I wonder how long we can continue doing just this for.

CHAPTER TWENTY-TWO

MAX

I didn't think it was possible to be with a woman I'm lusting after and not have sex, but this is how it is for me with Trinity.

There's something going on between us, but it's not sex.

We make out. *A lot.*

I'm a good kisser, it's a fact. But that's all we've done so far.

My kisses make her wet, and horny, and I can see she finds it hard to stop.

I do too. I want to do more than kiss, but I have to move *real* slow, otherwise I will spontaneously combust from being around her.

Who knew how exquisitely torturous it would be to be around a woman who is determined to never have sex before marriage?

I try hard to leave it at just kissing, and not move on to

something more. It's manageable, so far, but I'm not sure how much longer I can keep it at this.

We've met at her place a few times. We've talked, and found out about one another, and kissed. Problem is, I'm so wired for sex that it's almost impossible retraining my body to go slow.

Hot Gina hasn't called again ever since I never picked up her last call. Sadie also hasn't called me. I guess she finally got the message. We only saw one another occasionally, and more recently it was for me to get Trinity out of my system.

Each time I met her, I'd be so desperate for release, I needed someone and Sadie was that someone.

But now I have Trinity, only not in *that* respect. She's in my skin and under it. She's in every cell, in every fiber. I can't stop thinking about her, but I'm not sure if it's because I can't have her or because she won't put out. I'm not sure if she's a challenge, or someone I should treat like delicate china.

It's not even as if I want to make her change her mind. I'd love it if she changed her mind—I'm a hot-blooded guy—but, somehow, I don't want to be the one to make her do that.

I've never had a relationship quite like this one before and I'm having to step out of my comfort zone.

We hang out like this for a few more weeks and when I'm with her, when I lie on her bed with her beside me, holding her hand and just talking, it feels like enough. Ordinarily, I don't have much time for conversation, especially with the others. It's always been purely physical, but this *feels* different.

My heart feels fuller. She calms me. She makes me feel as if I've had a big, hearty dinner.

She has a way about her such that she makes me feel better about things, and I have no idea why. I complain about Enzo, and the customers, and how I work my butt off for such little gain, and she listens, and asks me what I want to do about it.

It doesn't matter that I'm not getting laid. All that matters is that I'm being heard.

It's not until I catch Al looking at me oddly at work one day that I stare back. "What?"

"You're singing."

I immediately stop, not realizing that until he pointed it out to me.

"What's the matter with you?"

"Nothing," I state calmly, then lie down on the car creeper. I'm about to slide under the car when he puts his foot in the way so that I can't roll back.

"Is Hot Gina coming this weekend?" Al asks.

Lying on my back staring up at him leaves me feeling slightly vulnerable. "No."

Al tilts his head as if he's trying to figure out what it could be. "One of the others?"

I can see what's coming. I'm almost tempted to tell him 'yes,' and that would shut him up, but I don't want to lie and taint what me and Trinity have, which, if I'm honest, I have no label for at the moment.

"No." I press my feet onto the floor in an effort to propel myself under the car and disappear from Al's interrogation, but his foot is still in the way, acting like a brake and preventing me.

"I'm in a good mood, dude," I say in a final attempt to get away. "I sing when I'm in a good mood."

"No, you don't. Anyway, I have to ask you something."

"What?"

"Wanna go to dinner with me and Sammy?" He looks a little embarrassed.

I don't know what I'm more amazed about, the fact that he hasn't interrogated me further about my good mood, or that he's asked me to go to dinner with him and his fiancée.

"*Dinner?*" Al and I have never done dinner. It's always the bar and a few drinks. Maybe some snacks, if it's a night out with the guys from the garage and if Enzo's paying.

"It's Sammy's idea," he says quickly, holding his hands up as if to distance himself from the idea. "She wants to get to know all my friends." He grins. "She said for you to bring your girlfriend."

As far as Al's concerned, he thinks me hitting on Trinity was a one-time thing, so I'm pretty sure he's talking about me bringing Hot Gina or Sadie. He also knows that I don't take these girls to dinner. I sit up and expel my breath slowly. "Not gonna be possible," I answer.

"Why not?"

I look at him and wonder why the hell I have to explain, but then I remember this guy is all loved up right now. He got engaged, and he's thinking of the future. He lives in a different world than me.

He doesn't live in NoHopesville like I do.

"It just isn't."

"But you and Hot Gina, you've been together a while now..."

"Not *together*," I correct him. Only on a need-to-fuck basis.

Al opens his mouth. "You've got no feelings for her?"

I have a lot of feelings for her. Sure, I do, but Gina doesn't want to settle down and that makes what we have so easy. I don't want to settle down either, and what the hell does settling down mean anyway? Why should anyone have to *settle*?

My real mom settled.

"Nah," I say, shaking my head. "It's not like we're going to have a church wedding, and buy a little house, and have kids. That's not going to happen." Gina says she's seen and heard enough things during her time in the army—she's been deployed to a few war zones—and it's made her never want to have kids and settle down.

"It *could* happen," says Mr. Loved-Up.

"Gina isn't the settling down type, and neither am I, and that's why we're so good together."

"But when you meet the right woman, you'll fall in love and change your mind," Al insists.

"What's the point of falling in love with someone when all they're going to do is leave you in the end?"

"Why would they leave you if they love you?" Al asks, shaking his head and staring at me as if I've gone insane.

"It happens." What does he know? That's exactly what I think because it's exactly what I've come to know.

"You have a warped sense of relationships," he says.

"I have my head screwed on just right. I get to have a good time without anyone messing with my head."

"What about Trinity?"

I wave my hand dismissively and lie. "That was a one-time thing, like I told you."

"Thank goodness, for her sake," he mutters. "Well, can you just think about it, for me? Sammy's not going to stop asking me until we get together." He throws his hands up in the air in a gesture of defeat.

I hiss out my irritation. "Why?"

"I don't know. Seems like getting engaged has gone to

her head. She wants to do all these coupley things all of a sudden. I wish she'd stay the same."

I can't say I know Sammy very well, even now, but I guess it's nice that she wants to get to know his friends. I relent. "Tell her I'm busy for a few weeks, and maybe we can get together sometime next month."

Al looks as relieved as I feel. "Are you sure?"

"She's never going to stop going on about it, you said. Have you set a date for the wedding yet?" I ask him.

"She wants a summer wedding, and we're looking at next August."

"Next August, huh?"

Al nods. "Gotta start doing lots of overtime so that we have enough to pay for the damn thing."

I snicker.

He turns to go. "I'll tell her that you'll be free next month."

"Next month for sure." The idea already seems weird to me because even though he and Sammy have been together a few years, I've never been out on a double date with them before.

My girlfriends in the past have never been the type, but the idea of taking Trinity suddenly appeals. I can see me and her going out with Al and his girlfriend and having a good time.

He moves his foot away and the creeper is movable again. Except that I don't lie down and slide under the car just yet. I'm trying to get my head around the fact that I'm starting to see Trinity as girlfriend material.

We've been seeing one another for the past two weeks. An evening here and there and on weekends.

A couple of times we've gone out for a coffee. We even met someplace for lunch.

It's weird for me, to be with a girl and not want to rip her clothes off, and to not want to get her into bed. Don't get me wrong. I do think about that stuff, but I don't dwell on it for too long. I don't have an ulterior motive for being with her. If anything, her not having had sex makes me hesitant.

I'm not sure Trinity feels the same way. She's turning into a bit of a tease. I knew there was a minx hidden underneath all those loose-fitting clothes of hers, but even I am surprised by how she reacts sometimes. It's like her sexy inner goddess has suddenly been unleashed.

When Friday comes around, I call her. I don't have overtime this weekend, because I'm going to let Al have it, and so my weekend is free. I'm hoping to see her tonight.

"Hey," she answers with a smile. I can hear it in her voice.

"Want to meet up?" I ask. Though maybe this weekend she can come over to my place? She's never been before, and I would like her to.

"When?"

"I was hoping tonight," I reply. Just talking to her makes me want to be with her. With her, it's so different. It's not only about desire.

She's a great listener, and maybe she has to be because she's a teacher, but after years of being around people who want to talk all the time, it's refreshing to be around a woman who listens.

Trinity isn't all about herself, and that's one more thing I like about her. Seems to be that the more I find out about her, the more I like about her.

"I can't do tonight, sorry. I've got my crochet class."

She showed me her crochet stuff the last time I was over. She's making some big-ass blanket. "You're going to pick your *crochet class* over me?" I cry in disbelief, wondering how it is that this woman still manages to surprise me each time we talk. "What is it about that goddamn hobby that you like so much?"

"It's a creative outlet for me, and I happen to find it relaxing."

"*Relaxing?* How?"

"Uh," she pauses, as if she's stopped to think about it. "I'm not sure. It just is. Maybe because my fingers are doing the motions, but my mind is free to wander. It's automatic, like breathing."

I can think of finger motions that I'd like to do on her; ones that would blow her mind. She's probably wearing a blouse with the top two buttons undone, as always. The thought of it makes me even more desperate to see her. I hiss out a slow and steady breath, as something twitches in my pants. I try to wipe that thought away.

How is it that this woman gets me so aroused and I haven't even seen her naked yet?

"Can we meet after?" I ask.

"Uh..." She hesitates, and the fact that she has to think about it puzzles me. I'm not used to being so low down on someone's list that they have to think about seeing me.

"I'm meeting Christina for dinner."

I've heard about her friend. "Ditch her. Tell her you have a better offer."

"I can't do that."

"Really? It's bad enough that I come second to crochet, but now I have to slip lower down the list?"

"I haven't told her about you yet."

My silence fills the air. I don't expect her to rush around making an announcement. I haven't told Al, and he's one of my closest friends. I guess we're just trying this out, seeing what happens.

"Christina and I always meet after crochet to catch up."

"Wait," I say, trying to get my head around it. "Your friend crochets too?"

"Yes, and then we—"

"She gets to see you for crochet *and* dinner?"

"Pretty much."

"Maybe I should join your crochet class."

Trinity laughs. "You could. We have a guy who comes."

"That's sad."

"We can meet tomorrow," she suggests.

"Okay." Tomorrow will have to do.

"Could we maybe go shopping? I need to buy a shelf for my books."

"You don't say." She has books all over the floor, some lined up against the wall neatly. They get in the way.

"I keep putting it off," she says.

"I noticed."

"So, will you come with me?"

I would love to come with her.

"I can go shelf shopping with you," I reply. Words I never expected to hear myself saying.

What in the world is happening to me?

CHAPTER TWENTY-THREE

TRINITY

It's the weekend and I'm out with my boyfriend. It feels weird to be thinking of Max like that, but he is. What else can he be after spending time together the way we have these past few weeks?

I'm also wearing a new wrap-over top which hugs my body, instead of floating around me. I'm so used to wearing loose, baggy clothing that having something a little figure hugging is scary, but it actually looks good. The sales assistant told me that this style really suited my curvy figure. It was a new buy, a daring buy for me.

Something new. Something different. Just like being with Max is something new and different for me. My top was the first thing he commented on when he saw me.

He's been over to my place a couple of times, and we've been out a few times for coffee and food.

It makes my heart lift that he seems so eager to want to see me. He asked if we could meet yesterday, but there was no way I was going to ditch Christina just to be with him, even if I am desperate to see him again. I couldn't do that to Christina.

I still can't bring myself to tell her about him, and I don't know when I will. I haven't said anything further to Ed about him, either, but he's obviously seen us together and knows that there won't be any more dinner dates for him and me.

"What about this one?" I show Max a dark wood bookshelf.

"Do you like it?" he asks, tracing his hands along the wood. Then he raps it with his knuckles. "Sounds hollow."

"I don't care what it sounds like," I tell him. "It will look nice in my bedroom."

I've been meaning to buy a good bookshelf for ages, but never saw one I liked, and also, many of them come flat-packed and need to be assembled.

I kept putting the task off, the thought of lugging the huge package in and out of the car, and then the headache of assembling it, was enough to put me off the task.

But being with Max has its advantages. I watch him walking around the showroom, checking out bookshelves for me, and my heart feels light and airy, as if it's going to float right out of my body.

I walk towards Max and examine the bookshelf he's showing me. The wood isn't so dark, but more a reddish color. The bookshelf is slightly taller, and it has an old-style look about it.

I like it.

"This one," I say, running my fingers over the wood.

Max knocks his knuckles on it again.

"Does it pass your test?" I ask him.

"It's better than the other one. Do you like it?"

I nod. "I do."

"You sure? I don't want you to say just because I picked it out."

"I wouldn't say that just because you picked it out," I retort.

"Why don't we look at a few others?" he suggests. I find it surreal that we're having a conversation about looking at bookshelves so early on in our getting-to-know-one-another phase. It makes me realize how I was so wrong about him from the start. He's thoughtful, and caring, and decent.

I shake my head, not keen on the idea. "We've already been to two department stores." I'm bookshelved out. I'm hungry and tired of walking around, and I want to get something to eat. "I'm going to get this one," I decide.

Luckily, they have it in stock. It comes in a great big box, which looks really heavy.

"I've got this," Max offers, when the shop assistant fetches the flat-packed package and puts it into our big shopping cart.

He wheels it to the checkout where I make payment. Then he picks it up out of the cart. I widen my eyes in alarm. "Shouldn't we wheel the cart to the parking lot?"

He rolls his eyes. "I can carry it. It's not that heavy."

I don't fully believe him, but if he wants to help, I'll let him. We walk away, with Max carrying the package under one arm. He hikes the long, thin slender box higher so that it sits on his waist.

I make my admission. "I've been meaning to look for a bookshelf for ages, but I kept putting it off because I knew it would be too heavy for me to carry by myself."

"So you waited for me to come along?" he asks, grinning.

"You don't have to put it together for me," I say quickly. "I'm good with instructions and a screwdriver."

"I can give you a hand. What else am I going to do at your place?" He throws me a look that could melt my panties. We grin at one another. I'd take his hand, if it wasn't for the way he was holding the bookshelf box in his arms.

We walk through the bedroom section of the store to make our way towards the exit doors, when I catch sight of someone who looks familiar. At first, the sight is so unexpected, that I blink a few times, and then I squint.

It's Ed. I watch dumbfounded as he lies on his back, then turns to one side, then rolls over to the other, then sits up and bounces some more on it.

He's still trying to find the right mattress. I'm sure we discussed this weeks ago, if not more than a month ago.

I suddenly decide that I don't want him to see me, but it's too late for me to suggest to Max that we go around the table lamps section and leave the store that way. Max would get suspicious.

I look away, and hope that Ed doesn't see us.

"Isn't that your friend?" Max asks.

I force myself to turn and look. Except that Ed is lying on a different bed this time. And he's going through the same procedure of testing the mattress out.

I don't say anything at first.

And I hope Ed doesn't see us, especially given the way he's bobbing up and down on a mattress.

Unfortunately, he sees me, and stops, mid-bounce. "Trinity?"

His gaze switches from me to Max and back to me again. He doesn't speak at first. But I can see the look of annoyance all over his face. Then his gaze drops to the large package Max is holding. I'm not sure if Ed can see the picture of the bookshelf, but the fact that I'm out with the mechanic seems to be enough to render him speechless.

"Hey, Ed," I say, forcing my voice to be brighter and perkier than I feel.

"Hey," Max pipes up. Ed slowly gets up, still continuing to stare at us, and then the package. I bet it's killing him, trying to figure out what that is.

"What are you doing?" I ask Ed, despite it being so obvious.

"I'm trying to find the right mattress."

I flash him a smile, as if this is entirely normal. "You still haven't found one?"

Max waits and listens, and I'm so thankful that he hasn't said a word.

"I like the memory foam ones, but there are so many of them. I have problems with my back."

"Oh, yeah?" Max starts up. "What kind of problems?"

I glare at him, because I don't want to stick around chatting for too long.

"Stiff lower back," Ed replies, actually holding his lower back as if he has a pain in it right now. "What's that?" He jerks his head towards the package Max is holding.

"A sex swing," Max replies, pokerface. My stomach empties into my mouth as the color on Ed's face drains.

I don't know how to salvage this, but I'm going to try. "He's joking," I say, forcing a laugh. "It's a—"

"It's a sex swing," Max repeats before I can finish. He winks at me, as if this is a big joke. I want to hit him in the center of his balls.

This isn't funny.

I work with Ed.

Ed knows about me, and what type of person I am.

What the hell is Max doing?

Before any of us can say another word, Ed's cell phone rings, and he excuses himself to take the call.

"See you on Monday," I mouth to him, desperate to get away.

I walk off quickly, fuming inside. "What did you go and say that for?" I hiss at Max when we're out of earshot.

"It was funny, no?" He's grinning like a hyena.

"Funny? Are you serious?" I snap. "I work with him. He knows I don't do things like that..."

"Do what?" Max stops in the middle of the department store.

"That...." I roll my eyes at the package in his arms and look away.

"Trinity, we both know that this isn't a sex swing. It was supposed to be a joke."

"Ed doesn't know that."

He narrows his eyes. "Why the fuck do you care what he thinks?"

"It matters to me when you slander my reputation."

Max looks at me as if he can't quite believe what I'm saying. "Reputation? Does he know about your V-card?" he asks.

I'm so mad at him that I don't answer. I'm also not sure that my anger is entirely about Ed, but I can't put my finger on what it is exactly.

"Did that come up in a conversation?" Max asks. "Because I didn't think you and he were all that close."

"We're not, and it didn't come up," I throw back.

"Then why are you so worried?"

I don't know the answer to that myself. I don't care what Ed thinks, but at the same time, I don't want him thinking

I've bought a sex swing with Max when I clearly haven't. I don't even know what a sex swing is.

"Are you the master connoisseur of all sex toys?" I shoot back. Just like I saw Ed bouncing around trying to find the right mattress, I imagine Max going shopping for the right gadgets to spice up his love life. Jealousy stabs at my heart like a pick-axe.

"I'm sorry that you don't think it's funny," he says, his voice turning softer. I look away, feeling silly myself.

"Okay," I say with a shrug. "Let's forget about it."

We carry on walking. I'm not sure where we're headed, but we walk past a lingerie shop. A huge poster of a voluptuous model with her breasts almost spilling out of her bra is stuck on one floor-to-ceiling window.

I glance at the mannequins in the shop window and the scanty, pretty and delicate lingerie they have on.

Max also sneaks a look. When I catch him doing it, I want to rip his eyes out. His gaze shifts to me, and I quickly look away.

The strength and intensity of my emotions when I'm around him frightens me.

CHAPTER TWENTY-FOUR

MAX

I was only joking about the sex swing, and I don't understand why Trinity's so angry. I do know one thing for sure; that Ed dude pisses me off.

After our encounter with that guy, we didn't even stop off for something to eat. And when we walked past a lingerie shop, Trinity had a face like thunder when she caught me looking at the sexy poster.

I saw the picture of that model and I imagined that Trinity would look as good, if not better, than the model because she's got that type of figure.

It breaks my balls being with her and having to hold back. The truth is, I'm not sure what to do. I love sex, and she's never had it. I don't want to make any rash moves. I don't want to do anything that she might have regrets about later.

Can I, Sex-Crazy Max, be with a woman like Trinity? I should walk away, but I can't. I want to be around her for as long as I can, even though I'm not sure what we're doing together.

It pisses me off that she's so concerned about what Ed thinks, she can't take a joke.

I walk into her tiny apartment, but I'm not sure if I should stick around given that there's a cloud of tension hanging over us. I was hoping to put the bookshelf together for her but I'm having second thoughts about that now.

"Are you still mad at me?" I ask, setting the package down in her living room.

"No, why?"

"Because you've been quiet the whole way back."

She looks at me.

"Want me to stay?" I ask, when she doesn't answer. My gaze falls to her top. If that were Hot Gina or Sadie, I'd have unwrapped her like a Christmas present by now. Instead, I have to look away when the top gapes slightly, and she keeps adjusting it and then redoing the bow so that it doesn't gape open.

I'm sure she didn't wear this to tease me, but I have to look away, otherwise I'll be in trouble.

"I was going to make us some lunch."

This sounds hopeful. "Yeah?" Maybe she wants me to stay after all. "That sounds like a good idea." Because I'm starving.

I can't believe how fast the situation has changed between us. I don't know how it happened, but all of a sudden it seems like Trinity's the one in charge and I'm suddenly not feeling so confident. Everything about Trinity, everything about us, has changed. I once thought I had the upper hand, being the one who was so cocksure of himself, but I'm not. Experience has nothing to do with it.

I want Trinity to be happy, and when she's down, I

want to cheer her up. When she's angry, I want to know why so that I can fix it.

All these feelings and no sex makes this a whole new level of relating and being for me.

"What would you like?" she asks.

I'm in no place to make any demands. "I'll have whatever you're having. Thanks."

She disappears into her kitchen. I follow her, placing my hands on the doorjamb above me. It causes her to turn to me and stare, but not before her eyes sweep over me from head to toe. "I was going to assemble your bookshelf."

"You don't have to. I can do it later," she replies.

"I know you're capable of doing it yourself, but if you're making lunch, the least I can do is to get started on the shelf."

"Well, sure. If you don't mind," she says, taking the salad out of the fridge. Of course I don't mind. She's fixing me lunch, and I'm making her bookshelf. This is a cozy setup. Al would be proud of me.

"I don't mind." I start to step away, but first I have something to say. "I'm sorry, about making that joke. I didn't realize you were so uptight about that stuff."

"I'm not uptight. I don't even know what it is."

Oh. Right. *Right.* I open my mouth, to explain, then see the hard expression on her face and think better of it. She doesn't seem too eager to want to know.

I slink away and get started on the shelf. With the planks of wood, screws and instructions out of the box, I'm about to start putting it all together when Trinity announces that lunch is ready.

We eat quickly, talking about our shopping trip, and Ed. Trinity tells me about his mattress saga. The dude seems kinds of sad, bouncing around on the bed by himself like that. Must be the height of his weekend. I can't talk; I'm putting up a bookshelf, but I've got Trinity and he doesn't.

After lunch I resume putting the rest of the bookshelf together, and she helps.

"What's a sex swing?" she asks suddenly. I almost drop the screws she's handing me.

I slant a quick look at her. Something darts across her face. It's like she has questions for me, but she can't bring herself to ask them.

I tighten the screw in place, thankful to have something else to focus on, and I pretend I haven't heard.

"Have you ever used one?" she asks, clearly not giving up. I've usually answered this question with glee. With a certain amount of bravado, yet I don't want to do that now. I can feel the heat of Trinity's eyes on me, and I don't want to lie to her, but it's going to cost me soon if I'm not careful. "Yes."

"Yes, what? With all of them?" she asks, as I get busy again putting more screws in place. My insides churn as I level my gaze to her face. "With all what?"

"All of your girlfriends."

I bite down on my teeth. Hot Gina introduced me to this amazing contraption. She has one at her place and we've had some great times with it.

But I don't know how to answer Trinity. A flush creeps across her face, and she looks away. I can't tell if she's embarrassed asking me about this stuff, or embarrassed for me. And at the same time I wonder why she's asking.

"Just one of them," I reply, and then I cough lightly to clear my throat. She gives me a slight nod, then turns her back to me to pick up some more screws.

"It will be safer for me to anchor the shelf to the wall so that it doesn't fall over."

She looks at me oddly. "Fall over?"

"If it becomes unsteady, it will be a safety risk. Can I secure it to the wall?"

"You can do whatever you like."

We work together silently after that.

CHAPTER TWENTY-FIVE

TRINITY

I Google 'sex swing' on my phone in the bathroom while Max is finishing off the bookshelf. I'm curious to know what it looks like and what he might have done with it.

When the website page loads, I find out. And now my head is up there, in a place where it's never been before; imagining Max and his last girlfriend using that contraption.

I stare at the picture. It looks like a harness that's suspended from the ceiling, or attached to a door. I sink lower as I see diagrams showing how it's used. An arrow of electricity darts upwards from my belly. My mouth falls open as I flick through the diagrams showing a woman sitting in this thing with her legs apart, suspended above the floor, and the man...

Heat coils between my legs. I wish I was on that swing with Max doing those things with me.

I go into the kitchen, instead of returning to him because the spike of jealousy in my gut twists inside me.

I'm not used to feeling like this, out of control, and as if I want to lash out. It's like he cast a bad spell on me, and I can't undo it. I want to return to normal; to the happy and ignorant and uncomplicated me.

I start to clean up my kitchen, even though the tiny space is pretty neat and tidy anyway.

"I was wondering where you were." Max comes up behind me as I empty my cutlery drawer. He puts his arms around my waist, and the smell of mint and freshly cut grass floats around me. I sink back against him, because it's automatic. He is what I crave.

His mouth nuzzles my ear, and I instinctively giggle, tilting my head, and squirming because it tickles. "What are you doing?" I squeal, and his hands slip and slide over my belly.

"This looks good on you," he says, tugging my blouse gently from the bottom.

"You already said," I reply, "but thanks."

He's silent as he hugs me tighter. We stay like that for a long moment until, eventually, he says, "I've finished putting up the bookshelf. Come see." But he doesn't grab my hand and lead me to the bedroom to take a look. It feels like he's trying to gauge my mood.

"What are you doing?" I ask him.

"Just holding you."

I wonder if he feels sorry for me.

"Let me see the finished product." I move out of his embrace and walk into my bedroom expecting to see the finished bookshelf. And I do. But he's also picked up all my books from the floor, and he's put them on the bookshelf which he's pushed up against the corner of the room. There is no more clutter. My room looks so much bigger, and cleaner. The bookshelf looks as if it was made for my room.

I clasp my hands together as I walk towards it, my heart racing at his thoughtfulness. "You picked all my books up."

"Like it?"

"Love it. Thank you." I trace my fingers across the books on the shelf, and then across the wood. I know he didn't chop the wood from the trees or anything like that, but my heart is so full right now knowing that he put this together for me.

"Thanks. I love it."

"Now you won't trip over your books when you get out of bed."

I'm so grateful, I reach out and put my arm around his waist. "Thanks."

He snakes his other hand around me, and pulls me in.

It's no surprise when we end up on my bed, locked in a deep kiss seconds later. Everything about this morning seeps out of me, seeing him, and being around him, and running into Ed, and reading up about the sex swing.

I want to touch him, and I suddenly have a deep desire to feel his skin on mine. When I tug at his T-shirt and lift it up, he looks puzzled for a moment. I've never done this before. I've never led. Max has always, but the more we've kissed, the more curious I've become, and this time, I want to feel more than just deep kisses.

He gets the message and takes off his T-shirt. I see his scars, the raised pale pink welts and while I don't purposely run my fingers around them, I feel them when I place my hands on his body. He shifts his body so that he's lying on top of me, supporting his weight on his elbows.

I hold in a breath, waiting for him to untie the bow on my wrap-around top, but he doesn't.

Seeing that he's not going to undress me, possibly because he doesn't know how far I want to go, I undo the bow and the top falls open slightly, enough to show off the top of the brand new bra I bought. It's a new bra; pretty instead of functional, and I hoped he would get the hint.

I hoped he would appreciate it, but he looks at me as if he's not sure of what I'm doing.

"Don't you find me attractive?" I ask, when he does nothing further.

He seems to be having trouble answering because the vein on the side of his head is slightly raised.

I wriggle out of my sleeves, so that I'm only in my bra and jeans. I stare at him, at his bare chest and long to feel his skin against mine. When he doesn't make a move, I lift my hand to his chest, and lay it flat against his skin.

He hisses out a breath, and then takes my mouth hard, as if he's tried to hold back and failed.

It is exactly what I need.

We kiss, tongues thrashing, hands all over one another. He showers me with kisses along my jaw and down my throat and lower, coming to a rest with his face buried between my breasts.

I want him to take my bra off. I want him to undress me. I want more. But I don't want to lead, I need to know that he finds me attractive and that he wants this as much as I do. I hate that he has done things with other women. It's a ludicrous thought, but I can't help it. I wonder if he's toying with me. But if he is, why isn't he doing more?

Our kisses grow longer and more sensual. I can feel the throbbing between my legs, and I moan in delight when he buries his face between my breasts. I claw my fingers through his hair, loving the way he runs his tongue along my cleavage, loving the feel of his hardness against me.

I can't think of a better thing to do on a Saturday afternoon, than this.

"Trinity," he groans, then lifts his head and looks at me. I love the sound of my name on his lips.

I shift beneath him, making sure I rub against his erection, trying to tease him further. Surely he can also hear the pounding of my heart? I'm so hot, so desperate for him, that I can no longer wait for him.

I lift myself slightly, then undo my bra from behind. His eyes shift to mine for the briefest of seconds, before my bra falls away, and I'm topless.

This is the most brazen thing I've done and my reputation, along with my embarrassment, hang together on the frayed thread of my being.

"Are you sure?" He blinks.

"Do you have to ask?" My breasts are already pebbled, and he hasn't touched me there yet.

Without answer, he takes my breast into his mouth and sucks. I sink back on the bed, a feral sound coming from my lips. This feels beautiful. His mouth feels divine. I sigh and squirm, and get even more aroused as Max sucks hungrily, giving me the attention there that I have craved for so long.

He grinds his hips into me, and I immediately reciprocate and push my hips up against him. I can't reach my hand down there because he's lower down my body, still sucking my breasts, and driving me slowly crazy.

We carry on like this for the longest time, and then he rubs me over the fabric of my jeans, there at the right place where I'm a bundle of nerves. I try to reach for him again, spurred on by the heat of my desire, but I can't quite get my hand there.

"Kiss me," I beg, and he shifts up, his lips on mine. Now

I can touch him too. We rub one another, kissing deeply, our bodies hot and sweaty and deprived.

I moan as he rubs me harder, and I can feel my release building, elevating, until it reaches a precipice.

And then I tremble and fall. It's something, but it's not enough. I slowly turn to him and rub him. His jaw hardens, and then he lays me on my back and presses his body against mine. I hear a grunt deep in his throat, as he presses his hardness against me. Then he flops down, his head lowered and resting on my naked breast.

It's a release for both of us; a letting go, but the deeper yearning is still there.

My insides are in an uproar, and the nerve endings in that sweet spot between my legs are almost ready to riot.

I *need* him.

"I want you, I want all of you." I tell him as I stroke the back of his head. He lifts his face, his fingers tapping gently across my chest.

"But you said..." His tapping is distracting. It mirrors the throbbing between my legs. "You're a good girl, Trinity."

"I don't want to be a good girl, not when you're around. I want to know what it's like, going all the way."

His fingers stop, and he takes my breast in his palm. "And you want to go all the way with me?" His voice is raspy, filled with need, and his eyes are dark. I want him so much that I can hardly breathe. I have never been in this situation before. I have never let things get this out of hand before.

I want all of him, and I want to give him all of me. My ideals and my values slide away, like the skinny straps on sexy lingerie pieces.

He must surely see his answer from the way I look at

him, because it's impossible for me to mask my desire any longer.

"You're the sexiest woman I've ever met," he says, making me chortle, because I don't believe a word of that.

"You are," he insists, when I remain silent. He shifts on the bed, adjusting his posture, then winces. "I came in my pants." He makes a face. "This is uncomfortable."

I smile at him in understanding.

"Maybe I should bring a spare pair of boxer briefs next time."

"Or you could take them off," I offer, boldly.

His hooded eyes snap wide open and he stares into my eyes, left to right, and back again, as if he's making sure I haven't turned delirious. Making sure I mean it. "I'm struggling to resist you fully clothed. If I get naked, I won't be able to hold back."

"Then don't."

He cocks his head, and starts to squeeze my nipple between his fingers. The motion arouses me again. "You don't mean that."

I lick then bite my lower lip. "I do mean that."

His Adam's apple moves.

"What would you do to me if we had a sex swing here?"

"Here?" he asks, his voice croaky.

"And if I was completely naked and in it?"

His eyes begin to shine. "Damn it, Trinity. Don't tease me like that."

"I've never had sex, and I can't stop thinking about it now, not since I met you. *You* make me think about it."

He swallows again, the telltale motion of his throat clueing me in on his uneasiness. I reach down and feel between his legs. He's hard again. And right now, I consider pulling down his zipper and touching him. I want to, but I don't.

"What would you do?" I ask him again.

He moves his hand away then sits up. Affronted, so do I, holding my top together so that it doesn't gape open. "You didn't answer the question."

"I can't answer the question," he says, getting up off the bed. When he turns his back to me, I see the pattern of burns on his back, a clump of ugly welts going across from one shoulder blade to the next. I wince involuntarily, not because they look unsightly, but because I don't want to think about the pain it must have caused him when his flesh burned.

"I don't want to take something so precious away from you," he says, putting on his T-shirt still with his back to me.

I can't help but go up to him and hug him from behind. He stops for a moment, then exhales.

"They're war wounds," he tells me, knowing exactly why I threw my arms around him. I kiss his back, over the T-shirt, but don't let go of him.

"Hey," he says, turning around, his hands falling to my shoulders. "Let's not rush into anything." He kisses me on the forehead, leaving me more confused than ever as he walks away.

"Where are you going?"

"I think I need to go see my dad."

His dad? We've shared an X-rated moment, and he's thinking about his dad?

"I don't want you to do anything you're not ready for."

I blink, and blink again.

"You don't think I'm old enough to decide when I want to start having sex, and who with?"

"I don't want us to move too fast." He comes over and

kisses me, on the nose this time. "Trust me, it's better if we go slow."

I can't stop myself from thinking what it would be like to have sex with him. It's something I've always held dear, something I've never been tempted to want to give up, but now it's like a dead weight that needs to be shifted from a sinking ship.

My desire to save myself isn't born from any religious sentiment, nor is it to do with the way I was brought up. It's something I've wanted to do for myself.

Now, I'm not so sure.

CHAPTER TWENTY-SIX

TRINITY

E
d has stopped coming to my classroom for our end-of-day chats. If this goes on any longer, it will become even more awkward between us, so I decide to knock at his door.

He looks up and his face hardens.

"Did you find the right mattress?" I ask, walking towards him.

He doesn't answer right away, but chooses to focus his attention on the paperwork in front of him. "Ed," I say, finding his behavior childish. He gives me a cold look. He and I aren't even dating, and he's behaving like this. "The mattress?"

"Didn't find one I liked." He taps his red marker pen on the table. An uncomfortable silence swirls around us.

I feel so uncomfortable that I'm tempted to turn back around and walk out, but he's a work colleague, and his classroom is next door to mine. We have another two semesters of school. I can't have this awkwardness between us. "Ed, can we stop this, please?"

"Stop what?"

I stare at him directly in the eye. "We used to talk every day. I've barely seen you lately." Ever since Max and I saw him testing the mattress.

"I don't understand how you've ended up with that guy."

I stare at him, not quite liking the way he said 'that guy.'

"Someone who crashed into the back of you and trashed your car," Ed says.

I consider it to be a brilliant story for telling people how we met. "It was chemistry," I reply, trying to keep a straight face.

Ed doesn't look amused. "A sex swing?"

I take a deep breath. "He was joking."

Ed gives me a mistrusting look. "I didn't realize you were that kind of woman."

"He was joking, Ed! It was a bookshelf."

But Ed doesn't look convinced, and that angers me because what on earth does any of this have to do with him?

"You surprise me, Trinity," he says. "I thought better of you."

I detect an undertone of righteousness in his tone. "Then you don't really know me at all." I'm so incensed by his words and his attitude that I have to take a long slow breath outside his classroom, out of his sight.

I miss Max, and wish he was here. Usually he calls me when he's free, but he hasn't so far this week. It's the longest we've gone without seeing one another.

Things got heated the last time, and I wonder if that's why he's been quiet lately. The roles seem to have switched between me and him. I'm the one who wants more, and he's the one who's taking things slow.

I start to wonder if he's getting bored with me. I start to wonder if I'm too nice for him, and that's why he doesn't want to take things to the next level.

Just as I think about him, he texts me out of the blue to ask me when I'm coming out. Before I can text back, he asks me if I'm ready for a ride? He says he's waiting outside on his motorbike and that he has a spare helmet for me.

I thank the lord that I'm wearing pants and not a skirt.

I rush out and see him through the school fence. He's waiting on his bike and my heart lifts in happiness at the sight of him. I practically fly across the parking lot to get to him.

My car is here, so I'm not sure if it would be better if I follow him, rather than get on his bike. Just as I get near to the school fence, a guy deliberately stands in front of me, blocking my path. He's come out of nowhere, and takes me by complete surprise.

"Miss Weldon?" It's an angry voice, with a pissed-off tone. I don't recognize him, and the more I look at his face, the more I know I've never seen him before. The smell of alcohol rolls off him.

"I'm Dylan Church's dad." I open my mouth in surprise. Dylan hasn't been in school for a few days, and I'm even more worried now.

"Is he all right?"

"He would be, if you stopped interfering."

Simmering resentment spills out of him, and it scares me.

"Mr. Church, I don't think we've ever met." I hold out my hand for a handshake, but he doesn't take it. Come to think of it, the more I look at him, the more I see that he's not happy. Not at all.

"Stay away from my kid." He pokes two fingers in my shoulder.

"Excuse me?" His threatening behavior shocks me.

"You heard me. Stay away from him."

"Mr. Church..." I start to protest.

"You've been giving him food and sneaking and asking him all sorts of questions. Stop poking your nose into our business."

I can hear him talking, but my mind is on Dylan and I'm suddenly worried about him. This man looks unsteady and angry, and when he pokes me again, I raise my voice. "Will you stop doing that?"

"Stay away from my kid." He jabs me again.

"Will you stop doing that!"

"Hey!" Max's voice reaches my ears at the same time as I see him marching towards me.

"Quit poking her," Max snarls.

"Yeah? And what are you gonna do about it?" Dylan's father spits back.

"I'm gonna send you flying, dude," Max threatens. In my periphery, I see a crowd of astonished parents and children forming in the distance around us.

"Mr. Church," I say, trying to appeal to the man's senses. "If you have a complaint to raise, I suggest you do so with the—"

"I'm telling you," he says, pointing an angry finger at me. "Keep away from my kid," he jabs a finger into my arm, and this time it hurts. Max pushes him away.

"What did I tell you?" he roars.

This inflames Dylan's dad even more, and he charges at Max, until I stand in the middle of them and take the full brunt of his hand, which shoves me hard into Max. He holds me, his arm around me protectively, before he quickly pushes me behind him.

"I fucking warned you, dude." He holds me at a distance behind his back, and his other hand and voice and posture tell me he's about to hit Dylan's dad.

"Stop!" I yell, trying desperately to free myself from Max's hand. I look around me, trying desperately to locate a staff member. Incredibly, I see no teacher, but a crowd of shocked parents and children.

"Max!" I say, pulling him away. "Max, NO! I will get into trouble," I hiss. This seems to have a sobering effect on him, and he moves towards me.

Dylan's dad stands there, ready, eager to lash out. He probably would have, but I sense Max might have scared him off.

"Mr. Church," I say, raising my voice. "If you have a complaint to make, I suggest you raise it with the principal."

He throws me one final death stare, and points his finger at me. "Keep away from my boy."

I watch him leave, then raise a hand to my forehead. I steal a glance around the playground and see parents look away, then continue about their day.

"The son of a bitch," says Max.

"Shhhhh," I say. He's quickly forgotten he's in a school playground and not a garage.

"You okay?" he asks, putting his arm around me. "Can't believe that fucker pushed you."

"Max!" I put a finger to my lips. "We're in a school."

"Just as well that I was here," he says. "Who the hell was that?"

We walk away from the school, and I look around, wondering if Dylan's dad will suddenly reappear. "Dylan's dad. I'm worried about Dylan. He hasn't been in school for a few days now."

"What's wrong?"

"His mom said he had a stomachache."

"What did his dad want?"

"I'm not sure. We can't talk here." I'm still in shock because I'm not accustomed to physical or verbal abuse. I'm shaking.

"Hey," Max blankets his arms around me, and I let him. I don't care who sees. I need this comfort. I bury my face in his arm and breathe in, not wanting to move. There was so much rage inside that man. I think of Dylan, and his tiny mom, and I shiver.

"You're still shaking," Max says, stroking my hair.

"I've never had that happen to me before." I look up at him.

"Let's get out of here."

I feel as if I need to take a moment and think about what's happened. I feel like I need to tell someone. Another teacher. Maybe Marshall.

Max's hand on my lower back relaxes me. Soothes me.

"Come back to my place," he says.

"How come you came?" I ask, remembering that I've told him not to come to my classroom, since it's not really permitted. And kissing is definitely not permitted anywhere on school premises.

"I wanted to surprise you," he says.

"You did."

He touches my face lightly. "I missed you."

I smile. I wasn't sure. Doubt crept in when I hadn't heard from him. Seeing him just now was the best thing, until Dylan's father raised his ugly head.

"I missed you," I tell him.

"I hate to think what might have happened if I hadn't shown up. I hated that dude talking to you like that."

"Things might not have become that confrontational if you hadn't been here."

"I wasn't going to let him lay another finger on you."

I'm too deep in thought, too worried about Dylan, to respond when Max kisses the back of my hand.

"He's the father of that little boy, the one you've seen a few times."

"Dylan?"

I'm surprised he remembers his name. I nod. "You're good that you've noticed stuff isn't right for that kid."

"You get an eye for these things, being a teacher."

"Come home to my place," he says. "You're too shaken up to go home alone. I've missed you. Need to see you again."

These words wrap around me like a thick woolly blanket.

I want to be with him. It's that simple. "Okay."

I leave my car at the school, and get on his bike, and we speed away.

He takes me into his place. It's the first time I've been here. It's slightly bigger than my place, and the layout is almost similar. But, surprisingly, it is neat and tidy. I'm not sure why I expected anything less. Maybe I'm more judgmental than I like to admit.

After a day like this, it's nice to come back home to Max. Although this isn't home.

"That kid is lucky he has a teacher like you."

"Is he? What if I've gotten him in more trouble?"

"You care too much." I'm resting on Max's chest, leaning against him on the couch.

"I'm supposed to care. I'm his teacher."

"His old man reeked of alcohol," Max comments. "Poor kid."

"Poor mother," I say, recalling Dylan's harried mother. "I'd hate to think he'll take his anger out on them when he goes home."

"You can't go to the kid's place, Trinity. You can't get that involved."

"I wasn't suggesting that." I wipe my hand over my forehead.

"If you want to go back to the school, I'll take you back."

Now that we're here, I'm not so sure. I could call Mr. Marshall and update him on events but chances are that he might have left for the day. I let out a loud sigh. "I'll go see the principal tomorrow."

"My dad was like that," Max says suddenly.

I want to turn my head to look at him, but I'm scared that he might stop talking. So I listen. "He was?"

"He was an asshole."

I let out a breath as silence falls. I suspected something like this.

"I don't remember much of my home, except that it wasn't a nice place. I remember being terrified of my father, and finding refuge in my mom." I stroke his hand as I listen.

"Moms are the backbone of many a family. People think women are weak, but we're not."

"She took a lot of crap from him," he says. "He'd slap her around some. I can't remember it all, except he'd get angry, and then when he was really angry, he'd stub his cigarettes out on me."

I suck in a breath. I want to turn and hug him. I want to hold him, but he's never opened up like this before, and I don't want to interrupt now that he's finally telling me. So I stay put, and stay very still, and I listen with my heart.

"Didn't your teachers ever notice?"

"I didn't go to school. Not then. So he could do what he wanted and there was nobody to notice, except my mom."

"She must have been scared of him."

"She was, I guess. But she picked him over me."

"How's that?"

"One day he went absolutely berserk. He got badly drunk and turned me into a human ash-tray."

"Max," I say softly, my heart bleeding for him.

"Usually, she'd hold me and try to make my burns better, and give me chocolate. But on this particular day, the old bastard was so drunk, he passed out stone cold on the floor. She packed my clothes and said we were going on a trip." He stops for a moment, and I seem to have lost him.

"A trip where?" I ask, when he doesn't speak.

"She made me sit on the steps of this place, told me to stay there, and sit still, and that she was going to buy me some donuts, and she would be back soon."

My heart lurches as I imagine it. "And then?"

"I sat and waited, and waited, but my mom never came back."

I am horrified. "Never?"

"Never." His voice is croaky again.

"And then this woman opened the door and found me, and took me inside."

A gasp escapes my lips. I am horrified, unable to speak.

"My mom had left me outside the steps of a children's home. I never saw her again."

I jolt forward, then twist my body so that I can see his face. "What do you mean you never saw her again?"

"She deliberately left me there because she wanted me to be found. It was Grampton House. It's shut down now, but the building's still standing."

"Here in Chicago?" I clutch at these pieces of his life story, as if they're sharp pieces of glass. Everything I imagined about him is so wrong, so different. "You said your mom died when you were a teen."

"I'm adopted. I was adopted a few months later. My birth mother was the one who abandoned me."

His birth mother left him, and then his adopted mother died.

My heart begins to bleed for him. I'm not a mother, but what I feel for my students is the fiercest love and devotion. I get sad each time the school year ends and I have to say goodbye to my class. I cannot in the darkest creases of my mind imagine what it must have been like for Max's mother to give him up the way she did.

"My adopted parents were the best. They showered me with love. Maybe I was young, and that helped, but I still remember fragments about my real mom, like her soft hair, and her hugs. She was always hugging me."

"Oh, Max." I put my arms around him and hold him. "I'm so sorry."

He doesn't say anything.

"So they never tried to find your parents?"

"No, but she left a note." He lets out an exhale, and I don't let go. I still have my arms around him. "She said she couldn't keep me safe, and that this was the only way she knew to give me a decent life. She knew I would get taken care of here and she hoped I would understand. She said she knew what she was doing, and that she'd left me there on purpose, and that it was the hardest decision she'd ever had to make."

I want to cry for the four-year-old sitting on those steps, alone and abandoned, and still waiting for his mother to come back. I clench every muscle in my body so that I can hold it together, so that I can be strong for this man that I care so much about.

"My adopted parents told me later that the woman who found me outside the children's home told them my mom had packed me with a small bag of clothes and a fabric book that I loved. My mom used to read it to me every night, when she could. They said I had bruises all over my body, along my back and thighs, as well as the burns."

"Why didn't they track your parents down?"

"Because they probably moved out of state."

I lift my head and stare up at him. "And your mom never wrote to you after that?"

He shakes his head. "My adopted parents were good, after I went to live with them, they still checked in with the children's home from time to time in case my mom might have written, but nothing ever came. My mom told me she kept checking in, right up until she got sick and died. I don't think my dad, my adoptive dad, kept on checking. I suppose there was no point. He's never quite been the same since my mom died."

I bury my face in his chest again. My forehead rests on his T-shirt and my arms wrap around him. I have no words. There is nothing I could say that would take away his pain. I have no words of wisdom, no profound saying. No uplifting quote.

I hug him harder than ever, because this man has seen so much pain, and he has become an expert at hiding it well.

"My real mom picked my dad over me. She gave me up so that she could spend her life with him."

I twist around some more, and then climb over him so that I'm straddling him, so that I can see his face.

"Hey," I say, laying my palm against his face. "Maybe your mom loved you so much that she wanted you to live.

She gave you up so that you would have a chance. Maybe she was scared to confide in anyone, maybe she was scared that your father would come after you both if she tried to run away with you. Maybe that's why she did what she did, Max. It's the ultimate sacrifice. The poor woman must have been terrified, and had nobody she could go to."

Max blinks at me, as if this is some new way of looking at it, as if it's something he has never thought of before. I want to reframe his past for him, because it doesn't seem hopeful that he will ever find out the truth.

"That doesn't make sense."

"She loved you, Max. Even now you remember the good things about her. You said she always hugged you, and you read together." I bet he's put that fabric book away somewhere safe. "Maybe you wouldn't have lived if she'd picked a life with you in it. Maybe she tried to leave with you but couldn't walk away. Not all women can. Some have no choice but to depend on their men in order to survive. It shouldn't be like that, but maybe your mother didn't feel she could survive on her own, or have the help and support she needed. You don't know, Max. You'll never know, so why not think of an alternative ending?"

His eyes tear up, and it looks as if he's considering it. "It's weird not knowing, and then it's also weird that my adopted parents gave me such a great start to life, they saved me. They rescued me, and I fit into their family as if I'd been born there. But when my adoptive mother died, it ripped my heart out and I felt lost all over again. It was harder the second time around, because I was older, because I'd come to know what real and unconditional love is."

I kiss his hand. It must be strange, to have such gut-wrenching memories of his childhood, to not know the reasons for his birth mother leaving him, for having her severed out of his life. Max's life is made up of shattered fragments of his past, from memories that cut deep. He has scents, and stories, and hugs and kisses, and he has scars as daily reminders, too. My life is nothing like that, and I can't truly begin to imagine what his loss must feel like.

"She sounds like a woman who loved you more than life itself," I tell him. He's been let down all his life. My heart is breaking when I think of the women he has lost and the pain he has gone through. "Hey," I say, lifting his chin up and making him look me directly in the eye.

His lips start to move upwards at the corners, but it's a flimsy attempt at a smile which never reaches his eyes. I don't expect him to smile, I don't expect him to put on a brave façade for me.

His eyes are sad and shiny, and all I want to do is to put a smile on his face. I want to hold him, and love him, and make him feel not so sad.

So I kiss him.

CHAPTER TWENTY-SEVEN

TRINITY

is lips crush mine and we kiss so hard that I won't be surprised if we have bruises tomorrow.

He gets up slowly, with our lips still joined, breaking the kiss a little to adjust himself until he's sitting up; his back ramrod straight against the couch. I move so that I'm straddling him, and our kiss lengthens and deepens, and maybe it's the way we're sitting, the way we're face-to-face now, and maybe it's because he opened up and bared his heart to me, but I kiss him as if my life depends on it. His hands slide under my blouse, his fingers skittering over my stomach, tickling me.

I can feel his hardness between my legs, and I instinctively press against it. He is hard and needy, and I am soft and wet.

I get up off him, then stand in front and start to undo the buttons of my blouse. He will go too slow, hold back, make excuses. It's odd how I've become the seducer, and he's the shy, hesitant one.

"What are you doing?" he asks, even though it's perfectly obvious. His eyes shift from my fingers to my eyes.

"Take me to bed," I whisper, remembering a line from a movie. I don't know where his bedroom is, otherwise I'd lead the way, but knowing me, I'd probably accidentally end up in a closet. And there's a questioning gaze on his face, as if he's not sure I know what I'm doing, and for a microsecond I feel slightly embarrassed, knowing how I must look; knowing how this must sound to him. But a throbbing deep in my sex keeps me in the moment.

Max gets up, then takes my hand and leads me to his bedroom.

We fall onto his bed, kissing and rolling around like animals. Energy surges through my veins as his strong body sends a signal deep inside me. He kisses me again, and my no-sex stance disappears into a fog of desire. He presses harder against me, there's no mistaking the size or hardness of his erection as it sears my stomach.

I'm suddenly desperate to touch him. I want to examine him, and run my hands all over his body.

Desperate for more than kisses, I shrug out of my blouse.

"Aren't we moving a little too fast?" he asks, sitting on the bed, his lips wet, his eyes shiny.

"I want you, Max."

He lifts his head up, his eyes darting across my eyes as if he's trying to uncover something new, as if he's trying to decipher what I'm doing. "But you're..."

I place my hand over his hardness and squeeze gently, then hold my breath because I don't know how he'll take it.

In answer, he pulls me down towards him and seals my

lips with his then thrusts his tongue into my mouth. This kiss is different; it's carnal, dirty, deep. He sucks my tongue long and hard, and a pulsating, throbbing sensation steals my senses. I feel ready. I *am* ready.

I have never been this aroused before, and I shake and shiver with giddy anticipation.

"We should…" he lifts his head, "We should take this ….slowly Trinity. We don't have to rush."

He's talking too much. I don't know how much slower he wants to go, but this is agony. "I *need* you," I moan. "I need more."

"I don't want you to do something you're not sure of," he tells me.

"Don't you want me?" I ask. Maybe he doesn't want this? The thought stabs deep in my chest, lacerating my heart.

"Of course I want you. It's killing me to not be able to…"

He does want me.

That's all the reassurance I need. In my desperation to have him inside me, I stroke him again, and try to lever my hand so that I can pull down his zipper, but I can't quite do it.

His mouth dips down and he kisses me again, and somehow, he's managed to unhook my bra too. While he moves lower and showers my breasts with kisses, I try to shrug off my pants, which isn't easy given the way we're lying.

I accidentally kick him.

He yelps in agony and rolls away from me, lying on his back, his hands over his package. I raise a hand to my mouth in shock and watch his face contort with pain.

"I'm sorry," I gasp in shock to see him grimace in pain. I don't know what to do, so I lean over him. "Max."

He pants out loudly. "I'll...be...fine," he bites out.

I want to touch him, and kiss him and make him better. More than anything I want to touch him where it hurts.

We stay like that, me on my side wincing, because I can see his pain, and him on his back, breathing through his pain. "Aw... shit...that hurts," he wails, lying there in agony. I wince, and think how constrained he must feel, so I gently lower his zipper, then pull down his boxer brief enough to free his member.

It pops up. Straight as a rod. Purple, and engorged, and so *big*. I've never seen one so close up before. Previous boyfriends have tried to thrust my hand down there. I've fooled around with guys before but not to the point that I ever had this staring me in my face.

My insides turn to hot liquid.

"I'm sorry." I reach out gingerly and touch the tip.

He groans.

"Does this hurt?" I ask, sliding my hand lightly over it. He laughs, then pants out and lifts up on his elbows. "It doesn't hurt."

I touch him again, rubbing his silkiness over him. He lets out a low guttural moan. I grasp him in my hand. I've never done this before, but I can't seem to stop now. I stroke him gently, up and down, with my thumb sliding over his tip, because he seems to like it.

I want him to put it inside me, but I also have an urge to put him in my mouth.

It scared me that he will see how inexperienced I am on both accounts.

"You're going to make me come, Trinity," he says, his voice tight.

"Sorry." I stop stroking, but my fingers still remain around his shaft. I pump him gently.

"You're killing me softly." He sits up, then lifts his arms and takes off his T-shirt. Then he stands up, and my hand falls away. I'm better positioned, sitting on the bed, so I peel his jeans and boxer briefs all the way down.

I look up at him, and he's completely naked. An inferno rages through me.

"I'm sorry if I hurt you." I don't know what to do next. Maybe it's about time *he* made a move and took things over from this point on.

He crouches on the floor, flicks his finger over my hardened nipple. His mouth is so near to me that I'm breathing in his breath. "You have to stop apologizing, Trinity."

I look at him, not knowing what happens next.

"Seems a little one-sided to me," he says, "Me being completely naked, and you only half-naked."

"How did we end up like this?"

He reaches for my hand and pulls me up. "You tell me," he whispers. "Fuck." He cups his hand around my neck.

"No swearing."

"We're in the bedroom, not your classroom," he reminds me. "And I recall you asking me to take you to bed."

Yes, please.

"You're so damn sexy, so damn sweet, I don't deserve someone like you."

"I want you to make love to me. I want you to be my first."

His thumb glides over my lips. "Are you sure?"

I'm sure, surer than I've ever been. We kiss deeply again, our bodies pressed tight against one another. His hardness jabs me in my belly, and I love the feel of it.

His hands shuffle around with my zipper and button, and I shrug off my pants. Then he hooks his fingers on either side of my panties and rolls them down. I forget to breathe. It's intimate, and makes me feel vulnerable. And nobody has ever done that to me before.

Nobody has ever seen all of me.

"You're beautiful," he murmurs, kissing the top of my thigh. Another first for me. My breath turns shallow, and it becomes harder to breathe. Max's fingers skim along my thigh and come to a rest on the part of me which no one has ever touched.

Embarrassment courses through me when his fingers slide lower. I am slippery wet, and he can feel it.

"Lie down," he says softly, and I obey him, scooting up on the bed. He lies down so that he's on his side, staring at my nakedness. I can't cover up. There are no sheets, because we're lying on the bedspread. It's just me and him, no clothes, no barriers, skin-to-skin.

I can't hide anymore.

"Are you sure?" His lips brush mine and our breath mingles. It's intoxicating.

"Can't you tell?" I ask him. His fingers dance around below and I let out a gasp. He slides them over me.

"So wet," he murmurs, pressing his lips to mine. Then he dips a finger inside me and I mewl in delight.

"You're so tight," he says, as if it's a problem. His finger stills. Being tight is a good thing, I thought. If anyone should have any hesitation, it should be me. I've seen the size of his erection.

When he slides another finger in, I let out a sound I don't recognize as mine. His thumb slides easily over my folds and I almost lift up off the bed. It feels...divine, as if my nerve endings down there leapt up and jumped for joy.

My heart races.

The pulsating beats are as loud as a drum, and I'm

convinced he can hear them. He gives me another long, drawn-out kiss, and I start to buck against him. He immediately stops. "Slow down."

"It feels so good," I moan softly.

"I've got something that will feel even better."

I arch again, because his words are so potent, the promise so great, and my ache is so deep.

I reach down and touch him again, and he lets out a groan, then rewards me with his finger again. We pleasure one another slowly. It's sultry, and sensual, and deliciously dirty. I don't want to ever stop doing this. He draws sounds out of me which I don't recognize as my own. I pump him gently, my eyes on his face, observing his reaction as he grows harder still in my hands.

I've imagined these moments before, before Max came along, but so much more vibrantly and in detail ever since he collided into my life.

Now I get to experience it all for the first time and I'm a bundle of highly excitable nerves.

My legs fall apart as he rolls on top of me and we become a tangle of wet mouths, hot tongues and roaming hands. He touches me everywhere, leaving a trail of fire as he moves all over, sucking and licking my breasts and my neck. We do this for the longest time, until I feel as if I might explode. Or he will. Each time his fingers move, I'm closer to the edge. Everything is so new, so heightened, that my senses feel as if they might overload and combust. I can only take, and absorb, and feel so much.

And then he stops. He rolls off me and reaches for a something in his bedside cabinet. Then he returns to me, and kneels on the bed. His erection is practically inches from my face, and I'm oddly excited by it. I reach out to touch him when he rolls the condom on.

He lowers himself down on me, and I feel him poised at my entrance. "I don't want to hurt you," he murmurs, sucking my lower lip. And then I feel him moving slowly inside me, feel my body stretch as he fills me.

I sigh in gratitude, unable to contain myself as he slowly slips and slides his way deeper, inching into my slipperiness. I'm so wet that it doesn't hurt, and when he gives me a slobbering wet kiss, I am so aroused that I buck my hips.

"Are you okay?" he murmurs, his lips skimming over my cheek. I respond with a smile, and a sigh, my eyes almost rolling back into my head. I don't see, as much as I *feel*, and what I feel is being filled to the hilt. The slow-burn friction sends shockwaves through me.

He thrusts into me then, a short sharp pain pinches me. It barely registers before a tsunami of pleasure rolls through me. I hear a sound, like a wounded animal, and then I realize it's me, crying out in ecstasy.

My brain short-circuits as my inner muscles clench around him. My back arches, and I jolt and jerk in a spasm. It's involuntary, but Max sliding in and out of me feels so, so good.

I have no control over my body, and when he plunges his tongue into my mouth, mimicking the motion of his member deep inside me, it blows my mind.

I feel completely claimed by him.

CHAPTER TWENTY-EIGHT

MAX

She picked me to be her first. Me.

She's snuggled up against me, her arm over my chest as if she's claimed me. I want her to claim me. I want her to feel that way about me, because it's dawning on me slowly, that I want her in my life, not as a friend-with-benefits—she's not that kind of woman—but because she makes me feel whole again.

"You waited all this time, and you were saving yourself," I say, running my fingers through her hair. "I'm not the marrying kind, you know that, don't you?" I have to say it, because I need her to know. Maybe I should have told her before, but it honestly didn't come to my mind.

She holds a finger to my lips. "I don't expect you to marry me, silly." Then I need to know if she took pity on me.

"It was because of what I told you, wasn't it?"

She lifts up slightly, puts her hand to my cheek. "What

happened to you is heartbreaking, but us making love just now has nothing to do with pity. I'm falling for you."

I let her words sink in.

What is she saying?

She lifts up the sheet that covers her, and holds it tight against her so that it doesn't slip. "I want you to know that I love you, and I wanted to make you feel happy. I can't sleep at night because I think of all the things I want you to do to me." She drops a quick kiss on my lips, then snuggles against me again, leaving me to savor her words.

She's lying naked in my arms and she thinks I'm the best thing she's ever had. She thinks I deserved to be her first one, and she thinks I can give her a happy-ever-after. I don't want to hurt her, but I don't do happy-ever-afters.

I want to tell her that I'm not boyfriend material. That I have done things she would disapprove of. I wanted her to know about me, and I started to tell her the truth, that one time, about how I treat women, but she looked so disgusted that I had to pretend I'd been joking.

But today I told her stuff that nobody knows, not even Al, definitely not any woman. The fact that I could tell Trinity already tells me that she's special to me.

And now this. I never intended that our evening together would end up like this, with her in my bed.

I don't want her to go.

We snuggle together in our little bubble. I feel complete, in a way I never have after sex. This didn't feel like *only* sex. It was something more.

Trinity makes me feel calm.

She grounds me.

I like her being around, and I want to hold onto her for as long as I can, even though she deserves someone who can give her more, someone who can be more.

"Are you sore?" I ask, looking down at her.

She grins happily. "No."

"I didn't hurt you too much?"

She shakes her head.

I shift away from her, and lie on my side so that I can see her face.

She turns to her side too, with her head propped on her hand, so that we're facing one another.

"You have a gorgeous figure," I tell her, and rest my hand on her hip. Sure enough, the expected frown lines appear on her forehead and she squirms, as if she's not sure if I'm saying it because we just had sex.

"It's true," I insist, resisting the urge to sneak my head under the covers and sprinkle her with kisses. I'm ready for more, I always am, but with Trinity, it's more than sex and making out. I don't want her to leave.

"I need to lose some weight."

I give her a look of displeasure. "You don't need to lose anything." I cup her buttock gently. "You're perfect and beautiful exactly as you are."

"What were they like, your past girlfriends?"

She always wants to know about my previous girlfriends. I try not to think about the conversation I need to have with her when I tell her that they weren't exactly girlfriends.

I don't want to have any secrets between us, yet telling the truth might be the thing that pulls us apart.

"We can talk about that another time. Now that I have you in my bed, I want to make the most of it," I say. "Ready for round two?"

Her eyes widen, her lips curve into a smile. "Could we have round two?" she asks, as if she's Oliver Twist asking for more porridge.

"You can have anything you want." I feel myself harden again, just thinking about it, and all the things I can teach her, and do for her, and how much more satisfying it is to have someone for whom everything is brand new.

"I like the idea of round two, but I should go. I have some work to prepare for tomorrow." Her face turns somber. "I can't believe this is a school night."

Damn it. Tomorrow is Friday, and I lose her to her crochet class and her friend. I won't get to see her again until the weekend.

"Stay," I say, the word falling out of my mouth without thinking.

She gives a surprised laugh. "I can't stay. I have school tomorrow."

"And you can't go to school from here?"

I snake my hand gently along her waist and hips. My cock hardens some more. We kiss again, because I want to make her not think, because I want her to stay.

I feel as if I've just won a major prize, and I want to hold onto it as long as I can. I love that I was her first.

"I don't have a change of clothes," she says, giggling as my fingers skate over her warm skin.

I lean in for another kiss that can only lead to one thing. She pulls away, her hand lowering under the sheets to my cock. She wants more, and I intend to give it to her, all night, now that she's mine. School night be damned.

"Stay with me." If it sounds like I'm pleading with her, I am.

"Okay," she says, holding my chin gently. "But I have no change of clothes."

"You won't need any clothes tonight."

She giggles. "I'll need them for school tomorrow."

"Your car's at the school. I'll drop you at school or at

your place, tomorrow as early as you want." I graze my lips over her ear, and she squeals and squirms just as I expected.

"I need to take a shower," she says. "I'm all sweaty."

My stomach rumbles, reminding me that I'm hungry. The night is still young, we need to get these little things, like food, out of the way. I climb out of bed. "You take a shower, and I'll get some food on."

"You're going to make dinner?"

"I'm good with my hands."

"I noticed." She stands up then bends over to pick up her underwear, and my brain overheats and has other ideas.

"I'll get you a towel," I say, moving towards her. My hand skims her waist as I walk past, then come back to her. "How hungry are you?" I put my arm around her stomach from behind. She feels my erection jab her from behind.

"I'm not that hungry for food," she answers, pushing back against my cock.

There are so many new things I have yet to introduce her to, so many things I want to do with her, and sex in the shower can be our next lesson.

CHAPTER TWENTY-NINE

TRINITY

I'm late for school. It's only a few minutes, and the school day hasn't officially started, but I'm always here extra early. Max drops me off around the block from school because I don't want him to ride right up to the gates where all the parents dropping off their kids will see me.

I'm still in yesterday's clothes, and I feel dirty even though I showered this morning.

I'm tired, because we didn't sleep much. My mind is filled with our night together, and I can't stop thinking about all the things we did. Max's kisses are still imprinted on my mind, and I can't help the stupid smile that is permanently stuck to my face this morning.

I pray I make it through the day quickly.

I breezily say "Good morning," to Ed as I walk into my classroom.

The school bell hasn't yet sounded, and I quickly sit

down and try to prepare the things I need to for today's lesson.

Principal Marshall sticks his bald little head through the door. "Can you come see me immediately, Miss Weldon?"

I open my mouth to protest, when another teacher walks in.

"Helen will cover for you."

I rise from my chair, wondering why this can't wait. It's only when I follow him into his office that it all comes back to me.

So much happened yesterday, and all my brain can think of is what happened between me and Max. I've completely forgotten about Dylan's dad.

"We've had a complaint," he says, sitting down. I sit down opposite him. "Dylan Church's father made the complaint. Do you want to tell me what happened?"

The guy made a complaint? I should have told Mr. Marshall yesterday. I should have forewarned him.

I tell him what happened, that Mr. Church was threatening and aggressive. I tell him exactly what happened, but I leave Max out of it.

Mr. Marshall surveys me in silence for a moment. "He said there was someone else. Someone who walked in and threatened him."

I scoff in surprise. "Nobody threatened him. I mean," I try to remember how it happened. "My friend saw the commotion and came to my assistance. I tried to find a teacher, I wanted to go get someone but it happened so fast."

"Who threatened him?"

"Sean, I could smell the alcohol on that man's breath. He was looking for a fight."

"He says you've been giving his son food at the end of the day. Is that right?"

My mouth twists as I think of something to say. "Is that a crime?"

"You're not supposed to have favorites."

"It's not about having favorites. That child looks malnourished."

"His father said you give him fruit most days."

"It's not a crime. I'm worried about Dylan."

"You should have come to see me."

I swipe my hand across my forehead in consternation. "I didn't want to cause undue problems."

"Are you worried about the child or not? If you were concerned, you should have raised those concerns with me."

He's right. I should have. I should have called it in to the CPS because of the bruises I saw. I failed. I've not had my head in my work as much lately, and I'm failing children like Dylan. I feel something heavy land in my stomach and weigh me down.

"Also..." Sean clears his throat, narrowing his eyes at me. "I don't know how to say this, so I'll just come out with it..."

I sit up, in worried expectation.

"Kissing your boyfriend is not allowed on school premises. In fact, your boyfriend shouldn't be on the school premises in the first place."

I have nothing to say in my defense, except, "I'm sorry."

Sean looks at me, and I feel extra paranoid, hoping he won't know that I'm in the same clothes I wore yesterday. Or that I've had sex. I sit up straighter and smooth down a crease in my pants.

"This isn't like you, Trinity. This behavior isn't what I expect from you."

"I know. I'm sorry. It won't happen again. Is there anything else? I need to get back to my class."

He looks surprised, but I have nothing further to say, and I want to get back to the children. "There's nothing else. But, remember, if you have concerns about any child, about Dylan Church, you need to be certain, and you need to tell me."

"Yes. Of course."

I return to my classroom and the children are all looking up at me, as if something is wrong.

Helen stands up as soon as I walk in. "I got them to read the next chapter of their book."

"Thanks, Helen." When she leaves, the children stare at me, wide-eyed.

Dylan is the only one who avoids looking at me. His eyes are on his book, unlike all the other children. This is a break from the norm, and it is usual that they will automatically assume I was in trouble.

Why else does anyone go to see the principal? This is a blip in their little organized lives so I say something light and breezy. "I was sorting something out for our fieldtrip next week," I lie, convincingly. I do not lie to my children, *ever*, but in this case it is justified.

Their faces melt into little smiles.

"Carry on reading, please, for a little longer."

I slide into my chair and prepare for the rest of the day. I need to catch up on work I should have done last night except that I was busy with Max.

My day resumes as normal, even though I have difficulty focusing on anything for too long. It's just as well that I'm teaching seven-year-olds, and not older children studying for their high school diploma.

Dylan avoids eye contact for the entire day. He doesn't

look as bad as I had feared he might, given that he's been off school for a few days. I feel relieved. There's a note on my desk and when I open it, I see that it's from Dylan's mom, explaining the reason for his absence.

"I hope you're feeling better now, Dylan," I say, as I later walk around the class handing out papers for a spelling test.

"Yes, miss," he replies, as if he didn't really hear what I said. He still doesn't look at me. I decide to give him his space and, of course, I won't be giving him any more fruit from now on.

I'm not angry with him, but I am still concerned. I've seen enough of his drawings and paintings to still harbor the same level of concern, but I have to watch myself.

I'll still continue to look out for him when he changes into his gym clothes but now that I've met his father, I'm extra alert. Some scars—the mental scars—are invisible.

I think of Max again and blush. I think of how we spent last night, that I spent the night with him, that I had sex for the first time. That I'm no longer a virgin.

My long-held resolve vanished into thin air. It wasn't completely because of him opening up to me, it wasn't pity I felt, but sadness. A deep, gut-wrenching sadness for the abandoned boy he was.

I have no regrets. I'm glad Max was my first.

As the day ends, I am grateful that it's Friday. I have crochet class and then dinner with Christina, but I am tired and in need of more sleep. I want to get out of these clothes and lounge around at home, preferably with Max, but I also don't want to be one of those friends who drops everything because she suddenly gets a new boyfriend.

I also feel as if I want to tell Christina, even though I know already that she won't approve.

I haven't completely decided what my plans are for this evening, but as I rush to leave, Ed walks into my classroom, the way he used to do before Max came along.

"What's going on?" he asks.

He knows, but I don't know how, since he couldn't have heard anything in the playground that day when Dylan's dad confronted me. But maybe some of the children said something.

"What did Marshall want?"

I stare at him, trying to figure out what he knows. There were no teachers around yesterday when I needed them, but there were plenty of parents picking their children up. I can only imagine how fast the rumors must have flown. He knows something.

"I heard that an angry parent came up to you."

"If you know that much, then you probably know everything, Ed."

"That's all I heard. I don't want rumors, I want to hear the truth."

I tell him, as briefly as I can, about Dylan's father, and his aggressive behavior, about him shoving me hard, and about Max coming to my rescue.

"You have to be careful," he says, "You've always been concerned about that kid, but sometimes you can't become too involved. These things have a way of biting you back."

"You can't expect me to close my eyes and look the other way when I suspect a child is being neglected."

He cocks his head and shrugs.

"By the way, thanks for snitching on me," I say, sounding not unlike a seven-year-old.

Ed looks at me as if he doesn't understand.

"The other day when you saw me and Max in here." I recall Ed sticking his head in and catching us.

He frowns, making crisscross lines appear on his brow. "Marshall knew?"

"Don't pretend to be surprised."

He points a finger at himself. "You thought I told him?" There is outright indignity in his voice, and I start to wonder if I had it wrong.

"Didn't you?"

"It wasn't me. I'd never do that to you." He studies my face because I'm too shocked to say anything. He wouldn't lie about something like that, and now I'm the one who feels bad.

"There were other kids walking past your door that day." I remember, and now I want to take back my accusation. Things are definitely awkward between us. I'm starting to miss that easygoing camaraderie we used to have.

"But your choice of boyfriend surprises me."

"You don't know Max," I say, feeling defensive. He scoffs, and it annoys me.

"I hope he's good to you. I hope he makes you happy."

I'm trying to think of something to say when Ed leaves without giving me the chance to.

I head home, glad that it's the end of the week. I change out of my two-day-old work clothes, feed Benji and get my crochet bag ready.

I haven't done much crocheting lately, and my blanket is still the same size. Christina is almost done with hers. I'm suddenly looking forward to seeing her. I think I'm going to tell her about Max. About me, and how I've finally lost my V-card.

Just as I'm about to head out of the door, my phone rings. It's Max. Seeing his name on the caller ID makes a shiver roll down my spine, and when I answer and hear his sexy voice, I want to see him again.

"Hey, stud." I say, in my most provocative voice. I have no idea where this came from, but this is the effect Max has on me.

He laughs. "Hey."

"I was on my way out."

"Crochet and Christina?"

"Unfortunately, yes."

"Unfortunately?"

"I'd much rather be seeing you again." After yesterday, spending all night with him, I find myself wanting that all over again.

"Me too, babe. Me too."

It's the first time he's called me that. I set down my crochet bag and flop onto the couch again.

"Come over," I say.

"What?"

"Come over. I want to see you again." I want him again. I want sex, and to make love, and to feel his lips and fingers on me again.

"What about ... you know...your crochet, and your friend?"

"I'm having impure thoughts about you."

"Yeah?" he says. "You have no idea of the thoughts in my head."

His voice is low and seductive, and I picture him with a sexy smile on his face as he speaks.

I want him. "Come over, *please.*"

"On my way."

I text Christina and tell her that I'm not feeling well and I won't be coming tonight. It's easier for me to text than to blatantly lie on the phone.

CHAPTER THIRTY

MAX

Things are moving so fast between us. It's like I have Trinity overload on my brain. What I didn't expect was for her to give up her regular Friday night plans for me. But she's discovered sex.

I'm falling for her, and maybe she's falling for me. Maybe I can dare to think about being with a woman like her, having a girlfriend instead of a fuck-buddy.

She's loyal, committed, and caring, and she makes me feel as if we belong together. What we have didn't start with the need for sex. It was based on attraction, and friendship, and maybe even a hint of something taboo.

But it evolved over time, and what we have is a beautiful thing.

When I go over to her place, she jumps me the moment I walk through her door. I wrap my arms and lips around her, and when I draw back, her cat bares its teeth at me as if he wants to claw me to death.

"He hates me," I tell her, pulling away from her and slanting a sideways glance at the beast.

"He does not."

"I'm not risking it." I scoop her up in my arms and head for her bedroom. "Jealous much?" I say to him, before I close the door on the cat-beast. At least this way he won't come in and rip my back to shreds while I'm going down on her.

I push her back on the bed and slowly peel her jeans off, making her giggle. I tell her to relax. She stares back at me as if she's unsure, and scared, and excited. I stare down at her, feeling the most turned on ever.

"What are you doing?" she asks, when I drop to my knees, my hands on her thighs.

"Wait and see."

I love being the first to show her things. I love being the first to witness her reactions. I love watching her shiver and quake. I love hearing her cries, and her shivering sighs. I love my name on her lips when I bury my cock deep in her pussy.

And now I'm going to show her what it's like to pleasure her with my mouth. She resists at first, but I slowly win her over.

And win her over I do.

She mewls the loudest I've ever heard her when my face is buried between her legs. Her back arches off the bed when I tunnel deep with my tongue. When she comes, writhing and moaning uncontrollably, it is a beautiful sight to behold.

I strip off and watch her come down from her orgasm, her face all hot, sweaty and flushed.

"What do you think?" I ask her, as if she's tasted a new dish from a menu.

"Oh..." she sighs, her hand over her head, her eyes like liquid. Her breaths are starting to still. I drop a kiss on her shoulder, because that simple 'Oh' is enough.

We climb under the covers, and I hold her in my arms, thinking how complete I feel. I haven't come yet, but I get as much pleasure giving and seeing her come as I do from my own release.

"Spend the weekend with me," she says suddenly, tracing her fingers lightly down my chest as she lies in the crook of my arm.

"You sure?" I like the idea of that, and how quickly things are changing. I never used to stay over, and I've never wanted anyone to stay over at my place, except for Hot Gina, but that was purely due to scarcity and time, and yet I'm breaking all the rules for Trinity.

"I wouldn't ask if I wasn't sure."

She lifts her head and rests her chin on my chest. "We won't have to get out of bed much."

My cock hardens with her words. I push up, so that she feels it. "That's a yes."

"I felt it loud and clear." Her eyes light up as she stares at me. "Do you have to work this weekend?"

"No. I'm letting Al do as much overtime as he needs on account of him getting married."

I told her he got engaged recently. Hopefully she can come to the wedding with me. I don't ask her yet, though.

One thing at a time. I'm scared of tempting fate, of thinking that far in the future. I'm not used to dealing with having a woman in my life.

"Do you have any plans this weekend?" I ask.

"Just Sunday dinner with my mom and dad. You?"

"Me and my dad don't have stuff like that."

"And you have no siblings?" she asks.

I shake my head.

"Me neither," she tells me.

We're both single kids, but I bet our lives are so different. Our families, our upbringing. I skim my fingers up and down her back. "I have you until Sunday?"

She digs her chin into my chest. "Yes." Her lips widen to a smile I feel in my stomach. This makes me happy, her lying close to me like a second skin. There's no other place I'd rather be.

"Any other family? Cousins? Aunts or uncles?" she asks. This is weird, her wanting to know about my family and other stuff.

"I have a horrible cousin, Rufus, on my dad's side. They moved out of state years ago, so I don't have to see that idiot anymore."

"Idiot?"

"He didn't like me. Maybe because up until I came along, he was the only child. My grandparents doted on him, and my mom and dad did too. Apparently, they'd been trying to have children for a long time and gave up. And then, they adopted me."

"You stole his thunder. He was jealous." She kisses my chest and it's like a reassuring full stop at the end of my sentence.

"I reckon he was. He was a shit."

Thinking about it now, given my circumstances and how I was found, my mom and dad who adopted me showered me with love, as did everyone else in my extended family. I was loved so well, so deeply. Rufus had been the only child until I came along.

"Why? What did he do?"

Trinity drops another kiss on my chest, this woman who

completes my world, and makes me feel good again. This woman who isn't a quick-fix, insta-love experience for me.

"My parents had a huge party for me. I think it was my eighth birthday, with all of my school friends, and Rufus. He was a year older than me, so in a different school year. Anyway, there was a bouncy castle, and an entertainer, a piñata, and a blow-up paddling pool. I remember balloons, and chocolate cupcakes, and I remember feeling incredibly excited and really happy.

"Then Rufus, my nasty, jealous, malicious cousin, said to me, right in the middle of my party, but away from the adults, he said, 'your mom never loved you and she gave you away.' I can still hear him saying those words right now."

Trinity lifts her chin and stares at me in shock.

"He messed up my party, one hundred percent."

"What an evil, nasty, horrible child. Did you tell your parents?" she asks.

"They found me crying in a corner of the garden, and I told them what had happened. Rufus got a huge lecture from everyone but the damage was done."

"You didn't believe him, did you?"

I nod my head. "I did. I was a kid, what was I supposed to do?"

I wasn't able to shake my cousin's words away. I remembered as if they'd been printed on a billboard in the center of town.

"Did you know you were adopted?"

"Not really. Nobody used those words. It was just...weird. One moment I lived in a rundown place that was sad, hard and miserable, and then the next moment, I'm with parents who love me, and I live in a big house where everything is warm. It's soft and bright. I don't remember the change. I might have blocked it out. Tried to forget about it."

"Children are adaptable," Trinity says softly. "But it would have hurt deep down, when your cousin said that?"

"Being reminded that the people you think are your parents aren't your real parents sucks. At some deep level, it sucks because you start to think of your life as not real. I started to think I was living a lie, that this was temporary and my mom might come back. Or my dad. I love my adoptive parents—to me they're my real parents because they cared for me, and loved me, but my cousin's words have stayed with me. He reminded me that I have no sense of where I came from, no sense of belonging."

"Don't let a bitter child's jealousy taint your memories, Max. Don't let him change what you know."

"And what's that?"

"That your mother loved you enough to give you up in the hope that you would be cared for and loved. That's the biggest sacrifice she could have made."

I say nothing.

"And you *do* belong. You belonged with the family who adopted you." She winces. "I'm sorry that your mom died, but you have your dad, and..." she pauses, and her eyes turn glassy.

I get it.

She wants to make me feel better. The thing is, when my adoptive mother died from cancer when I was in my teens, it only served to reinforce that loving someone leads to heartache.

Loving someone isn't guaranteed forever. Even after you come to love someone, they can still let you down.

It's why I decided from a young age to not let love in. It's why my encounters are only surface level.

It's why I won't allow myself to fall in love, but to fall in lust and stay there until I get bored.

She looks at me as if she wants to say something, but her phone starts ringing. She bites her lip. "It's Christina," she says apologetically as she answers.

And then her voice changes. She sniffles, and coughs, and pretend-sneezes. "Ahhh, that would have been nice," she says, looking at me with big eyes and making a face. She sniffles some more. "You don't want to catch what I have, trust me. I feel awful. I'm going to bed. Thanks."

She hangs up.

"What was that about?"

"Christina was going to come over with chicken noodle soup and see how I was."

I raise an eyebrow.

"I told her I wasn't feeling too well and that's why I skipped tonight."

"You changed your plans and you lied to your best friend to accommodate me." I rest my hand on the curve of her back as she lies back down against me.

"You belong to me," she says.

This warms my heart. I think I love her. I roll her over so that she's on her back, and fill my hand with her breast. There is so much flesh here that I can't hold all of it in one hand. I love the feel of her. Lowering my head, I take her breast into my mouth and suck hard.

She lets me suck for a good few seconds, before rolling me over on my back. "My turn," she says, reaching for my cock a little more roughly than I need her to. I wince in pain. "Too hard?" she asks, like Goldilocks checking out the three bears' beds.

"Just a little," I choke out.

"Then how should I do it?" she asks, innocent as a lamb.

She wants to know how to stroke my cock?

If my insides could smile, I would be a walking, talking bag of joy right now. I've truly hit the jackpot with this woman. "I can train you in the dark arts," I say in a mock-horror voice.

"Dark arts?" she asks, tightening her grip around my cock. "Some of us waited for the right person to come along before we gave up our V-card."

She thinks I'm the right person for her? My expression turns sober, and she notices.

"What?"

"There are a million reasons someone like you shouldn't be with someone like me," I say, looking for an opening, for a chance to tell her about my past. I hate lying to her but I don't want to spoil this.

"You have to stop talking like that." She rewards me with a long, slow kiss, then loosens her grip a little and starts to pump me faster.

"Better?"

I grunt my approval. I love the feel of her hands, the way she moves her thumb over me. I love her naked and in bed and in my arms. I love that we have days and nights of this.

She stares into my eyes as she says these beautiful words. The combination of that and her hand on my cock are enough to make my eyes almost pop out of my head. I clench my teeth in an attempt to hold myself together. I'm so used to ripping my partner's clothes off and getting right to it, but I need to go slower with Trinity.

"Maybe we should get a sex swing."

Her suggestion comes out of nowhere. "You want me to get one for us?" I picture Trinity in the sex swing, and me fucking her while she's sitting in it. She would love it, but now I have a picture I can't get out of my head.

She giggles. "I'm curious to see what it is."

"I guess we're just going to have to try it out, then," I manage to say. She strokes me faster, and I'm in pure sex heaven, and any moment soon, I'm going to flip her back onto the bed and bury myself inside her.

CHAPTER THIRTY-ONE

TRINITY

"You sound so much better," Christina notes when I call her a few days later. "You sounded so sick last time."

"I am better," I tell her, feeling guilty about my constant lying.

She asks me to come over one evening, and I do, showing up at her doorstep with a big box of her favorite chocolates.

"What's this?" she asks, taking it.

"An apology."

Her brows push together as she lets me in. Now that I'm here, I can't hold it in any longer.

"I'm seeing someone," I confess, excitedly.

Now her eyes light up. "We need wine." She rushes to the kitchen, leaving me to close her door.

Soon, we're sitting on her sofa with the wine and chocolate on her coffee table.

"Go on then," she says, sitting back expectantly. "Spill all."

"It's Max."

"Who?"

I'm not sure that I've ever mentioned his name to her before. "The mechanic, the guy who crashed into my car."

She sits forward, sets her huge wine glass on the coffee table, and puts her hands on her face, as if the news—or her face—is suddenly too hot to handle.

"You're going out with *him?*"

I nod my head vigorously and can't stop myself from smiling.

"Since when?"

"Since...since I bought the car from him. I told you about my car, didn't I?"

Christina scoffs. "You did, but you didn't say you got it from him." She doesn't look too pleased. "How did you buy a car from him? I thought he had a bike?"

I start to explain. "It started when he fixed the damage to my other car, the one he crashed into."

"You told me all about that, how he fixed it for you, but you didn't mention any of the other stuff."

"I didn't know how to."

There's a hint of accusation in her glare. I've wanted to tell her, but I was always afraid she would tell me to steer clear of someone like Max. She doesn't know what he's like, she wouldn't understand him. She would judge him, and I didn't want to hear her say anything negative about him, so I never told her, but now that I have, it feels good not to be sitting on this secret anymore.

"Are you going to tell me now?"

I proceed to tell her how he came to my rescue when my car broke down on Jefferson Street, and how he kept saying I needed to get rid of it. I tell her about our strange and slow attraction, and she listens, although her face could be softer, her expression could be friendlier.

"And then I bought the car, and we kept running into one another, and one thing led to another." I can't quite gauge her reaction, and when I announce, "And I've had sex!" with all the excitement of a teenager who's been in the back of a car with a spotty, gangly boy, a part of me wishes I haven't told her at all.

"You've had sex?!" It's the first smidgen of surprise I've had from her. But I'm not sure if it's shock I detect in her voice or disappointment. She gives me a what-were-you-thinking look.

The moment seems to fizzle and flatten, despite the exciting lead-up to it. In my head, anyway.

I sense Christina's disappointment and maybe even a hint of disapproval.

"I really like him," I say, setting my wine glass on the table, and wringing my hands together.

"So, you were with him?" she says. "Last week when you said you weren't well?"

My happiness sinks like a lead balloon. I hadn't expected the evening to turn out like this. I hadn't expected Christina to be anything but happy for me, especially after I told her how happy I am with Max.

While we both had similar ideas and views about sex, about wanting to hold onto our virginity, it wasn't a lifelong pact.

Things changed.

I changed.

I met Max, and I fell for him.

I wanted to take away his pain. I wanted to make him

happy because he made me happy. I wanted to have more of him.

I don't understand Christina's reaction.

"I'm sorry I lied to you about that. I didn't mean to."

"Where were you?" she asks, and then nods her head, as if the obvious answer has flashed into her brain. "How long has this been going on?" She's sounding more like a parent, and less like a friend.

"A few weeks."

"A few weeks? I thought we told each other everything, Trinity. It hurts that you didn't want to tell me sooner."

And this is why I didn't, I think to myself. I feared she would be judgmental, and how right I was.

The air prickles, not with excitement, and girlish banter, but with an awkwardness I wasn't prepared for.

"Well, no wonder you found Ed so boring," she says, suddenly perking up as she refills our wine glasses. "So... what's it like, the sex?" She hands me my glass.

I had envisioned that I might share a little, and tell her about how I've suddenly turned into a sex-crazy fiend, tell her how Max makes me feel, and of how I can't get enough. A broad brush picture rather than intricate details, but I no longer want to share anything.

"It's...uh..." I take a sip of my wine, buying myself some time. "It's... it's better than I ever imagined."

She sits on the couch, then leans forward, waiting for my next word.

"That's all I'm saying on the topic, Christina."

"Poor Ed. He seemed to like you."

"You've never met Max." I resist the urge to describe him in glowing terms.

"He's obviously got something that you found impossible to resist."

She's not wrong.

"But, do you trust him? You can't have known him for too long after he crashed into you."

"I do trust him. He's ... he's a great guy." When I think of the things he's done for me, I know I can trust him.

"But you've already had sex, and you've hardly known him long. This isn't like you, Trin."

"You'd understand if you met him."

"And when can I meet him?"

I stutter and scoff at that request. "Give me some more time to get to know him better."

"So you don't know him that well?"

"I do," I protest.

Christina shakes her head as if she has difficulty understanding what I've done.

I don't stay long after that. Things are a little strained. I decide to give Christina time to get over my wrongdoing.

I expected more enthusiasm, more happiness on her part for me, and when I didn't get it, it tainted the mood of the evening for me.

I'd made my peace. I had apologized, and if she wanted to judge me, that was her problem.

The rest of the week is busy. Max has a lot going on at the garage, and I have the school trip to the museum on Thursday, and that tires me out.

Dylan no longer stays around at the end of school, and Ed doesn't come in to see me. With things being odd between Christina and me, I decide to give my crochet class a miss for the second Friday running, only this time I don't bother to call Christina to tell her.

She doesn't call me to find out why I missed it.

I suppose she can figure it out.

Instead, I call Max and ask him if he'd like to come over.

I'm aware that I might come across as clingy and needy, but I love being with him. Of course, the sex is new, and he's a good teacher. A great lover.

I'm different when I'm with him.

"You come over," he tells me. "Your cat scares me."

"Benji?" I laugh at the absurdity of his comment.

"Have you seen the way he looks at me when I'm with you?"

The idea of Max feeling cautious around Benji is funny. "Are you working?" I ask him, since I'm not sure if I'm going to stay at his place for the night, or the entire weekend. A few weeks ago this would have been unheard of for me, yet Max not only crashed into my car, he crashed into my life, and now I can't imagine my world without him in it.

"I might have to go to work for a few hours at some point, it depends, but bring clothes for the weekend, not that you'll need them."

I smile.

It hasn't been more than a week since I last saw him, but I miss him so much it hurts. I'm turning into one of those women who become so dependent on her man, it's embarrassing. But it doesn't matter, and I don't care as long as I'm with him.

CHAPTER THIRTY-TWO

MAX

She comes over on Friday again, missing crochet and dinner with her friend for the second time.

I feel like I've struck gold.

I don't want to make it always be about us spending hours in bed, so I plan a movie and dinner on Saturday evening.

I see she's brought a small overnight bag. "You didn't bring many clothes," I comment.

"I packed tightly. I didn't bring my entire closet. Why, are you used to girls bringing suitcases over?"

It's the first time in a while that she's asked me about other girls. Her question makes me think of Hot Gina. She brings a slightly bigger bag, but I'm not about to tell Trinity this.

I answer her question with a kiss, which will soon lead to something else if I don't watch myself. I have plans to take her out tonight, and we have all night to do everything else.

On Al's suggestion, I take her to Waquito's.

"What?" she says, when I tell her we're going out.

"Waquito's. Al recommended it. It's a bar where his hero, that boxer, Elias Cardoza, used to work."

I tend not to hang out in bars much, and now that I'm scrambling for places to take Trinity to, I discover how much my life revolves around the garage, or lounging around at home, playing pool or being in bed with a woman.

I never do much else. I never entertain, never go places, never think to take a woman out to have a good time.

I have never been with a woman with whom I might want more than the sex.

I want things to be different with Trinity, hence why I had to tell Al.

"You told Al?" she asks, sliding her hands around my back. "About us?"

"I wanted recommendations, places of interest to take you, and wine and dine you."

"You don't have to wine and dine me. I'm already yours."

I dip my head and kiss her as a 'thank you.'

"What did Al say?"

I recall his reaction when I told him.

"You sneaky little rat," he replied. "I knew there was more to it than you recommending a car for her to buy."

"He was happy for me. Which reminds me. Al and his fiancée want to go out to dinner with us. Will you come?"

"Dinner?" she asks.

I nod. "You and me and Al and Sammy."

"Sammy's short for?"

"Samantha."

"Samantha," she echoes. Women are weird like that. I'm asking her about a dinner date and she's more interested in Al's fiancée's name.

"What shall I tell him?"

"Tell him yes, we can."

"Yes, we can," I repeat. She has no idea she's the first girl I'm taking out like this. She knows I was her first, but she is as many firsts for me.

We go out later that evening to the bar where Elias Cardoza used to work. Rumors are that he still comes here on rare occasions. We don't see him, but we have a great time. We drink, eat, listen to the music and talk.

Later we go home, and make love for a long time.

The next day we wake up late, make breakfast at home, then end up in bed for a few hours where I show her the benefits of sensual massage. It soon leads to other things.

In the evening, we catch a movie, and go to dinner at a place she recommends. Someplace called Nino's.

When we're there, she tells me that this is where she had that date with Ed, a date she instigated because she wanted to get me out of her system.

"You used to squirm," I say to her, when she refuses to admit that she ever felt anxious around me.

"You were overpowering."

"I gave you The Max Factor." I mention my proven tactic for hitting on women.

"The Max Factor?" she cries in amazement. "You have a name for it?"

"You mean for the way I made you tremble at your knees, and grow all hot and flustered just because of the way I stared at you?"

I remember those early days well. It was so easy to make her blush, to have her get all flustered. I'm glad I persevered, because I can't see how else we would have ended up together.

I'm lucky I found her, and I'm lucky she's mine. I'm lucky I get to spend the entire evening with her, and then take her home with me.

TRINITY

"I have to go in for a few hours." Max's lips skate down my back. It's a delicious way to wake up.

"Aww, what?" I turn around and look up at him. "You have to go in now?"

"Only for a few hours."

"Why didn't you wake me earlier?"

"I did."

My lips form into a smile as I remember exactly how he woke me up in the early hours of the morning, with his lips skating along my thighs.

I stretch out like a super-contented cat. He lifts the covers up and slowly takes in my naked body. "Don't move," he orders, bending down to drop a kiss on my lips. "I'll be back."

And with those famous words, he leaves. I curl up again, but I can't sleep. The bed smells musty, and I wonder if I should change his sheets for him before I leave.

I wouldn't have to leave, but my parents will be expecting me at their house for lunch. I consider not going next week.

I consider the subtle ways in which my life has changed.

I feel ecstatic, incredibly happy, and I don't even feel that upset about Christina.

I will get up and shower, and maybe change the bedsheets, and then I'll get ready to leave to go to my parents.

I hope Max will be back before I go.

It's with a shock that I wake up and see that it's noon, and that I must have fallen asleep--hardly surprising given how little sleep I've had these past two nights.

I smell like sex, and jump into the shower, and when I come out, he calls on my cell phone to tell me to wait, that he got held up but that he's on his way home.

I decide to surprise him with a goodbye present before I go. I slip on one of his T-shirts. It doesn't quite hang on me, not like it would some slim slip of a woman, but I do fill it out well enough.

I decide that it doesn't look sexy enough, so I go through his closet and pull out a formal shirt, he doesn't have many, and this is a pale blue one. I slip it on and it makes me look sexy, which is the effect I wanted, and which the T-shirt didn't give me.

By the time I've changed the sheets on his bed, and tidied up his place, I have doubts that he'll be here soon. If he doesn't get here soon, I'm going to have to leave. My mom and dad are very particular about their timings for lunch.

I call Max, but he doesn't answer and so I go into the bedroom and start to get changed into my own clothes when I hear the door slam. "I'm back!" he shouts. "Where are you?"

I walk out, and smile, but tap my wristwatch. "You're late."

"And you're looking so damn sexy." He comes towards me and right away his hands slide around me.

"This looks better on you than it does me," he kisses the side of my neck, moaning in appreciation as he slides his hands under the shirt and feels me over. "You smell nice," he whispers, as he nibbles my ear, his hot breath tickling my skin.

"I wanted to leave you with a goodbye present."

His hand moves lower, slides in between my leg. "No underwear. Best present you could have given me." There's a hint of naughtiness in his eyes.

"I've been waiting for you for over an hour."

He dips his finger inside me. "And I can see that you're excited to see me." He rubs my clit gently, touching me the way I've come to love and crave.

He smells of oil, and sweat and dirt, and this combination, far from turning me off, makes me want him even more.

Now that he's here, in the flesh, so hard, so big, so desperate for me, I dismiss plans to get ready to leave. My need for him clouds my shyness and inexperience, and I push him back onto the couch and I kiss him as if I haven't seen him for a year.

It's not that he's been away long, but that my mind has been full of dirty thoughts while I've been waiting.

Max is imprinted on me. Waking up in his bed, showering in his bathroom, changing his sheets and now wearing his shirt, all of these things have done this. They have reinforced my feelings for this man I have come to love. To lust. I can't differentiate between the two.

I pin him down, straddling him with my knees on either side of his hips. He looks up at me with dark hooded eyes.

My own Hemsworth.

He begins to unbutton my shirt, but I am so desperate for him that I can't wait for him to finish. I've lost the patience to have him pay lip service to my body. Instead, I reach for his zipper, surprising myself with the speed at which I free his great big, throbbing cock from his jeans.

"Whoa, babe—" he manages to say, before I slip my tongue inside his mouth. I'm not sure what's come over me, but I need to feel him inside me again. I raise myself to my knees and reach for him, positioning his member at my entrance.

A sigh escapes my lips.

A growl escapes his.

I sink down a little, the first touch is sublime. Then I inch down slowly, savoring the friction as I slowly impale myself on his shaft. It fills and stretches me, and I groan, the sound of pleasure dripping from my lips as I swallow his cock whole.

"Fuck, Trinity," he moans, his hands all over my breasts.

"No, fuck you," I say, so consumed with need, and desire, and lust, that I use a word that is never in my vocabulary. "I want to fuck you ..."

Max gazes at me in surprise, his mouth open. This is how I feel, dirty, and hungry, and desperate for him. I kiss him, hard and long and start to ride him, slowly at first, then my desire makes me speed up.

Excitement races through me because I know what lies ahead.

"Oh, baby," he growls. His magic thumb circles my clit, and I start to shudder and convulse.

The feeling is too intense. It shoots straight through me from my toes to my stomach to my breasts.

I sink my mouth against his, our kiss intensifies just as I increase my pace. It's beautiful, me sliding up and down on him, feeling him fill me to the hilt, then slide out. It slowly starts to build, pleasure waves spiraling out from deep in my core.

I feel as if I'm going to implode. Just the feel of his cock is enough to make me come, but with his thumb working like magic, it's delicious, and intoxicating, and starts to become too much.

I try to move his hand away because my body is on fire. All the sparks and vibrations are concentrated in one tiny place; it overloads my senses. But I can't move his hand away. He circles, and tweaks, and the intensity deepens. I feel as if I'm slowly dissolving into a vat of pleasure.

I clench muscles I never knew existed much, and come hard on him, feeling a release that is new to me. He murmurs sexy little words to me, strokes my hair, my skin, holds me, as I give in to him, lost in bliss, as my face drops to his shoulder. I suck in air as if there's a short supply of oxygen.

He lets me rest for a few seconds before he tilts my face towards him, then moves my hair away, holding it back from my face as he cups the sides of my head. "You liked that, didn't you?"

I moan in answer. He sucks my lower lip, making shivers shoot up inside me again. I don't know if I have the energy to move my hips like before. "Let's try something else," he says, starting to shift. He stands up with me still on him, then he pulls out. He spins me around, and pushes me forward so that I'm kneeling on the sofa with my back to him. My stomach is flat against the sofa back and my arms rest on top of the headrest.

"My turn," he whispers in my ear, so close that his breath kisses me. Without warning, he lifts my leg up, and thrusts deep inside me from behind.

I cry out because it is deep, deep, deep, and it feels so, so good. He rams into me, then pulls out.

Then he does it again and again and again. Not only does his cock thrust into me like a heat-seeking missile, but his fingers circle my clit hard. I can't breathe, and I jerk involuntarily, my fingers digging into the sofa because I need something to hold onto.

He gives me two searing thrusts, and fondles my clit.

I see stars.

I become white light.

I want to cry and laugh, and I can't do either, because I come undone again, convulsing and crying out in pleasure as the shock of my orgasm crashes through me.

I collapse, sighing and hugging the sofa with my stomach as Max continues, short, sharp thrusts before he presses against me, shooting his release inside me.

I've never come so hard before, even in the short time I've been having sex. This is my most intense orgasm.

We're glued together, sweaty and sticky, and we stay like that for the longest time, neither of us wanting to move.

Eventually he slides out of me, and I realize that I have to take another shower. I turn around, trying to find my legs. He reaches out his hand and helps me to standing. We hug one another, and hold one another, and stay like that.

"Do you have to go?" he asks.

I don't want to. I want to stay here, curled up in his arms. I want to get into the bed with him and stay there, lingering in our post-sex haze.

"No." I bury my face against his chest. He strokes my hair, makes me feel wanted, makes me feel loved.

I sigh. "I should go. It's … it's like a ritual."

"A ritual to have lunch," he mumbles. "I don't want you

to leave, but you gotta go." He drops a kiss on my head. "Come back after."

I lift my head and stare at him. "It's a school day tomorrow. I have to prepare."

He kisses me on the lips. "You can do that here."

He doesn't want me to go. I'm reminded of that child on the steps waiting for his mother to bring him donuts. I have to come back to him.

I give him a slobbery wet kiss, in answer. "I'll be back."

Just then his doorbell rings and he lets out a groan. I can hear the irritation in his voice.

I head towards the bedroom, and hear a commotion at the door. It's a woman's voice.

"Gina?" I hear Max say in a voice that is full of surprise.

I step away from the bedroom door and shift towards the hallway, holding the ends of the shirt against me so that it doesn't gape open. I peek my head around the corner.

"I've *missed* you," the woman says, lunging for him. She's pretty, and tall and slim, and wearing a stylish beret—something I could never pull off. Her coat is open, and it's hard to miss her tight jeans and figure-hugging top.

"What are you doing here?" I hear Max say.

"What do you think? Sex-Crazy Max. I'm on leave this weekend and I *need* your cock."

My breath escapes, as if I've been punched in my stomach. It's loud enough for them to realize I'm there, still in the shadows with my head peeking out a little. The woman turns and stares at me, and then so does Max. I straighten up, even though I want to curl up and die.

I muster what I can of my dignity, while trying to hide the shock, anger and betrayal that swirls inside me like pig swill in a trough.

"Who's that?" the woman asks. I stare at them both, then look at Max as a piece of my heart breaks away.

"Trinity," he says, moving towards me. There's an urgency in his voice, but I back away.

"I can explain," he says, reaching for my arm, but I swat his hand away.

"*Please* explain," the woman demands.

There is nothing to explain.

Max is cheating on me.

Or he's cheating on her.

He has a girlfriend.

I don't want to hear anything he has to say. I turn around and rush into the bathroom.

"Trinity, wait!"

"Don't." I bite out behind the closed door. I need to shower. I am covered in the smell of sex, but I don't want to be here another second.

Luckily, my clothes are here, so I quickly get changed.

He bangs on the door. "I can explain."

"Leave me alone, Max." I employ my best, sane, calm teacher voice. "I do not want to hear anything you have to say."

"What's going on?" I hear his girlfriend's voice, and then he must have stepped away because I can hear them talking, but I can't hear what they are saying.

I don't want to hear what they're saying because I've already heard and seen enough.

She said she needed his cock.

This tells me everything I needed to know.

CHAPTER THIRTY-THREE

MAX

Talk about fucking timing.

Trinity is dressed and has her bag in her hand when she sweeps through the living room. She's angry, too, but it's the hurt I can see more clearly.

"I can explain," I say, standing in her path, trying to block her exit.

"Leave me alone," she says, when I make one final attempt to grab her arm. Hot Gina stands by the wall and watches, her arms folded as if she's watching a fucking soap opera.

My hopes crash and die as Trinity slams the door shut behind her.

I should have spoken to her sooner. I should have told her the truth about my past, about my life.

Damn everything.

"Does this mean I can't have your cock anymore?" Hot Gina asks, summing up the entirety of our relationship. I turn around slowly, even though my mind is elsewhere, trying to figure out how to fix this shit.

We are done. "We had a deal," I tell her, trying to keep my voice calm. "No showing up unannounced, remember?"

She takes her coat off, throws off her beret and runs her hand through her hair, shaking out the ends. My world has splintered, and she's making herself at home as if nothing happened.

"You didn't return my calls."

Fuck. Yes. I wish I had now. I wish I'd spelled it out to her that I no longer needed our arrangement. "I was busy."

"I can see that. Who is she? What's the deal with her? I know we're not exclusive." She waves her hand at me and her. "I don't mind sharing, but I really need your cock right now."

I shake my head. "She's my girlfriend."

Gina folds her arms. "As in what? What does that mean?"

"As in my *girlfriend,* not a friend-with-benefits. You should have called."

"I did!" She shouts back. "I know we always called first before we met, but I called you. I was worried about you. I'm allowed to be worried about you, aren't I?" She looks at me, and the hardness that is so a part of her slips for a moment. Her eyes soften, and a telltale line crosses her brow.

"Is she good in bed?"

I grit my teeth because I don't want to answer that question. Because our sex life is none of her fucking business.

I can't believe the mess I'm in, and I hate the idea of losing Trinity.

"Is she good in bed?" Gina asks again.

I stare at her in contempt. I know one thing for sure, though. We are done. Me and Gina. Done, done, done.

"Don't ask me about her. I told you, she's my girlfriend, and I'm not interested in our arrangement anymore."

"How convenient for you," she hisses. "Where does that leave me?"

"We said we could opt out at any time."

"Opt out?" she cries. "I'm not a goddamn magazine subscription."

Her behavior startles me. I expected aloofness. I expected her to not care. "That's what we decided from the start. We were free to leave at any time. I'm sorry I didn't tell you sooner."

"I can share you," she says, as if this has any bearing on our future. "I don't mind sharing you, because, let's face it, your cock is big enough to satisfy an army." She attempts a laugh but I am so not in the mood.

"No, Gina. This is it. No more."

She moves towards me. "It's not like you get to see me every week. We can still have our sexathon weekends."

Her hands move to her hips. She looks fearless, not like someone who's ruined my day. She looks like she's ready to dive into bed with me.

Once upon a time, that's what I wanted. Once upon a time, that was enough.

Not now.

I need to talk to Trinity. I need to explain everything but she's gone to see her parents. I won't be able to contact her until this evening, but I need to fix this as soon as possible.

I love her. I love her and I need her, and I hate that she found out the way she did.

I can fix it, and I will.

"I don't want to do this anymore," I say. "It's over." Gina opens her mouth, and just like that, the suggestiveness of her pose disappears.

She opens her mouth. "But..."

I'm not interested in her buts. "We knew what this was, right? We knew it was only sex and nothing more."

"That's what I mean," she says, closing the distance between us, and putting her hands on my arms. "I can do *just sex*. I'm happy to share you with her."

I shrug her hands off. "I can't."

"Why can't you? You always told me you didn't want a connection, that it was only sex. Why the hell can't it be only sex now?"

"Because I don't want to hurt her." Because I care about Trinity. I think I love her, I think I'm falling for her, but I'm not sure. I don't know what love is. All I know is that it's a scary thing that leaves you feeling hurt at the end.

I'm too caught up in my concern for Trinity that it takes me a while to understand Gina's reaction. Her eyes have glassed over, and I see the hard set of her jaw.

"You... you don't want to hurt her?" she asks, her voice so low it sounds like a whisper.

I'm taken aback because I've never seen Gina like this. She seems less hard, and more brittle. "Do you have feelings for her?"

I don't want to discuss anything about Trinity with Gina.

"You were the only constant I had," she says when I remain silent.

"We had an agreement," I insist. She moves towards the sofa and picks up her coat and beret. She looks at me with sad eyes.

"I always hoped that one day, you and I...we might lead to something."

I feel as if she's thrown a grenade at me.

She had feelings for me?

All along, I assumed it was just sex. It was for me. I thought she felt the same. I thought she could handle it.

She told me she could. She told me that she wasn't like most women, and she wasn't. Plus, I've mostly only gone for women who didn't have more than physical needs.

Gina lied.

Now I feel like an asshole. I've let down two women in one day. Great going.

I reach her as she opens the door. "Hey," I say, grabbing her arm. I don't want her to leave feeling as if I didn't care about her. I did care. But it wasn't anything deeper than that. "You mean something to me."

"I don't mean enough." She pulls her arm away and walks off, and I know, because the hard Gina is back, that nothing I say will soften the blow I just gave her.

I'm at a loss for what to do for the rest of the day.

I count the hours, and try to estimate what time Trinity might have finished lunch with her parents.

I send her texts, and leave messages on her phone. I'm not a clingy kind of guy. I don't beg women or chase them for a response, but this situation is new and different for me.

I even consider going to her apartment later in the evening, and confronting her. I text her and tell her that I need to talk to her but she texts back and says that she's not ready to talk to me, and she asks me not to show up at her apartment or the school.

She needs time to think this through, so I decide to let her have a few days.

I don't want to lose Trinity, and I haven't cheated on her, I just haven't told her the truth.

TRINITY

My mom noticed that I was subdued. I told her that I had things going on at work. I struggled to get through lunch, and I struggled to keep up the pretense. I had to turn my phone off while I was there because Max kept calling and texting me.

When I get back home to my place later in the evening, he texts me to say he needs to talk to me. He threatens to come to my apartment, but I'm not ready to see him.

I can't see him. I don't want to face him because all I can think of is that woman and Max, and my head has been exploding with so many questions.

I want to know how long he's been with her, and why he came after me. Why did he cheat on her? And why did he get involved with me?

Was it to claim my V-card?

I feel used and stupid, and I hate myself for getting carried away.

I take a long bath, sitting in the hot bubbles, willing the water to wash away all signs of Max.

I think about the day again—the images are on auto-replay in my head, of me and Max, and then that woman.

It smacks into me like an arrow, the initial shock making me sit up straight before I crumble, then sink back into the water; we never used a condom. In my moment of need and desire, when I sank onto him, I didn't remember. And later, when he thrust into me, we still forgot.

And now I'm terrified, because of his cheating, that I could have caught something.

But more than that, I'm terrified that there's a chance I could be pregnant.

CHAPTER THIRTY-FOUR

MAX

I don't know what to do. I want to give her the time she needs, but I've given her a few days and now I'm scared of losing her, that is, if I haven't already lost her.

Al notices that I'm unusually quiet, but I'm in no mood to talk about what happened, and he knows me well enough to know when I need my own space. He leaves me alone.

I wait a few more days. I leave more messages on Trinity's phone, and I send her more texts.

I get nothing back.

I feel like shit, and I need to see her. I text her and say I'm coming to see her at school. She calls me back within the next few seconds.

"You can't. You can't come to the school. You'll get me in more trouble."

Her voice is cold and hard, but it's *her* voice, and I haven't heard it for days. I miss it. I miss *her*.

More trouble? What kind of trouble is she in? "We need

to talk, Trinity. We can't go on like this. I can explain everything."

To my surprise, she agrees. "I'll come over to your place."

My heart starts to sing. This has been easy. "Thanks. Thanks a lot." I'm overcome with happiness. She's giving me a chance to explain myself. I haven't cheated on her. I'll explain the situation with Hot Gina. I'll tell her I'm sorry, and I will win her back.

I go home early, and clean up. I light a few candles. I've never had candles in my place, but Trinity mentioned that she liked them, so I got them. I light them up and my place soon smells like a warm and cozy lodge.

She didn't say what time she was coming, but I presume it will be after school. I don't know whether to make something to eat, or get takeout.

I'm so nervous that I can't concentrate on anything. All I can do is wait, and I can't even sit still and do that.

I wonder if this is how Gina felt when I told her we were done. All of a sudden, I understand what it feels like to be rejected by a lover, to be told that you are no longer in favor.

I barely have a moment to dwell on this further when my doorbell rings.

I rush to open the door, and my heart leaps when I see Trinity. She's wearing make-up. More than I've ever noticed on her before. Her face looks a little gaunt, as if she could do with more sleep, but otherwise she looks fine. I expected her to be in pieces, somewhat downcast, but she looks fine.

Better than me.

"It's good to see you again," I say, wanting to take her hand and pull her towards me. I want to put my arms around her and kiss her, but I can't do any of those things.

She walks in, her silence unnerving me. I'm surprised she suggested coming over here to my apartment, which probably holds recent bad memories for her.

"You two-timed me," she says, not wasting any time.

"Shall we at least sit down?" I offer.

She shakes her head. Her handbag still hangs from her shoulder, and she hasn't taken off her coat. I never expected her to make herself comfortable, but this upfront coldness, from Trinity of all people, isn't something I was expecting. "I don't plan to stay long."

"I didn't two-time you. In all the time we were together, I never saw Gina."

"But she's your girlfriend, isn't she?" Trinity tosses back. "She walked in and told you exactly what she wanted from you."

I swipe my hands over my face. "She's not a...a... girlfriend. She and I had...uh....we had an arrangement to meet for... sex." The truth is out in the open now, and I can't take it back or cover it.

Trinity's face hardens, and I'm scared she'll tell me to go to hell. I'm scared she'll storm out and leave forever.

I'm in a race against time to get my words out. "You remember once I told you that I phoned a friend for sex? You were disgusted. I was trying to tell you the truth."

She looks to the side, at a place far beyond my face, as if she's trying to remember. "You said you were joking."

"I tried to tell you the truth but you were so disgusted, so I lied. I wanted you to see me as someone worthy, not as someone who disgusted you."

"What we had has been based on lies," she states.

"I was going to tell you. I tried to tell you." I shake my head, step towards her, but she steps back, repulsed.

"You met only for sex?"

I nod.

"How often?"

"Whenever she was home on leave from the army."

Her face clouds over. "All those times, when we first met, when Al was talking about you being *busy*, is that what he meant?"

I don't remember the exact conversations she might have overheard, but I assume she's close enough to the truth. Al has a tendency to talk about stuff, even if he thinks he's being discreet and talking in code.

"I had an arrangement with Hot Gina, and it was a mutual arrangement, but I last saw her that weekend I crashed into you. You and I weren't together then."

"Hot Gina?"

"She knows I called her that, because...."

"Because she's hot."

Trinity says it as if she's jealous.

"I wasn't looking for a girlfriend. I didn't want to get close to anyone. I didn't want to give anyone the chance to get close to me. I didn't want to take that risk."

For a moment, it seems that she's listening to me instead of being hung up on Gina and what she thinks Gina meant to me.

I sense my chance to win her back. "I'm sorry. I wanted to tell you, and I tried, and then I got scared of what you would think. You see sex as something precious, something to share with one person forever...and I see that now, but I didn't then. I needed comfort, a connection, and sex was the quickest and easiest way to get those things."

She presses her lips together, as if she's trying to come to terms with what I've said; as if she understands why I did this.

"You found comfort in meaningless sex?" she asks.

"Yes." Surely she can understand why? "You know about me, Trinity. I've never opened up to anyone the way I have with you. With Gina, it was purely physical. Other women don't know about my past. They don't know about my scars, they think I got them from the army, or from mixing with the wrong people, getting drunk and hurting one another. I don't remember what I told them, but I know I told you my truth." She says nothing, and I pray that my words are getting through, that she will believe me, because this truth, the way I feel about her, is all I have left to give her.

"I don't feel that way about you," I say. "What you and I have is like nothing I've ever had before. I don't want to lose it, and I hate that I messed things up."

"It was only you and Hot Gina?"

Her question is like a dagger through my heart. Her hopes are wrapped up in that question, and I can either lie and make good on that hope, or I can tell the truth and have her see me for the type of debased and sex-crazy guy that I am.

That I *was*.

I'm different now that I have her.

Each second that she stares at me, each second that I prolong a reply tells her that I'm hiding something.

I can't lie to her, because I love her. She has to see the real me, and I'm afraid that revealing the real me is the thing that will cost me her.

"There were others."

"Others?" She looks as if I've slapped her. My heart sinks further into my belly. I hate this. I hate that every truth I tell her makes her hate me. "At the same time?" Her voice is hoarse.

I hang my head in shame. It sounds worse than it

seemed at the time. "Hot Gina didn't come home for months...and so..." I let her paint her own picture.

"And so what?" she snaps.

She's going to make me spell it out for her. I bite down on my teeth.

"Are we talking a couple of women? A handful? A harem?" she spits the words at me.

"Maybe a couple."

"A couple? At the same time?"

"No. One woman at a time. We all had the same arrangement. They weren't girlfriends. They were just..."

"You're disgusting."

It's like she threw a spear right into my stomach.

"I should never have trusted you from the start. Every single thing I did ever since I set eyes on you has been to my detriment."

I can't deny this. She took a lot for me, protected me, covered up for me, helped me out of a hole.

And I swept into her life like a tidal wave and trashed everything she had to offer.

"You made me a better man, Trinity," I say, needing her to know.

"I can't say the same about you. I don't want to see you again."

She's not only speared me, she's ripped out my guts. I hold steady, because she is right. I've done wrong by her. She's never done wrong by me.

But I try one more time. "I've changed. You made me change, because you made me see that I was worth loving."

Her eyes widen, and curiosity slants across her face.

"That's right," I say, grabbing the moment. "I never thought I was lovable. I never thought I could have that, have someone want me and love me and stick around long enough to make me feel as if I mattered."

"Oh, for goodness' sake, save the excuses."

The what? This isn't the Trinity I know. She snarls at me, dismisses everything I tell her.

"It's true. I stopped seeing the others once you came on the scene. I swear to you it's the truth."

"I can't believe you. I don't and won't believe you."

"I've always tried to tell you the truth."

"Except when you've lied."

"I lied because I didn't want to scare you off. I tried to tell you, but I was afraid it was too soon."

"Is there ever a right time to tell someone that you're sex-crazy and you need more than one woman? That you have an arrangement for sex instead of a relationship?" she asks.

I feel the force of her words as if they are hammer blows to my head and my heart. She's rendered me speechless.

"The last time I was here, when we had sex, before your friend came..." She pauses for longer than I expect.

"What about it?" I wonder why she insists on plunging the knife in deeper.

"We didn't use protection."

I don't have to think back far because that moment is still fresh in my mind.

She's right. Trinity mounted me, and I completely forgot. We were so caught up in the heat of the moment.

"With everything you've now told me, I have something else to worry about."

I raise an eyebrow.

"I'm scared that I might have picked up something nasty from you."

I snort. "I've always been careful. I've *always* used protection."

"Well, we didn't that last time. And given your track record and your history, I shiver to think what I could have caught from you."

I should be hurt, but I'm too stunned by this turn of events. She's worried for no reason. I might have had my fuck-buddies, but I've never not used a condom. She was my first.

"And you know what else?" she says, with venom in her voice.

"You have no reason to worry, Trinity. I promise you. You haven't caught anything." Then I stop. "What else?"

She gives me a look that could make my balls shrivel. "There's a chance I could be pregnant."

The words fall on me like an atomic bomb, causing mass destruction and vaporizing my thoughts.

"It's a small chance, but..."

Pregnant.

Trinity, and my baby?

I have never worried or ever thought about anyone I've slept with being pregnant. Surely, there's only a slight chance of that happening?

"I'm keeping it if I am, and I don't want you anywhere near me."

I open my mouth to say something, but words fail me. "Pregnant?" I've never allowed the idea of a girlfriend in my world, let alone a baby, and this news lifts me up like a helium balloon.

"Are you?" I ask her.

"I don't know. I hope not."

I don't take that in a bad way. I don't take it to mean that she doesn't want my baby, because I am still so surprised about the idea of Trinity carrying my baby.

For someone like me, whose beginnings are shrouded in bleak hopelessness, she's given me news that can change all that.

I can do things differently going forward, if it comes to that. "Whatever happens, I'll be here for you and the baby. I'm not going to turn my back on you. Just let me in—"

"I wish I'd never met you."

My heart sinks to the base of my stomach. "Forgive me. I never meant for this to happen."

"I wish I'd never set eyes on you."

CHAPTER THIRTY-FIVE

TRINITY

"Thanks for seeing me," says Dylan's mom.

She walks into the classroom at the end of the day with her son. Dylan has been avoiding me, and seeing him walk in with his mom at the end of the school day stops me in my tracks.

I brace myself. It's been weeks since Dylan's dad confronted me in the playground.

I suggest that Dylan play over in the corner while his mom and I sit at my desk to talk.

After the recent ups and downs in my life, it's a nice change for me to focus on something else.

But Dylan's mom surprises me by apologizing for her husband's behavior. She tells me that she wanted to explain to me in person, because he wasn't usually like that. She tells me that him losing his job has made things difficult.

It's good of her, and I know that she seems to be trying very hard to keep her family together, but I wonder why it's taken her this long to come to me, not that I was expecting her to in the first place, but I wonder why now?

While she's here, I ask her about something that has worried me.

"I couldn't help but notice that Dylan had some bruises on his arm."

Her sunken eyes flash with defiance. "He got into a fight at the park with his cousins. You know what young boys are like."

It's plausible. It could happen. I don't know what to say.

"You can ask him, if you want," she says. "We have nothing to hide. There's nothing going on that you need to report, Miss Weldon. We can't give our son as much as most parents might be able to, but we try to do the best we can. What we don't need is false rumors to make things worse."

I open my mouth to protest.

"I didn't come here for your pity, Miss Weldon. I came to ask for your help."

Her words disarm me. "What sort of help?"

She shrinks back a little bit, and her eyes lower to the desk. "I was wondering..." She seems to have difficulty continuing.

"Please go on, Mrs. Church. You can talk to me. Anything you say will be confidential."

"I heard that the janitor is leaving."

It takes me a moment to process what she's said. I blink at her. "The janitor?"

"I was talking to him on the playground. He's nice, but his wife is sick, and he's leaving."

I still don't understand what this has to do with her or me.

"I hate to ask this of you, but...do you think my husband

could apply for that position? He's done those types of jobs before, and he has the experience."

I was expecting something dark, something worrying. I was expecting the worst, but not *this*.

I'm almost relieved. "I...I'm...I'm not sure how I can help," I say. I have no idea. I assume there will need to be a background check done, and Mr. Marshall can be a stickler for rules and regulations.

"He can start immediately."

The urgency in her voice, the desperation and pleading is subtle, but it is there. She's asking for help, in a noble way. She's not asking for handouts or begging for money, she's asking for a chance.

"I think your husband should apply, or get in touch with the school. Maybe go see someone in the HR office, and..." I tap my fingers on the desk, conjuring up my own plan of attack, "I'll see what I can do."

"Anything you say will help."

"I don't know about that."

"How will you know unless you try?" she asks. Some would find her manner forward, but I see someone struggling to stay afloat.

"I will do my best, Mrs. Church, but I can't promise anything."

"I wanted to at least ask."

"I'll go speak to the principal right now."

Her eyes light up with a glow that wasn't there seconds ago. "Thank you."

I nod my head.

She rises and holds out her hand. "Thank you. Thank you so much." She seems so hopeful.

"I can't promise anything, but if you don't ask, you don't get, right?"

She nods and leaves.

Naturally, I can't stop myself from getting involved, or interfering, as Ed would say.

What would Max say?

I don't waste any time and go straight to the principal's office where I spend the next fifteen minutes pleading with Mr. Marshall to give the Churches a chance.

Being the rules-and-regulations guy, he comes up with obstacles, such as the need to go through the correct channels, and to do things in a certain manner.

"But I didn't even know the janitor was leaving," I protest.

"His wife has had a stroke, and he can't continue with the position."

"Perfect. Not for him, poor man," I hasten to add, "I'm not asking you to give Dylan's dad the job, I'm asking you to consider him. He can start immediately. He's been laid off, and the family is struggling—"

"I can't help him just because he's struggling. Everyone is struggling."

"But if he has the experience, if he pans out, if he interviews well, and he can do the job, can't you at least consider him? He can start immediately."

"You've already told me."

"Please, Sean. Please just think about it? One tiny thing could be the difference between a family that falls apart, or a family that manages to keep it together."

"I'll think about it."

"Good, because his father will likely enquire about the job as early as tomorrow."

"How can he enquire when I haven't even written up the job posting?"

"But when you do, it would be a gracious act of

kindness to consider Mr. Church." I smile at him sweetly on my way out.

"Was that Dylan's mother with him?" Ed asks, coming into my room for the first time in a while.

"It was. She wanted to apologize for her husband's behavior." I decide not to tell him about the other reason for her visit.

"It's a bit late for that."

"Better late than never."

"How are things?" he asks, as if things are back to normal between us. I'm glad they are. I've kind of missed talking to him, especially given the recent drama in my life.

"Fine. Same as usual," I say, forcing a smile, knowing the great lie behind my reply. There has been nothing usual about my life to date.

I have worries I can't tell my parents about.

I've lost a good friend in Ed, as well as Christina.

I've been conned, tricked and cheated on by a guy who might or might not have given me a sexually transmitted disease or two, and I am days away from finding out if I might be pregnant.

There has been nothing usual about my life lately.

Ed examines my face a little more intensely, to the point that I have to look away. He's probably itching to know why I've been quiet. Why I've had my head down for the past few weeks.

He hovers around, and because I know him so well, I sense he wants to ask about me and Max.

Thankfully he doesn't.

"Have you found the right mattress?"

"I certainly have, and I sleep like a baby these days."

"Good. Great!"

I remember him bouncing around on the mattress that day.

He looks at me then looks away. I wonder if he's remembered Max and his stupid sex swing comment.

"See you around," he says, obviously feeling the need to leave.

"'Bye."

I think about Max and wonder if Hot Gina was the one he used that sex swing with. There were others too. Maybe he's done all sorts, used all sorts of things with them all.

I don't want to think about it.

I've never had to think or worry about STDs and getting pregnant. These things were never a part of my world, and yet, here I am. Within a short space of time, everything has turned upside down.

I suddenly long for company, because I hate going home and moping around. It's bad enough counting the days until I hopefully have my period.

Between Benji and the TV, there is not much else to distract me from Max and all that's happened.

I'm not even in the mood for our crochet class tonight, so I decide to miss it yet again and stay at home and watch TV.

Benji is curled up on the sofa at the other end, and the blanket that I'm supposed to be getting closer to finishing stays still the same size and remains in my crochet bag.

I haven't touched it in weeks.

When the doorbell rings, I get up slowly, my heart starting to beat. I answer the door, and I'm relieved to see Christina, because the tiniest notion that it could be Max popped into my head.

We stare at one another for a few awkward seconds, and

I wait for her to say something, since she's the one on my doorstep.

"You missed crochet class again."

"I didn't feel like going," I confess.

"You haven't been for weeks. Everyone's asking me what's wrong with you. Is it because of me?"

"Uh...no." Not just because of her, but I don't tell her that.

I can't bring myself to feel happy or invite her in, even though deep down inside I need a friend to talk to. What I don't need is for that friend to be judgmental.

"Can I come in?" she asks.

"Sure." I open the door and let her in, because I can't tell her 'no.' There's no way I would turn her away now that she's here.

"How have you been?"

"Okay." I move into the living room and shove my hands into my pockets.

"I'm sorry. I'm sorry that I might have sounded a bit cold when you told me about your boyfriend. I should have been a better friend."

I wasn't expecting that from her. Christina isn't usually one to acknowledge her faults.

"Okay," I say.

"It's not so much that you're seeing someone, just that we used to tell each other everything. I feel like we're not so close anymore."

"Oh." Given everything going on in my life at the moment, I'm ill-prepared to accept Christina's apology with the graciousness it requires. She's come here and said her piece, and I ought to relent. "Thanks," I say.

"Do you want me to go? I'll go. This is weird." She turns to go. "I wanted to make sure you were okay."

"Yes, why wouldn't I be?"

"How come you're not seeing your boyfriend if you're missing the class tonight?"

"I wanted a night in by myself."

Christina nods. "Are you sure you're okay?"

"Yes," I reply, even though my world has turned upside down and I'm struggling to keep it all together.

"Good. I'll maybe see you next week? At the class? Maybe we can go to Nino's and catch up like we used to?"

"Sure."

I watch her walk towards the door.

"You were right," I say, as she opens the door. "You were right about him." Christina turns around and looks at me. The door is still slightly open.

"I was wrong to get involved with him. I didn't know him, and I fell for his charm, and now, well..." I slink down on the couch. "I put myself at risk of catching an STD, and I could be pregnant."

She closes the door and rushes to me, holding my hands as she sits down beside me.

"What?"

"You heard."

"Pregnant? STDs? Trin, what are you talking about?"

I look up at her, and though I don't feel like crying, I feel sad, as if I messed up my life. I glance at her nervously, trying to gauge her assessment of me.

In the next moment her hands are on my arms, and her face is lined with worry. "*He* did this?"

It takes a while for me to figure out what she means.

"No...he...it wasn't like that." An unwelcome advance, I bet that's what she's thinking. "He didn't force himself on me. It just happened. I got careless one time."

I let this happen, because I got carried away with the

moment, wrapped up in his spell, seduced by his Hemsworthiness.

I rub my arms as if to comfort myself. "He's got other women. Other girlfriends."

Christina's emits a shocked gasp. "What do you mean other *women?* Other *girlfriends?*"

"He owned up to it."

I ponder the wisdom of telling her, given the way she reacted before, but I can't keep this news inside me any longer. It's been churning inside me for weeks.

I need to get it out, otherwise it will continue to fill my head, obliterating all other calm rational thinking.

"One of them—his girlfriends—showed up unexpectedly when I was at his place." I leave out the details, the intimate things she doesn't need to know about.

"What did you do?"

"I left."

"Are you sure she was his girlfriend?"

How do I tell her about his arrangement?

"Yes."

"Oh, Trin." She tries to put her arms around me but I don't want to be smothered in her pity.

"I'm okay. I told him I never want to see him again."

"Trin," she says softly, and because I won't let her embrace me, she pats my knee.

"I know, right?" I say, forcing my lips into an awkward smile that I feel I need to give to show her that I'm okay.

But I'm not.

"What's this about an STD?"

I stare at the floor, as I tuck a lock of hair behind my ear. "We, uh..." I cough. "We forgot to use protection one time, and, uh..." More clearing of my throat. "And that's why there's a small risk, if I'm unlucky, that I might be pregnant."

She looks at me apologetically. She emits a long, drawn-out empathetic sigh. "Oh, no, Trin. Poor you."

I can see that she wants to hug me, or make me feel better, but she can't. I'm not letting her. She apologized for her previous behavior, but I'm the one who's feeling bad now because it turned out that she was right and I wasn't.

Max was a risk, and I should have known I couldn't trust him.

It's too late now.

"What was it about him that made you go crazy over him?" she asks.

"I felt sorry for him, I suppose that's what it was."

"Sorry for what?"

I tell her a little about how his mother left him when he was a child, and how he was adopted.

"You always want to make things right," Christina says.

"It wasn't pity. You have no idea how sexy that guy is..." I stop myself. It wasn't pity for Max that made me give myself to him. Maybe a little bit of it was me wanting to fix things, but it was his sexiness, and the way he made me feel without even touching me, that drew me to him.

I don't know how to explain such intense attraction to Christina when I'm certain she's never experienced it before. There's no point talking about that stuff now.

"I got involved and I gave my all to the wrong guy."

That's what I need to take into stock now. One day at a time. If it doesn't come tomorrow, then I'll be a day late for my period. I haven't had the usual pains and cramps which I normally get, so I'm worried, and my frayed nerves haven't been able to relax since that day his sex-crazy girlfriend turned up.

"His mother left him?" Christina asks.

I nod, not wanting her to fall for that same story the way I did. "Where?"

"She left him on the steps of a children's home. She told him to wait for her while she went to get him some donuts, and she never came back."

There's a flicker of sadness in Christina's eyes. "That's heartbreaking. Someone like that is going to be messed up. It sounds to me that he hasn't had the kind of steady upbringing that you and I have had. I feel sorry for the guy."

Great. That's all I need from my friend; her to feel sorry for the guy instead of feeling empathy for me.

"What are you going to do?" she asks. "When will you know, if you're …"

"I'll know soon. I could take a pregnancy test, but I think it might be too soon. I don't know. I don't know about these things because I've never had to worry about them. I think I'm going to wait and see, and if I need to, I'll get a test. It should be long enough by then to know for certain."

"And if you're pregnant? Will you keep it?"

I shoot a startled look at her. "Of course I'll keep it."

There's no way I would do anything else. My parents will be shocked. Mr. Marshall will be, too. And Ed? I hate to think what Ed would think.

But it's not time to worry about what everyone else would think.

Being as careful as I have been, I now can't comprehend the situation in which I presently find myself.

I often wondered how it was that people got themselves into such dire situations, and yet I find myself in a situation that is equally as bad.

It wasn't entirely Max's fault, but how much simpler my life would have been had I never met him.

CHAPTER THIRTY-SIX

MAX

I decide to go see my dad again. I've been visiting him a lot more lately, and he must wonder what's going on.

I don't usually go to my dad for anything, only because he hasn't been the same since my mom died—it's like she took the best part of him with her—but I'm not feeling so great lately.

Trinity hates me, and work holds no interest. I have no place to go, nowhere I need to be and no one who needs me.

That sucks.

As usual my dad is sitting in front of the TV, reading a magazine. My mom's picture is in the cabinet next to him.

On the way over, I called and asked him if he needed a few things, and he did. Lucky I asked. He asked me to get him a few groceries, and I did.

"Thanks," he says, when I start putting his groceries away for him. He tries to give me the money, but I refuse it.

"Everything, okay, son?" he asks, watching me empty the grocery bag.

"Yeah, yeah." I put the grocery bags away, and perch on one of the kitchen stools. I know what he's getting at. It's as odd for me to be doing this as I'm sure it is for him to watch me.

"Can I get you a drink or anything?" he asks. "A beer, maybe?"

I scratch my jaw. "No thanks. I'm not staying long, Dad. How are you doing?"

"I'm as good as I was the last time you saw me."

I smile at him, picking up on his comment because I only saw him a few weeks ago.

"Everything all right?" he asks again, presuming there's an ulterior motive for my visit.

Something bubbles up to the surface, and because I'd much rather focus on 'something' instead of my fuck-up with Trinity, I ask him without thinking.

"After mom passed, did you ever check in with the children's home to see if my birth mom might have written in?"

He stares at me silently, his thick white brows pushing together, as if he's trying to figure out why I'm asking him this, and why now?

"I didn't," he says slowly, then takes a deep breath in. "I didn't think to do it, son. Why are you thinking about that stuff now?"

"It's no problem." I rush to reassure him because I don't want him to feel bad. "I was curious, that's all."

It's something I've thought about on and off, but it's not something I've lost much sleep over.

Plus, my dad and I, we haven't really spoken much of things from the past.

"After your mom, things were never the same..." He can't finish the sentence, but I understand. After my adopted mom passed, he spiraled into the darkness.

"Your mom used to check in with them." He nods his head, as if he's remembering that time. "She used to say there might be a chance that your real mom would try to get in touch. A mother would want to know what happened, she used to say. She would check in at that home once a year, sometimes even twice, and then..."

He falls silent.

"It's okay, Dad."

"Are you wondering if your real mom's still alive?" he asks.

"My real mom passed when I was a teen, Dad." I don't want him to think that I'm not grateful for what they've done for me. I consider them to be my real parents.

I never forgot my birth mom, because she was good and kind to me, and because I still remember fragments of her.

But as I grew older, and she never came back, that hope died and the new life with my parents who adopted me was going so well that the image of my birth mom dimmed and died away.

But when my adoptive mother died, it left me feeling abandoned and helpless again, only this time I was older, and understood more, and felt the pain more.

"I was a mess, Max. Maybe I should have tried harder for your sake, but by the time I started to function again, that place had closed down."

"Hey, Dad. It's really okay," I insist. I wish now that I hadn't brought this up, and I'm not sure why I have. I don't know what's become of her, I don't even know if she's dead or alive. I know only that she gave me up.

Choosing to believe what Trinity said, that my mother

loved me so much she made the sacrifice to leave me at a place she thought would give me a better future, is a better way to think about it. And that is how I prefer to think about it.

"What's made you ask about the past, son?"

I shrug. "I just was, Dad."

Maybe it's because of the remote possibility that I might be a father.

It's a slim chance, but it's a chance I've never had before. It's something I never wanted before, and never thought of, only I'm forced to consider it now and with a woman who is the perfect woman for me.

But Trinity never wants to see me again. I don't believe that for one minute because I have come to know her.

She probably hates my guts right now, but in time, I'll be able to tell her how things were for me before she came along.

"Son?" My dad eyes me, his hands clasped together on the kitchen bar. I've never asked him these kinds of things before but I can't seem to keep it in any more.

"I sometimes wonder if she's still here and alive, or if she ... died." I shake my head once, wishing I hadn't brought it up. It's not fair, talking about my birth mother to this man who is still pining for his wife. "Sorry, Dad. Things have been crazy lately." I scratch my jaw. "It's made me think of stuff."

Not having a solid memory of where you came from makes you question where you're going.

"What's been going on?" my dad asks. I shrug.

"Work and stuff."

"How is that?"

"Okay," I reply.

"What's really bothering you, son?"

I haven't reached out to this man in such a long time, and it feels hard to hit him with all this stuff at once. "Nothing, Dad. I wanted to see how you were."

"I'm as fine as can be. It's you I'm worried about now."

I don't want to make the kinds of mistakes my birth father made. I don't want to be that kind of man, and the truth is, I don't know if these things are inherited or formed by the people who bring you up.

What if Trinity is pregnant, and what if she has a baby that's mine?

I'm secretly thrilled that she could be, even though I feel bad that this scenario wouldn't be so good for her. It would mess up her life and her career, being so unexpected.

She didn't envision any of this, but she also has to understand that this wasn't completely my fault. If I remember it rightly, she was the one who instigated the first moves on that fateful day.

CHAPTER THIRTY-SEVEN

TRINITY

Miraculously, even though I am late for my period, I manage to get through the next few days without falling apart. I had a blood test for the STDs, and all is clear on that front.

Benji is a great comfort to me in my dark moment, but even he can't know how topsy-turvy things have become for me. My life as I know it hangs in the balance.

I make it to my art class as usual on the following week, but by now I am days late for my cycle. Tomorrow, I'll have to buy a pregnancy test.

MAX

I need her to know that I'm here for her no matter what. I want to fix things between us, make her see that I wasn't technically cheating, but there are other bigger worries to deal with first.

She doesn't want to see me, I get that, but I *need* to see her. It's been weeks since she told me she never wanted to see me, but we have to talk.

I need to know that she's okay.

I was tempted to go see Trinity yesterday, but I knew she had her art class and she'd be back late, so I shelved that idea.

The next day, I am torn between showing up outside her school or going to her apartment.

I'm not expecting her to welcome me back with open arms, but Trinity isn't temperamental. She's grounded, sensible. I'll be able to reason with her sooner or later.

Plus, I need to know.

Is she pregnant?

If she is, I need to know so that I can be there for her, no matter what she decides.

I want to see her face-to-face, and I am tempted to go to her apartment and wait for her there, but I have to respect her wishes.

Instead, I call her.

"We need to talk," I say, rushing to get my words in before she hangs up. I hear a sigh from her.

"I know."

This is refreshing. I take it as a positive sign that she hasn't hung up, that she's talking to me. It lifts my mood.

"I was going to show up at your school or your apartment."

"I told you you'd get me in trouble if you showed up here." She sounds angry.

I want to tell her that I will support her no matter what, that I care for her.

I want to tell her that I want us to resolve our problem, that I never cheated, nor did I two-time her, though this would require her to understand the exact nature of a friends-with-benefits relationship, and I don't think she has the patience to hear me out on that note.

I want to remind her that I tried to tell her many times that I wasn't the right person for someone like her, but I wanted to be.

I want to tell her that I've never had a connection with anyone like I have with her, and I will beg, without shame, to be allowed to be a part of her life; whether she's pregnant or not.

I want to do the right thing.

"We need to talk," she says, cutting off my chain of thoughts. Those four little words are like a burst of sunshine in my dark little heart.

"I know. Let's talk. Let's talk now." I don't want her to say she'll come to see me in the next few days.

"I'll come over," she says. This is the second time she's asked me not to come over to her place. Dread starts to settle in my skin, as if this is a sign of her keeping me at bay and of cutting all connections.

"Cool." She can come over, and we can talk. "What time?" I'll finish up early, and go home and shower, make myself look presentable.

"I'll come over on my lunch hour." She hangs up before I've had a chance to protest.

Her lunch hour?

That gives me a limited window of time with her. A niggling feeling starts to worm its way out of my stomach, and then I figure it out. She's pregnant. That's the only reason I can think of her needing to talk to me and so urgently.

I don't feel worried, or sad, or disappointed. I've never had to think of a situation in which this would ever happen, because I've always been careful, but now that this has happened, I'm faced with a situation in which I could be a dad.

A huge grin spreads across my face as I walk back to the garage.

"It's back," says Al, his hands and coveralls all smeared with grease.

I touch my cheek gingerly. "What?"

"A smile."

I roll my eyes and get back to work even though I can't concentrate because my ears are on alert for a notification on my phone. I look around from time to time to see if Trinity has showed up.

A short while later, she calls me to say she's parked nearby, up the street.

"I'll be back," I tell Al and go out to meet her.

She gets out of her car the moment she sees me and waits on the pavement, her arms folded.

I feel sad that things have come to this, that we're meeting like strangers, as if she's someone who needs to ask me a question about her car, instead of someone who meant something.

I try not to look her over, to see if she's looking healthier, to see if there's a tell about her.

"Hey," I say, smiling, because it's so good to see her. I've walked out with a cloth in my hands, and I'm wiping my hands clean, as I try not to stare at her too intensely.

She looks good.

I've missed her.

I'm missing her right this moment even though I'm standing right in front of her. There's an iciness in her posture which wasn't there, not even that first day when I crashed into her.

"How are you?" I ask, wanting to tell her all these things and more. She definitely looks beaming.

Blooming, even.

Warm, and cuddly, and as curvy as ever. My eyes dip down to her stomach for the briefest of seconds. Could be my child she has inside her.

"I'm not pregnant."

Her words fall like a guillotine slicing my hopes to shreds.

"You're not...?"

I try to find more words but she's smashed my dreams with that announcement. Bludgeoned them, even.

"No." She looks calm. Relieved. "I'm not."

Until she spoke, I still harbored dreams that she could be pregnant. I can see that this is the best outcome, I can see that, for her and for me, but especially for her. The disruption, unpreparedness, and unexpectedness of such a thing thrust upon her would have been too much. It wouldn't have been fair.

But for my own sake, I feel a tremendous sense of loss. As if something precious has been taken away from me. This was the first time I had ever been faced with the idea of bringing a child into this world.

Me, Sex-Crazy Max, who wanted only a good time and an easy life. I was presented with the prospect of being responsible for a tiny person. I imagined doing the right thing by him or her.

I started to believe it might be true. I knew it was a slim chance; these things often are hit and miss. Like the good time in my life, lately.

"Aren't you going to say anything?" she asks, looking confused by my silent reaction.

"That's...that's too bad," I say, looking away, because I can't face her.

"Too bad?" Trinity snaps. "Too bad?" She springs forward like a Rottweiler. "That's because you're not the one whose life would have changed. You're not the one who'd have to explain to everyone what happened."

I'm too stunned, still, by her announcement. I can hear her, but I'm not taking her words in. I'm still standing in NoHopesville. I had been so prepared for her to be pregnant, because of her long absence from me, and because she said we needed to talk, that I'm just as ill-prepared to deal with the consequences of her not being pregnant.

And for me, I'm shocked by the realization that a baby was the thing that I'd been so looking forward to.

"Max," she says, looking at me. "Say something."

CHAPTER THIRTY-EIGHT

TRINITY

"Max, say something."

His eyes turn shiny. He's not about to cry, I don't think, but he looks...teary.

"What do you want me to say?" he asks. He starts cleaning his hands again with a cloth that he's pulled out of his pocket.

"I'm so relieved. It's been such a worry." He stops wiping his hands, a line appearing on his brow.

"Yeah. Yeah, it must be."

We stand like strangers in an uncomfortable, unfathomable silence.

"I'm clear too."

"Clear?" He can't even bring himself to look at me.

"My tests for the STDs," I whisper, but the moment I hear those words out loud, it occurs to me how insensitive I sound. As if I was blaming him for that.

"I told you I've always been careful."

"I wasn't sure whether to believe you." Now that there is no fear of being pregnant, and no worry that I've caught anything, I feel braver than I have in a while.

"Gina and I had a mutual arrangement, I don't know how many times I have to explain that to you."

His words jab me like a lance, so I throw the lance right back at him. "You always said you weren't the right guy for me. That's the thing I should have taken heed of."

"Yeah, lady, maybe you should have. You're talking as if I was the one who seduced you."

I'm about to say "Didn't you?" but it's not true. We're both adults. He might have tried his lines on me and his charms, and I noticed them enough to react, but he also gave me plenty of chances to not get involved.

I was the one who couldn't hold back a lot of the time. You could say I was the one who made a move on him and forgot the condom.

It was as much my fault as his.

I'm relieved that I'm not pregnant, because children are in my plan, but not just yet. If I had been, I would have made adjustments.

But I'm not, and I don't have to think about that now.

I'd be lying if I said I didn't feel a little sad when my period came yesterday. I didn't even need to buy the pregnancy test. I felt relieved, but also a little sad. But relief isn't the reaction I sense from Max. This surprises me even more than discovering that he had other women.

"I would have been here for you, no matter what happened, no matter what the result of that test was," he says.

"I didn't need to take a test." I look away. It seems much too personal to share this information with him, even though we've been so close and intimate with one another.

But now, we're like strangers again.

"Oh, I see." He opens his mouth as if he wants to say something more, but doesn't.

He looks like he hasn't shaved for so many days that he'll soon be in danger of sporting a beard. I prefer him more when he has sexy stubble.

I feel a pang of sadness crossed with guilt for him.

"I wanted you to know," I say.

He nods his head. "Thanks."

I sense it wasn't the news he'd been hoping for, and it surprises me. Of all the people I can imagine being upset by this news, I never imagined it would be Max.

"Well, you know where I am," he says, and looks as if he's about to leave. I'm unprepared for his abruptness, especially because I begin to see, to sense, to figure out that the chance of a new life might have meant more to him than I first thought.

"I do."

"Take care, Trinity."

I get into the car, but my immediate reaction isn't to sink back against the seat in joy. It is one of profound sadness.

***

MAX

It's not supposed to hurt like that. This is good news, she's not pregnant, and I have no responsibility, but it doesn't feel like good news.

Once I allowed myself to believe it, I let myself get used to the idea of new beginnings.

Of rewriting who I am, and where I came from, even though, as my dad told me, I didn't have to.

Life was easier before Trinity came along. I had Sadie and Hot Gina floating around in my pleasure-bathed existence. It was simple, uncomplicated, and empty.

Fuck, yes. It was empty, and meaningless, a series of orgasms connected one to the next. Hot Gina when she was in town, and Sadie when she wasn't.

Al can sense the drop in my mood when I return to the garage. I don't know if that's the last time I'll see Trinity. I don't want it to be, but we are in different places at the moment.

He tries to cheer me up, but I wave him off. Thankfully he gets it and backs off.

A week later, Al comes up to me looking like shit, and asking me if I've got time to talk.

I don't have time. Not really. I want to go home and get drunk. Shoot pool with the guys, but he looks like he could do with the company.

"Sure. Things okay with you and Sammy?"

He grits his teeth together. "That's what I need to talk to you about."

When he suggests Waquito's, I have no choice but to agree. The place where his hero, Elias Cardoza, used to work seems to have become Al's favorite new place to hang out in.

It's slightly extravagant, given he needs to talk, but he's a friend, and I'm here for him.

I order our beers, as we sit across the table from one another.

"What's going on?" I ask him.

"What's going on with you?" he asks me.

The server arrives with our drinks.

"You first," I say pointing the bottle at him. "What's going on with you and Sammy?" Seems to me as if the moment he got engaged, all his problems started.

"Nothing. Sammy and I are completely fine. What the hell's going on with you?" he points his beer bottle back at me.

I sit up, slamming my bottle onto the table. "You told me you needed to talk—"

"About you." Al points at me. "What's going on, Max? I let you have a few days of sulking and silence, but this isn't like you. This hasn't been like you for the past month."

I'm still mad that he's conned me into going for a drink all the way here, paying exorbitant prices for beer when we could have had something cheaper and nearer.

And all this to talk about me?

Fuck, no.

I press my lips together, rage bubbling beneath my skin. "Nothing's wrong."

"Nothing's wrong, eh?" Al nods his head, then whistles out an exasperated breath. "You don't talk, you don't laugh at my jokes—"

"I don't laugh at your jokes because they're not funny."

"You don't *hear* my jokes, I don't think," he throws back.

"No, I hear them all right." I gulp back two mouthfuls of beer, because I'm totally pissed about his underhanded methods to get me to open up. He raises his hand and orders another beer for me when I'm not even halfway through my current one.

"Drink up, buddy, we've got all evening," he says.

"There's nothing to talk about, Al."

"How are things with you and Trinity? Been a while since you mentioned her."

I swallow. The bastard. He knows me too well. "Things are good."

"Great," says Al, looking ridiculously happy. "I'll get Sammy to book a table for the four of us next week, before places start getting busy for Christmas."

"Book a table?"

"She wants to get to know you and your girlfriend, remember? I mentioned it a few weeks back."

I swipe my thumb across my brow. That's not happening. Ever.

"We broke up."

That was easy enough to say.

"You broke up?" Al's voice is softer now as he leans forward. Then he sets his beer bottle down. "When did that happen?"

"A while back."

"A while back? Yeah, that makes sense now. What happened?"

I tell him. I tell him everything, about Hot Gina's unexpected arrival, about Trinity seeing her, and hating me for that and my harem, as she called it.

"Damn, Max. You've got a whole soap opera show going on."

I snort. But he's not wrong.

"It's not my fault." I don't go into the specifics, but I've analyzed and cross-examined, and gone over everything between me and Trinity from the moment I met her to the moment we split up.

I don't truly believe it was all my fault. "It wasn't her fault either, it was just the way things were."

I miss having her around. I miss her in my life and in my arms. I miss her voice, and her touch, and her softness. I miss her care and concern, and her always putting a positive spin on things.

So why the hell can't she put a positive spin on us now?

"But you sound as if she means a whole lot more to you than any of the others," says Al. "I haven't even met the others, but you were willing to meet me and Sammy for dinner, and I assume you had Trinity in mind, because you'd usually say no outright?"

He's right. I did have Trinity in mind for that dinner with him and Sammy. Just like I had Trinity in mind to introduce to my dad.

"She does mean a lot to me, but she told me she never wanted to see me again."

"Over Hot Gina?"

"There was more to it than that."

"Thought there might be. Let's have it."

I tell him about the unprotected sex, and how, coupled with Hot Gina showing up, the whole thing became so messy. About Trinity's fears of catching something from me, and her worry over being pregnant.

"Yikes. That's a heavy load to get hit with in one go."

"Yeah." I lift the beer bottle to my lips and take a big gulp. "Especially when she's had nothing that intense to deal with before."

Al grins. "You think you were too much for her to handle?"

He doesn't get it, but he doesn't need to get all of it.

"Yeah, something like that."

"She means a lot to you and she told you she never wants to see you again, is that right?" Al asks.

"Yeah."

"As if that's ever stopped you."

"She means it." I feel as if she drew the line under me

once that whole episode concluded, when she found out she wasn't pregnant or at risk from catching any nasty diseases.

She realized how far out of her comfort zone she was with me, and she decided she never wanted to swim in those fast choppy waters with me again.

Because that's what I did to her. I took her from her place of calm tranquility and I threw her into my world of sex and recklessness.

I never meant to hurt her, but I made her feel the things she'd cushioned herself from feeling.

"Do you love her?"

I nod. "Yeah." I've been asking myself this very question lately, and I've come to realize that I do. "It's like I finally know what that word means."

Al almost chokes on his drink. He splutters around, reaching for a napkin to wipe his mouth.

"That, coming from you..." Al splutters.

I don't even have to think about it. Being with Trinity took me on a journey. For me, it was way more than sex. She made me look inside myself and want to be better. I didn't even realize I was experiencing little changes, but my dad mentioned last week that it was so good that I was coming over so regularly. We even had a small Thanksgiving dinner, just me and him.

I wanted to send Trinity a text.

In fact, over the weeks, I've wanted to send her many. I typed many of them out then deleted them.

I love her and I want her back, but she's the one who wanted to end it.

I've already put her through so much. She was doing fine without me. Her life was coasting along nicely until I came along.

"She's better off without me."

"You can't let her go."

"I can. If I love her, I can."

I love her that much to leave her alone, just like my birth mother did with me.

"This isn't a sad love story, Max. Where's that go-get-em guy gone? You lost your balls or something?"

I've lost more than my balls. I've lost my heart.

CHAPTER THIRTY-NINE

TRINITY

A restlessness hangs over me. Everyone around me notices it. Ed, Christina, even my parents when I went for lunch.

I think I managed to throw them off the scent.

Ed seems to stay around longer for his daily chats at the end of the school day. Maybe I'm imagining it but he seems to warble on, talking about nothing in particular, and I'm entirely happy for him to do so.

Christina is a little harder to throw off. I almost canceled my crochet classes completely because I'd lost the will to go back out on Friday evenings and sit in a room full of women.

But she convinced me to keep going. So my blanket with the waffle stitch keeps growing. And Friday nights, Christina and I catch up at Nino's.

I hate my empty weekends.

I didn't have them for long, but every so often I

remember my weekends with Max, drenched in sweaty sex and littered with a trail of our clothes.

Sensing my despondency, Christina attempts to get me out of the house, this time on the pretense of going Christmas shopping.

I'm in no mood for Christmas. I couldn't care less for the bright lights and the decorations which hang everywhere.

"What do you think?" she asks, holding up a dress which I know she will look beautiful in.

"Try it on," I urge her.

She disappears into the changing room, and I look through the clothes racks. I've been buying more clothes. Nicer clothes, more fitted, clothes which flatter me and show off my curves instead of hiding me. Clothes which no longer hang on me like sacks and make me look bigger than I really am.

I pick out a few tops and a couple of dresses in an attempt to make myself feel better, in an attempt to fill the huge gap I find myself staring into each day I wake up.

I love my job and the children, and that part of my day is a distraction, but it's the hours outside my teaching hours that are filled with nothing.

Retail therapy helps.

"Buy it," I say, when Christina comes out in her dress and turns around to give me a 360-degree view.

"I could wear this to the Christmas party."

"What Christmas party?"

"The crochet class one."

I blink as she disappears into the changing rooms again. She's making plans for the crochet class Christmas party?

Come to think of it, the teacher did mention something about it. It's at Nino's as usual.

"I should tell Ed to come," I say, when Christina is paying for the dress at the counter.

"To where?"

"To the crochet class Christmas party," I reply. "He came last year, and he said he liked it."

"He's coming," she announces.

"Is he?" We walk past the huge lingerie store where Max and I had walked past last time.

I look up at the posters. This time there's no voluptuous woman, but a skinny waif in a Santa Hat and Christmas-themed lingerie.

Everywhere I go there are reminders of Max. It's been weeks since I last saw him, when I announced that I wasn't pregnant. It's taken me as long to dissect and examine his reaction.

There are days when I miss him, and days when I desire him, and days when I consider calling him or texting him to see how he is.

Because the truth is, I feel like we are better together. I keep waiting for him to make the first move, but then I'm reminded that I told him to stay away. I'm the one who told him I never wanted to see him again.

Now that enough time has passed, and I've stepped away from the heat and lust that was us, I've been better able to think about things. I was so wrapped up in him when we were together. Being with someone that potent, that sexy, consumes you.

It was impossible not to get swept up in his pheromones and his sensuality. A man like that is hard to resist. Even I found him hard to resist, because I gave him something precious of mine. And then I remember he was hesitant to take it. He tried to stay away. Just like he tried to tell me about his girlfriends.

Just like he opened up and showed me his true self, and shared a part of his life he told me he hadn't shared with anyone.

Whatever Max has done, it's always been what I asked him to do. He's staying away because I told him to, and he'll stay away forever, unless I go to him.

"Do you want to come over to my place?" Christina asks as we reach the parking lot. Our cars are parked together.

She's helped me get out of a funk, and I'm grateful to her, but after a whole day of shopping, I'm not in the mood for more conversation.

At least, not with Christina.

"Thanks, I would, but we've been out the whole day. I should go home and see how Benji's doing."

Christina and I hug, and then get into our respective cars.

I do have plans to get home, eventually. It could be risky, but if I stop by Max's place on my way home and see how he's doing—would I risk showing up unexpectedly and ruining something? There's a chance he might have moved on, a chance that he might be *busy*.

At least it would confirm my need to put him behind me, because I haven't been successful so far.

I'm suddenly consumed by the thought of seeing him again, just to see how he's doing. Being at the mall today put me right back into that time he and I came here, when I bought the bookshelf and he carried it for me and put it together.

I see him everywhere.

Maybe I need to see how he is, so that I can put this behind me and get the closure I need.

CHAPTER FORTY

MAX

I bought Trinity a sex swing, but I won't need it now. I only got it because she expressed an interest in it. I ordered it weeks ago, but it only arrived last week, and it's been lying here in my hallway ever since. I'm supposed to return it and get my money back, but I keep on forgetting.

I've been at the garage working all day and I am glad to finally be home. It gets busy this time of the year, what with people getting ready to make long trips to see family and friends over Christmas.

My dad's coming over to my place this year. It's a first. I told him to, since he needs to get out and make new memories. Christmas at my place isn't going to be something to write home about, but it's a new thing for him, and for me.

I throw a frozen dinner into the oven, set the timer, then take a shower. By the time I come out, it will be ready, and I can watch TV for the rest of the evening.

Another exciting Saturday night.

No sooner have I showered and gotten my comfy clothes on than my doorbell rings. I'm not expecting anyone, and I answer the door, hoping it's not Al resorting to another tactic in order to draw me out of my 'new hermit shell,' as he calls it.

I wish the guy would let me have some quiet moments instead of trying to talk me into doing something.

I answer the door, praying it's not my good-but-trying-too-hard friend. Imagine my shocked surprise when I see Trinity standing on the other side.

I gasp as if she's punched me down below, because she's the last person I was expecting.

"Hey," she says, looking a little nervous. She's chewing the side of her lip.

"Hey." My mouth takes on a life of its own and breaks out into a nervous smile.

"Come in," I say, unable to dampen my enthusiasm. My mind is mentally calculating how long it's been since we last saw one another. Way too long.

"It's good to see you."

She walks inside and hovers by the door, as if she might need to run at any moment.

"It's good to see you," she replies. I can't help but notice that she's wearing jeans. Nice fitting jeans, and a long fitted top. A new coat, too. And her hair has been cut differently. It's shorter, layered. Frames her face.

She looks really good.

My heart sinks.

Not that I would ever wish anything bad on her, but it would have made me feel better to know that she was languishing the way I am. She looks at my hair, then looks around the room, as if she's looking for something.

"Uh...did I...have I interrupted something?"

I run my hand through my hair, self-conscious. It's wet.

"No," I say quickly. "I've just come back from work. Lots of overtime going on, and Al and I are taking advantage of it."

"Oh, good." She looks relieved.

"I was covered in grease, you know how it is."

She nods. "Yes, I know."

I am so happy to see her that it takes an almighty shift of concentration to suppress my happiness.

I don't want there to be any awkward pauses, I don't want us to stand here and have nothing to say, but I also don't want her to think I'm being too overbearing.

What do I do?

I have never known how to be around this woman, which is ridiculous given that I was once so proud of The Max Factor and my rapport with the opposite sex, given that one of my ex's used to call me Sex-Crazy Max, a badge I wore happily and with pride.

"I was passing by," she says.

"I'm glad you came. It's really good to see you." I frantically try to think of something to say. "I've got something in the oven," is the best I can come up with. "For my dinner. I can put something in for you if you'd like."

She looks at me as if I've asked her to eat frog legs. "Thanks, but no."

Fuck. This is awkward. There is so much I want to say to her, and at the same time I don't want to scare her off. But she came to me, I remind myself. She sought me out.

"What's this?" She stares down at the package by the door.

Talk about a way to break the ice. I cough lightly to clear my throat. "It's the sex swing."

She gawps at it, and she's probably wondering if Hot Gina is back, or her replacement.

"I ordered it weeks ago, for you. You remember we argued about it that time I put up the bookshelf? And then you suggested we get one, one time."

Her cheeks start to flush. "So you ordered it?"

I shrug. "You seemed interested, and I thought it would be fun to ..."

She looks away.

"How is the bookshelf?" I ask, as if it's a living, breathing human. I could kick myself.

"It's good," she replies. Her eyes dip down to the box again.

We stand apart, like wary strangers who want to talk, but have nothing to say.

I want to break this chill; this discomfort that seeps into my pores and dulls the mood. Luckily, my oven timer beeps, making a shrill, repetitive sound.

"Excuse me," I say and walk into the kitchen. I open the oven and stare at my rectangular plastic tray with my steaming hot chicken dinner.

"I miss you," she says as I'm about to take out my piping hot dinner. I swivel around to face her.

"What?" I'm not sure I heard her correctly.

"I miss you." Her voice sounds shaky, but there is nothing shaky about her words. That's twice she's told me. She really said it. Those three words that mean so much.

"I miss *you*," I mean it with every fiber in my body. If she came here to tell me this, and it means something; it means I get a second chance. I'm not sure why she's come to me now, but I am so thankful that she has, because I need to tell her how I feel about her.

"I've missed you ever since we stopped being together," she says.

I want to rush to her, and hold her, and touch her face and kiss her. I want to put my arms around her and feel her against me, but I make myself stay rooted to the spot.

Her face contorts, as if she's thinking carefully before she speaks. I want to get back to how we were before, when we spoke freely. When we were whole, and complete, and together.

"That means a lot to me," I say when she doesn't speak. "I've been thinking about you the whole time. Not a day goes by when I don't." I stop myself, because I might have said too much.

"I was scared, Max. I've never felt those emotions before."

"We moved too fast."

She shakes her head. "It's not that. We moved slowly, don't you remember?"

I do remember. I remember body heat and sexual chemistry. I remember wanting her and knowing that I had to hold back. I remember her first time, and how lucky I felt that she picked me.

I look at her, standing near the entrance to the kitchen staring at me.

Two strides is all it would take for me to clear the distance between us, but as always, I am reminded that this isn't one of my usual conquests, this is Trinity, and she's different. She's not here just for the sex.

And neither am I.

What we have goes deeper, beyond words.

"I remember," I say, only it comes out like a hoarse whisper. "I'm sorry, for the pain and worry I put you through, with the tests and all."

"I'm sorry too. I should have apologized sooner but I needed time."

"I understand."

"It wasn't your fault, Max. It was me who got carried away with you, that day you were late back from the garage. I practically jumped you." It's when she giggles that I allow myself to breathe.

"I loved you jumping me."

She chews her lower lip again, gives me that nervous glance, before her gaze drops and she seems to examine the floor. I turn around, feeling good, feeling as if we could be on the verge of a breakthrough.

My oven door has been open, and I reach out to grab the tray.

Holy fucking fudge sticks.

It's piping hot still, and I drop it instantly, then try to put on a brave face and not yelp like a howling chihuahua.

"You forgot the oven mitts." Trinity leaps into action, and turns on the cold water faucet. She takes my wrists and puts my hands under it. A sharp pain slices through my fingertips.

"Keep them there," she orders. I turn around to see that my hot dinner landed on the oven door, luckily. Only a little sploshed out, not that it looks particularly appetizing.

Trinity lifts out the hot tray and puts it on a hot pad, then cleans up the food that sloshed out.

She looks as if she belongs in my kitchen.

"Thanks," I say, watching her.

"That's okay." She turns the faucet off. "How does it feel?"

"Not too bad." I take the kitchen towel she offers me and wipe my hands.

My fingers are bright red, and I've lost my appetite, but

I feel as if I've won something a million times more precious. Something priceless.

I'm scared that she'll say she has to leave. Damn it. Where were we?

"I'm glad you came," I say, and then, because I feel as if we don't have much time, I throw it out there.

"Can we try again?" I have a sixth sense about her, and I can tell she's not as hostile as before. I dare to believe that she might even be interested in me again.

My next heartbeat depends on her answer.

"I would like that."

And that's all it takes for my heart to start up again. I resist the urge to take her hands and pull her into an embrace.

But she comes up to me and puts her arms on my chest.

I freeze, unsure how I'm supposed to react.

"Then can we start from here? Now?"

"You're saying all the right things? Is this a joke?"

She lays her hands flat against my T-shirt. I had forgotten how much I loved her doing that; how much I loved her being here. How much I needed her in my life.

"No. It's not a joke. I should have done this sooner, but I was waiting to see if you would."

"You told me you never wanted to see me again."

"I know." Her hands slip to my waist, then slide around my back.

"I knew it scared you, seeing Gina and being worried about no protection, but I'm not that kind of guy. I don't do risky sex. That was a one-time..."

"That was me, I know. I needed time to think." She smiles at me. It's a toe-curling smile, and I feel it at the tips of all my extremities.

"When you left, I figured that's what you needed."

"I didn't leave you," she says.

"No?"

"I needed to work through things. I've never had to think about stuff like that before."

"That's why I stayed away. I messed things up for you. Your life must have been smooth sailing, calm waters and all that, until I showed up."

"I've never had to think about STDs, or worry so much when I was late for my period."

I hear what she's saying. I wreaked havoc in her life. "I wanted to talk to you. Every day I wanted to reach out and make things better, but I also know that you're better off without me."

"But I wasn't. I'm not. I liked my life better when you were around."

She makes my heart fill up like a balloon when she says stuff like that. She gives me hope.

"You mean that?" Because my life is definitely better when she's with me.

"Yes, I mean that." She tucks a lock of hair behind her ear. "I love you, Max."

Her words reverberate through my soul, and I feel as if my heart is going to pop because it's so full.

"I love you." I reach out and tuck her hair back again, even though it's already in place. Our gazes lock and hold, and I know that if we were able to get through what we just did, we've got a good enough foundation to base our relationship on.

"We were at the mall earlier, Christina and I, and it reminded me of you, of the time we went there to get my bookshelf."

"I think about you all the time. Al says I've been a

miserable little shit, and it's driving him crazy. He wanted me to make up with you weeks ago."

"Why didn't you?"

"I didn't want to mess your life up again."

"You gave it color."

"Yeah?"

She nods.

I stare down at her, then lower my head. Her hands snake around my neck. Our lips press together, and our tongues meet. It's a sumptuous kiss. Deep, fulfilling, and hearty. A wonderful 'hello.' She sinks against me, and I hold her.

As if our kiss has touched a magic button, my body snaps to attention. My cells slowly wake up from their month-long slumber, and my nerve endings jump up full of energy.

She always has this effect on me, and any moment now, she's going to feel it, especially through these paper-thin sweatpants.

I can't help it. I can't stay away, I can't even maintain a slight gap between us. So I press against her, and she moans, low and throaty. When our kiss deepens, her sigh is almost guttural, and my cock is fully awake.

I pull away and stare at her, trying to gauge her next move.

"The sex swing," she says, pressing against me and setting my mind alight. "Why is it in the doorway?"

"I was going to return it."

Her eyes widen as if I've just told her that I've found hidden treasure. "Return it?"

"Or we can keep it. It's yours."

Her tongue slides over her lower lip, a move which I

find highly provocative. She looks up at me with dark, dark eyes. "I wouldn't know what to do with it..."

"I can show you."

"What *do* you do with it?"

"It's better if I show you," I offer with a smile.

"Tell me first, before you show me." Her voice is suddenly sexy and suggestive; as if my dick wasn't having a hard enough time.

"Well," I place a hand at the back of my neck, wondering if I can tell her without having a raging hard-on. "It's a harness, and uh, you attach it from somewhere—"

"But what *do* you do with it?"

"Well." My mouth turns dry. "You sit in it. *You*," I nod at her.

"Fully clothed?"

"No...naked."

"Naked?" The way she raises her eyebrow tells me she knows all about it.

"And then you decide how wide you want to spread your legs in the harness," I say, speeding up, because I know she knows.

"I sit in the harness naked?" She repeats, her voice is huskier than I remember it.

"Yes, yes..." I try to fight the pent-up desire which is threatening to burst out of me. "And I don't need to support your weight or hold you up."

"Which means what, exactly?"

I huff out a loud exhale. "It means I can sink my cock deep inside you, and use my hands for other things."

Our mouths are open, and I have a boner for her that isn't about to go down by itself. Or in the next week.

She's thinking the same thing. She's aroused, because

she hasn't said a word, and because I know her face when she's aroused.

"It's probably better if you demonstrate it," she says.

"I can, but it requires a willing partner. Are you up to the challenge?"

She answers me with another kiss. "I'm up for any challenge you have."

I scoop her up in my arms, and head towards the bedroom. Two seconds later, I rush back out to grab the sex swing, then decide that tonight we have a lot of catching up and talking to do.

The swing can wait until later.

TRINITY

"Well, thanks for the meal," Max says. We've all walked out from the restaurant, and we're standing around on the pavement, saying our goodbyes.

"It was lovely to meet you." I lean in for a hug and a kiss as I say goodbye to Al and Sammy. We finally got around to having that dinner that Max told me about so long ago.

I like these two. I like that Al kept an eye on Max. I like that Max has someone else who cares deeply about him, because I've come to see that he has a lot of surface-level friends, but not many close people in his life.

I understand it better now, his friends-with-benefits setups.

He has Al, but he also has me. I keep an eye on him too.

We say our goodbyes and promise to meet up soon, when Al suggests we come over to their place for coffee.

"Shall we?" Max asks, looking at me.

We've had such an entertaining evening, and these two

guys are jokers when they get together. Sammy was talking about their wedding later this year, and it's been a good evening. "Why not?"

"Why don't you guys come over to my place, it's closer?" Max suggests.

"Are you sure?" Sammy asks. "If you guys had other plans..." She looks at me, as does Max, as if he needs my permission.

"Come over," I say, liking the idea. "We can catch up some more." The restaurant was noisy, and it will be nicer talk in a quieter place.

"Follow us," says Al. "My car's parked further up, I'll wait for you."

They go off, and Max and I walk towards my car.

"Are you sure?" he asks me as we get in.

"Yes, I like them. I like them a lot."

"I like them too, but I was hoping we could get back to our business once we get back." Light from a street lamp falls onto his handsome face, and I catch the look of mischief on it. Max looks at me, and then his face takes on a shocked expression. It takes a moment for me to clue in.

"The sex swing!" I cry. "It's still hanging in the living room."

Max nods. "It's the first thing they'll see when they walk in."

I have had so many hours of pleasure in that harness.

"Oh, my goodness. We can't let them see that. What will they think?" I cover my face with my hands, dying from embarrassment. We used it earlier today, before we started to get ready to go out. We'd left it up, hoping to use it on our return. We never thought we'd have guests over.

"I'll race upstairs and take it down," suggests Max. "You keep talking to them in the parking lot."

"Now there's a plan."

I drive off, following Al's car. Max's hand rests on my thigh.

"Easy there," I say to him. "Don't make me lose focus."

His hand stays put, doing nothing, but I can feel the heat, and my body already knows what this man is capable of without doing much. A tingling feeling coils low in my belly.

We've been inseparable since I went back to him. We made up, talked all night. And he introduced me to the wonders of the sex swing.

These days I get wet just thinking about it.

Taking a chance on my feelings and getting back together with Max was a brave move for me, but it has changed my world.

It's changed *ours*.

I met his dad soon after, when Max had him over for Christmas at his place. I had Christmas lunch with my parents, then went over to Max's in the evening.

I could tell by the look on Max's face that it meant so much to him.

And last weekend, I took Max with me to meet my parents for Sunday lunch. He survived the initial grilling. My mom even told me she thought he was a fine-looking man. My dad liked the way Max fixed the windshield wiper on his car.

"I'll put the swing back in the bedroom," says Max, sliding his hand up my thigh a couple of sexy inches.

"Max..." I say in a warning voice. "I need to concentrate."

He presses his thumb and forefinger down. "This material is silky, I can't help it."

"Max!"

We hear an almighty crash, a deafening noise that scares me to death. I come to a sharp stop.

"Holy shit!" Max sits up and we both lean forward, peering out of the window.

Al has hit something.

MAX

One minute I have my hand on Trinity's leg, and the next minute we hear a loud crash. Sounds like metal on metal, and then some breaking glass.

Damn. I lean forward and see that Al has crashed into the back of a fucking limo.

What the hell?

I get out and rush to his car just as he gets out. "What happened?"

"I misjudged. I thought he was going to change lanes..."

It doesn't make sense. I survey the damage. It's doesn't look too bad. He's smashed into the side and broken the taillight, dented the rear quarter panel, too.

The great big shiny-like-a-beetle limo looks sleek and expensive. I dread to think how much this is going to cost.

"Tell me you've got insurance?" I ask Al.

"Of course I've got insurance."

I look over to find Sammy and Trinity standing over by Trinity's car talking. The driver of the limo gets out, and Al begins to apologize.

As Al and the driver exchange details, the back limo door opens and a guy gets out. He's built like a tank, and when I see his face, a "Holy shit," slips out of my mouth.

I look at Al's back, and my mouth curves into a smile. My friend is going to flip when he sees who it is.

"You guys okay?" Elias Cardoza asks me.

"Yeah, yeah, we're good." I hold out my hand and shake his.

"Are you okay?" I ask him, staring at this huge hulking figure of a man. He doesn't know me, but my interest in him shot up exponentially from the moment I found out that we shared a sliver of our past together.

He's similar in age to me, maybe a few years younger, and I'm not even sure we were at Grampton House at the same time, but I feel as if our shared history somehow bonds us together in a small sad way.

"We're good. What about your friends?" He turns and stares at Trinity and Sammy. I notice that both their jaws have dropped.

"They're okay," I say. "Seems as if Al just shaved the side of your limo."

"It's not my limo," he replies. "I'm supposed to be doing an interview. The studio sent this. Don't worry. I'm sure we can take care of it."

"*Elias Cardoza?*" Al walks over to us, his face is beaming like the full moon. He looks like a five-year-old who's just seen Santa for the first time.

"*Oh, man, oh, man, oh, man, oh, man!*" he screams, then wipes his hands over his face as if he can't believe it.

"He's a big fan," I say to Elias. "He's usually not this...insane."

"I love you, man," Al cries, unable to stop shaking his head. "You kick that Garrison butt real good this time. You show him who's the champ."

Elias grins and shoves his hands into his pockets. "Yeah. Thanks. I'm planning to." Then he peers at Al closely. "Do I know you? I feel like we've met before."

"He remembers me!" Al shrieks with delight. "Yeah,

we've met at Waquito's. At that party there. My fiancée got tickets. I've got a photo with you." He waves his hand at Sammy. "Sammy! Sammy, come over!"

"He's your biggest fan," I say to Elias. "He loves that bar, goes to it any chance he gets, especially if he thinks you might make an appearance."

Elias grins. "I thought I'd seen him before."

Al has beckoned Trinity and Sammy over and is making introductions.

"Boss, we've gotta get to the studio," the limo driver says. "We're gonna be late."

"I'm doing an interview," the boxer explains.

"Oh, man!" Al is still on his Cardoza-high and it doesn't look as if he's going to come down from it anytime this year. He's taking selfies with his idol, and he's gotten Sammy to get something out of her bag so that Elias can sign it.

Elias looks as if he can't keep a straight face.

"This guy loves you," I tell him again. "Trust me, he isn't this uncool normally."

"I'll take your word for it. Hey, would you guys like tickets to the match?" he asks suddenly.

Al's mouth falls open and his eyes go all funny. I'm worried he might have a heart attack.

"I think he would like that very much," I reply, speaking on behalf of my friend.

"We have to go, Eli," his driver says.

"Four tickets?" Elias asks us.

"Four tickets would be great, thanks," I say.

"Thank you, man!" Al looks as if he's about to hug Elias, but Sammy's hand on his arm stops him from making a complete fool of himself.

Trinity stands beside me, rubbing her arms and

shivering. "We should go. You've got goosebumps." I take off my jacket and drape it around her.

"Aww, thanks." She snuggles against the arm I put around her shoulder.

"Really good to meet you," I say to Elias, shaking his hand again.

"You're welcome, guys. Hope to see you at the rematch."

"We'll be there!" Al promises.

"He's got an interview, dude. You should let him get to it."

Elias laughs.

"Sure, sure. See you at the rematch," Al says, as Elias gets back into his car.

"We'll see you at our place?" I ask Al, but he shakes his head.

"We should catch up another time. I've had too much excitement in the last half hour. You guys go on and get home."

"All right. Goodnight, guys." I take Trinity's hand as we walk back to her car and get in.

"Four tickets to the rematch. Cool or what?"

Trinity's eyes are on the road as she drives off. "That fight better not be on his wedding day. Al would miss his wedding to be at the ringside."

"Who would have thought that crashing into the back of a car could be so life-changing?" I ask.

She's changed my life, and I can't imagine it ever being the same again. She changed it in a good way. She does that a lot, I've noticed.

She even managed it for that kid in her class that she was so worried about. She told me the kid's dad managed to get a job at the school.

"So...uh...Al and Sammy aren't coming over now," I say. I'm staring at her side profile and she smiles. "You know what that means?"

"We don't have to move the swing?"

"You could just slide right into it..."

She bites her lower lip and it looks as if she's thinking about it. "Mmmm. That *would* make a perfect end to the night."

"And then I could hold you in my arms and fall asleep," I tell her. "*That* would be the perfect end to *my* night."

Her smile is the widest yet.

I crashed into her life, and she saved me. She makes me happy. She loves me. She makes me feel whole. I'm lucky to have her.

Thank you for reading THE PROBLEM WITH LUST! I hope you enjoyed Max and Trinity's story.

There is more to come in THE SEVEN SINS series and **THE LIES OF PRIDE** is next. This is Nina's story. She's Eli's sister from THE WRATH OF ELI:

THE LIES OF PRIDE

The last thing she wanted was to fall in love with a movie star...

Nina Cardoza wants a simple life; no attention, no drama and no complications.

But one night she makes a terrible mistake. She saves a man who is being attacked.

Unfortunately, he turns out to be Callum Sandersby, one of Hollywood's hottest movie stars.

SIGN UP FOR MY NEWSLETTER to find out when new books release!
http://www.lilyzante.com/news

Read an excerpt from THE LIES OF PRIDE below.

Happy reading!

Lily

PREVIEW: THE LIES OF PRIDE

NINA

I hide in the kitchen, even though I'm aware that it is a silly thing to do, hiding in the diner at the height of the lunchtime rush, but I try anyway. I'm good at making myself invisible; it's a skill I've learned and honed over the years out of necessity. Call it a survival skill.

I hover around at the back, pretending to look for something.

Except that I'm starting to sweat.

I thought I was over this.

Palpitations pitter-patter in my chest. I remember this from before, needing to run for my life. It was flight or fight, and I couldn't fight, not as an eight-year-old. It happened a lot back then in that children's home. But I never managed to escape.

I used to be scared back then, except I'm not scared now, just anxious; I get like that when someone pays me too much attention, too much of the *wrong* type of attention.

I'm supposed to be used to this; getting hit on by

customers. It should be part of the job description of a waitress. A twenty-five-year-old shouldn't react like this just because a guy is hitting on her; and he's a nice guy, Office Guy, we call him. Frankie and Joni tease me about him because he comes in here regularly, and he always seeks me out.

I'm just not interested. I used to be able to handle this better, but ever since Elias's news surfaced, ever since I discovered what happened to him, I've started to fall apart again.

I pull down the cuffs of my long-sleeve turtleneck top. It's not part of the uniform. We have a maroon waitress dress with white edging on the collar and at the ends of the short sleeves, but I told Frankie that I feel cold. She's let me wear this long-sleeved top which is just as well because it covers my arms right down to the wrists.

Joni thinks I'm doing it to get attention. I remind her that I'm not like her. She's the queen of attention. She's already pissed that a lot of the customers often ask who Elias Cardoza's sister is. Ever since Elias won the boxing heavyweight title, Frankie's Kitchen has become a famous landmark in Chicago. My brother used to be a regular and he still hangs out here most weeks. People come here in the hope they might get a glimpse of him. It's the same story at the gym where he still trains. People hang out outside hoping they'll catch him going in.

It amazes me that people are that fickle.

Still, I get good tips at the diner on account of being Elias's sister. It makes Joni jealous. She doesn't even try to hide it. She hates that I get more customers asking after me, and that I get bigger tips. But if people think I'm going to give up any juicy nugget of information about my brother, they're wrong. I'm good at keeping things secret. I even hate the way people, celebrities especially, post boring facets of their lives on social media. As if anyone cares.

"What are you doing in here?" Frankie asks. "We've got four tables that need waiting on. Food's not going to come out of thin air!"

Most of the other waitresses would be scared of her, but I'm not. She's always got my back, and I've always done over and above what's needed. I turn around. "I just need a moment," I say, fanning my face.

"You take a moment, then." Frankie's voice is soft, just like her expression which has suddenly changed. She's never that angry with me, though, I've never given her any cause to be. But I've sensed that she's been watching me carefully lately. It's like she can sense that something is up even if she doesn't know what it is.

"Do you need to take a break?"

I shake my head.

"Who are you hiding from this time? Joni's friends again?" She puts her hands on her wide hips and looks as if she's about to go back out there and do something about it. She's protective of me and her staff, in the same way that I am protective of my brother. The customer is always wrong, as far as Frankie's concerned, though she might smile sweetly to them and then curse them behind their backs once they've left.

"No, they're not even here." Joni's boyfriend Rhys sometimes hangs around here and sometimes he'll come in with his friend, Scott. Apparently, the guy likes me, and Joni keeps trying to get me to go out with him. She says it would be fun for us to be a foursome. Scott's not so bad, I don't mind him, but I'm just not interested in him the way Joni says he's interested in me. It's Joni's boyfriend I can't stand. There something sick about him; something dark and menacing that takes me back to my childhood.

Frankie peers closer. "You haven't been in a good way ever since Elias won the fight."

I laugh off her concern, but I know what she's getting at, even if she doesn't. What happened to Elias shattered my heart. I don't like talking about it and there are nights when I can't sleep. I can't handle facing the past. All that time, growing up together, I thought I had protected him. I believed I was saving Elias by doing what the janitor asked and finding out that this hadn't been the case crushed me.

I thought I had finally put this behind me, thought I had fixed myself. Not *completely*, but enough to be normal. Now my broken past lingers in the periphery of my mind and I can't shift it. I don't think I ever will be completely okay.

I'm back to my old tricks again. Things I hadn't done for a long time.

"What's going on in that head of yours?" Frankie looks at me as if she's trying to X-ray into my brain. "Do you want to talk about it?"

I shake my head to try to indicate that I'm okay. I am. I really am. I get nervous when people want to get too close to me.

"It's Office Guy," I say in an attempt to derail her interest. I'd pulled out my pen and was about to take his order, and then he suggested we could go for a drink sometime. He's never been that forward before. Up until he made the drink suggestion, I was handling the easygoing banter just fine, and then he went and said that, and I clammed up.

"He's not so bad looking," Frankie says, a hint of a smile

curving out on her lips. "He's smartly dressed, handsome and polite too. What else are you waiting for?"

It's a going joke around here that I push all the interested guys away. I get asked for my number, more so since Elias won the fight, but I always say no, tell them that I'm too busy, or not looking for a relationship. The guys are easy to push away, but convincing Joni and Frankie isn't.

"You think you're too good for anyone 'cause your brother is the heavyweight champion?" Joni often comments. "What are you holding out for? A superstar?"

I'm not holding out for anyone. I can't handle getting close. Intimacy gives me the shakes.

But I hate being this way. I hate falling to pieces. It's a problem, especially with the job I have—facing customers all day long. Maybe with my latest course in interior design, I might actually do something with it. I should move on from waitressing. Elias is always telling me off. He wants me to work for him. I don't think so. I like it here. The diner might not be a great place for career advancement, but the familiarity of it all makes me feel secure. I take a long deep breath. "I'm going back out. I can handle him."

"It's not him I'm worried about," I hear Frankie say as I move towards the door and force myself to go back out onto the diner serving area. With a smile plastered to my face, I sail up to the table where Office Guy is sitting and ask him what he wants to order today.

"I didn't mean to cross the line," he says when I return. He seems sweet enough, the overreaction was on my part. Now that I'm back, I widen my smile—make it sweeter, make it count—the way I learned to do from way back; when I needed my little brother to know that I was fine, and that the world was a good place, and that we would be okay.

I shrug. "What can I get you today?"

"A cup of coffee, eggs, sausage and bacon. Maybe you sitting across from me and keeping me company," he adds with a wry grin that's enough to make me sprint back into the kitchen. But I stand my ground.

"I'm afraid I can't do that. I have to work. Frankie would fire me."

"You can always come and work for me."

"You don't let up, do you?" I say, with some of my old feistiness coming back.

"I'm a persistent guy."

"And I'm not interested," I tell him with a smile he buys. I rush back into the kitchen and pin the order along with the others.

When I come back out, I see another table that needs waiting on. The customers crane their necks in my direction and look eager to order.

Elias's win has almost doubled Frankie's customers to the extent that she's had to take on a couple of extra waitresses for when the place gets super packed.

I heave in a breath, and go deal with the other customers, while keeping an eye on the food orders I've already placed. When his order is ready, I give Office Guy his food, thankful that I can rush off because things are so hectic. I am rushed off my feet for the next hour.

"He seems like a nice guy," Frankie tells me as I pin another order to the board.

I almost roll my eyes but manage not to. "So do psychopaths."

CALLUM

"If you play things right, and don't mess up in your private life, this could be it—the role that catapults you to A-list glory," Rudy's voice comes through on my cell phone which I've sent to loudspeaker mode. I don't see him often. He's based in LA, but as my publicist, he touches base with me daily.

I stop flexing my muscles in front of the mirror and I briefly consider firing my publicist. "I *am* an A-lister."

"I mean, A-list *Oscar* glory," Rudy clarifies. "This could be the role to do it."

I smile at myself in the mirror and imagine myself holding that coveted Oscar in my hand. I even have the first few sentences of the speech floating around in my head. I'm trying to move away from my usual action roles and into something that's a little darker, a little different.

I've poured my heart and soul into this role. I want to be known as more than just a hunk. I want the Oscar and accolades, and I want to be talked about for decades. I want to do what De Niro did with *Raging Bull* even though *Death of a Legend* isn't as gritty and as hard-hitting as that classic, it's a step in the right direction and away from the formulaic action-packed movies I've been making so far.

I'm no De Niro yet, but that's what I'm working towards. I've been studying hard for this role, and I've gone through rigorous physical training and even taken part in a couple of real boxing matches. I even won one of them. It was good publicity for the movie, with critics talking about how I've been getting into character with this role. I've even read up about all the boxing greats, and I feel like I kind of understand them a bit more. Most of them were guys who need to prove themselves. Needed to get a one-up in life and fighting was the only way to glory.

Most of the filming has been done, there's a romance element to the movie, and all those scenes with my costar, Alyssa Watts, have been shot. The studio wants us to be the next romance in Tinseltown. We have a few sexy scenes. I wish we didn't. That shit takes away from the grittiness of the movie, but the people financing this movie say they need romance in it.

Now we're in Chicago in order to shoot some of the big boxing scenes as well as shooting those scenes that women like, the ones where I'm training hard. There are plenty of shirtless scenes, and I have to say, I'm pretty pumped by my physique. I've never looked better.

I puff out my chest again, posing once more like a bodybuilder so that the ridges and dips of my muscles are well defined. "I look the part." I nod approvingly at my reflection, and an image flashes through my mind again of me in a tux, raising my Oscar as I make my speech.

The door to my suite opens, and Dottie walks in. "Your dry-cleaned shirts," she mouths, seeing that I'm on the phone. She sets my healthy green healthy smoothie down on the table near me. I would be lost without my personal assistant. She goes over to the table, sits down and starts typing away on her laptop. She's staying at a cheaper place a few blocks from here, and we go through a few things once a day. She lets me know what interviews and meetings I've got, though now that I'm filming, this is where my focus is.

"Any luck with Cardoza's camp?" I ask Rudy.

"I'm working on it." That seems to be Rudy's stock response.

"How hard can it be?"

"I'll see what I can do."

I don't understand it. Rudy doesn't have much to do, it's not like he's the one getting into the ring and fighting. He's not the one who's had to get up at 4:00 a.m. most mornings and workout for six hours every day. "Did you speak to his manager?" All he has to do is set up one meeting with Elias Cardoza.

Just one. I've been trying to get Rudy to set up a meeting with the guy, but Rudy says Cardoza is hard to get a hold of. Even his manager doesn't seem eager. I get that the guy has a huge fight in a few months' time, but our coming together, even for a one-time meeting, would help us both.

"I'm having a hard time reaching him."

I wonder if I should put Dottie on the case. She's clever, quick-witted, and thinks outside the box.

Though this last part of filming is going to be intense, I feel prepared, but I want to have the edge. I've read about the boxing greats, legends like Calzaghe, Hagler, Chavez, Ali and Tyson, and now there's Cardoza. I want to meet with him and get inside his head. Maybe talking to him for a few hours will help get me even more into character. There's nothing like having a real-life boxing champion to talk to. This guy burst onto the scene back in the summer, dethroning Trent "The Tank" Garrison with his raw power and nimble moves. The world took notice. I read up everything I could on him. I watched the fight over at some big producer's house. We weren't expecting to see the fight of the century with this unknown underdog coming out on top. From that time on, I've been wanting to meet the guy.

It's weird how we've ended up filming these final scenes in Chicago because Cardoza comes from these streets. This is *his* city. This is where he trains. It's where he's lived all his life. I also been reading another biography on him, and I've found out about his terrible past. I see now why he was never going to lose, even to an opponent as formidable as Garrison. Cardoza's past is a bonus for me. All I need to do is to get some glimpses of his life which will help me with my role. I swear to god I can almost feel that Oscar within my grasp.

My movie, *Death of a Legend*, might seem as if it's based on Cardoza's life. It's not, but it so freakishly mirrors his story that critics might think we had hopped on the back of Cardoza's story. The truth is, this script came into my hands two years ago. They didn't want me for the role. The producer and director had someone else in mind, but my agent campaigned hard for me, and luckily, the guy they wanted was already signed to do another movie. They couldn't wait for him, so I got the part.

That part is similar to what happened with Cardoza. From what I've read, he wasn't supposed to fight Garrison, there were others in front, but for one reason or another, through injury or failing a drug test, they couldn't fight, and Cardoza got the opportunity.

We're not so different, Cardoza and I, in that respect.

His story, the fighting underdog pitted against the world heavyweight champion, who then goes on to win the title against all the odds—that's real. I admire the guy. Cardoza ignited people's hopes and dreams and went on to do the impossible. In a much smaller way, and less important, I want to prove to people that I can do parts that require depth. I am so much more than my action roles.

"What if *I* ask him?" I suggest. If Rudy isn't having much luck, maybe I should show up at the gym? Surely Cardoza wouldn't dare throw me out.

"I told you. Leave it with me."

I snort. "This is an important role for me. I only need one visit. You can make that happen, can't you?"

"I'll see what I can do."

I breathe out in irritation. I'm a famous actor, and this kid is new to his fame. I don't understand what damage a quick visit will do. This is my chance to prove to everyone that I'm more than just a handsome face, that I don't only have the body of a Greek god—thanks to my training—but I'm a serious actor as well.

"Try harder." I hang up.

Dottie looks up. "Do you want me to book you a flight back to LA on the weekend?"

"For what?"

"Rudy says there's a party you both need to be seen at."

I pull a T-shirt over my head. "I'm not going to LA until we're done filming." Screw Rudy, screw the studio and screw the fake romance. It's lucky I'm not dating at the moment, because something like this would piss me right off.

"You have to go back next month. Alyssa has a movie premiere and you're her date."

"Remind me closer to the time."

Alyssa's been working hard and done two movie back to back. Our sexy scenes in *Legend* worked well and now the studio wants us to pretend we're getting together. Rudy said it would be a good idea for me to attend the premiere of the movie she shot before *Legend*. I agreed only because I have no real-life girlfriend who might get pissed off about something like this, and I'll do what the studio wants me to do. "Anything else?"

She nods her head. "Do you need anything else?"

"My disguises." A fake beard, moustache and wig come in handy.

"In your suitcase."

Because we're shooting, I'm mostly going to be on set and in my hotel suite, but even I can get bored of being cooped up all day. I only have bodyguards when I'm attending an event where there are big crowds, but I hate losing my anonymity. Using disguises is my way of going out without fear of being recognized. Dottie picks up her laptop and moves towards the door. "You're not supposed to go out alone, Callum."

"I'll be fine."

"Don't do anything stupid."

"As if I would."

"You're supposed to be on set at four."

"Make sure you have my smoothie ready."

THE LIES OF PRIDE is available at all major retailers

**Buy Direct from Lily at
https://shop.lilyzante.com**

The Seven Sins:(New Series) A series of seven standalone romances based on the seven sins. Steamy, emotional, and angsty romances which are loosely connected.

Underdog (prequel)
The Wrath of Eli
The Problem with Lust
The Lies of Pride
The Price of Inertia
The Other Side of Greed

The Billionaire's Love Story: This is a Cinderella story with a touch of Jerry Maguire. What happens when the billionaire with too much money meets the single mom with too much heart?

The Promise
The Gift, Books 1-3
The Offer, Books 1-3
The Vow, Books 1-3

Indecent Intentions: This is a spin-off from The Billionaire's Love story. This two-book set consists of two standalone stories about the billionaire's playboy brother. The second story is about a wealthy nightclub owner who shuns relationships.

The Bet
The Hookup
Indecent Intentions 2-Book Set

Honeymoon Series: Take a roller-coaster journey of emotional highs and lows in this story of love and loss, family and relationships. When Ava is dumped six weeks before her Valentine's Day wedding, she has no idea of the life that awaits her in Italy.

Honeymoon for One
Honeymoon for Three
Honeymoon Blues
Honeymoon Bliss
Baby Steps

Italian Summer Series: This is a spin-off from the Honeymoon Series. These books tell the stories of the secondary characters who first appeared in the Honeymoon Series. Nico and Ava also appear in these books.

It Takes Two
All That Glitters
Fool's Gold
Roman Encounter
November Sun
New Beginnings

A Perfect Match Series: This is a seven book series in which the first four books feature the same couple. High-flying corporate executive Nadine has no time for romance but her life takes a turn for the better when she meets Ethan, a sexy and struggling metal sculptor five years younger. He works as an escort in order to make the rent. Books 4-6 are standalone romances based on characters from the earlier books. The main couple, Ethan and Nadine, appear in all books:

Lost in Solo (prequel)
The Proposal
Heart Sync
A Leap of Faith
Misplaced Love
Reclaiming Love
Embracing Love

Standalone Books:

Love Among the Ruins
Tomorrow Belongs to Us
Love Inc
An Unexpected Gift

ACKNOWLEDGMENTS

As always, I would like to say a huge 'Thank You' to my amazing group of proofreaders for their patience and support, and for calmly accepting my ever-changing deadlines. These ladies check my manuscript for errors, typos, inconsistencies and strange words and phrases which often find their way into my story.

Without them, I wouldn't have the confidence to release each book and I am eternally grateful for their help and support:

Marcia Chamberlain

Nancy Dormanski

April Lowe

Dena Pugh

Charlotte Rebelein

Carole Tunstall

I would also like to thank Tatiana Vila of Vila Design for creating the awesome cover.

ABOUT THE AUTHOR

Lily Zante lives with her husband and three children somewhere near London, UK.

Connect with Me

I love hearing from you – so please don't be shy! You can email me, message me on Facebook or connect with me on Twitter:

Website **|** Email | Newsletter sign-up

www.ingramcontent.com/pod-product-compliance
Lightning Source LLC
Chambersburg PA
CBHW061621210726
48287CB00001B/230